A Wrench in the Works

This Large Print Book carries the
Seal of Approval of N.A.V.H.

A FIXER-UPPER MYSTERY

A Wrench in the Works

Kate Carlisle

WHEELER PUBLISHING
A part of Gale, a Cengage Company

Farmington Hills, Mich • San Francisco • New York • Waterville, Maine
Meriden, Conn • Mason, Ohio • Chicago

This is a work of fiction. Names, characters, places, and incidents are either the product of the author's imagination or are used fictitiously, and any resemblance to actual persons, living or dead, business establishments, events, or locales is entirely coincidental.

Wheeler Publishing Large Print Cozy Mystery.
The text of this Large Print edition is unabridged.
Other aspects of the book may vary from the original edition.
Set in 16 pt. Plantin.

**LIBRARY OF CONGRESS CIP DATA ON FILE.
CATALOGUING IN PUBLICATION FOR THIS BOOK
IS AVAILABLE FROM THE LIBRARY OF CONGRESS**

ISBN-13: 978-1-4328-5700-4 (softcover)

Published in 2019 by arrangement with Berkley, an imprint of Penguin Publishing Group, a division of Penguin Random House LLC

Printed in Mexico
1 2 3 4 5 6 7 23 22 21 20 19

This book is dedicated with love to Chris and Claire. May you be happy ever after!

Chapter One

Two months earlier

"Shannon!"

I turned and saw my friend Jane Hennessey waving at me from halfway down Main Street. She ran to catch up with me, despite the fact that she was wearing a lovely dress and high heels. I guess when you owned the Hennessey House Inn, the most elegant world-class inn in Lighthouse Cove, you had to dress the part.

"Hi, Jane." I set my toolbox down on the sidewalk and gave her a quick hug. "You look so nice. Where are you headed?"

"I'm swinging by Lizzie's shop to pick up Mac's latest thriller and then we're going to have lunch at Emily's. You should come with us."

"What a coincidence," I said, gazing up at the clear blue sky. It was early fall and the weather was warm and sunny with a slight breeze. Perfect for walking along the town square. “I was just on my way to Emily’s to fix a stopped-up sink. I’ll walk with you.” I surreptitiously brushed my hand over my mop of curly hair, hoping to swipe away as much sawdust as I could. “But I should probably pass on lunch. I’ve been working at the old Parton mansion all morning, redoing the staircase. I’m covered in wood shavings.”

“We’re used to seeing you like that,” she said with a grin. “Emily won’t mind. We’ll just hose you down before we go inside.”

“That’s so sweet.” Our friend Emily Rose owned the popular Scottish Rose Tea Shoppe on Main Street, facing the town square. She made the absolute best sandwiches and tiny delectable pastries. My mouth began to water just thinking about them. And that settled it. “I’d love to join you if you’re sure I’m not interrupting anything.”

She laughed. “Since our whole point in having lunch is to talk about Chloe’s visit, you won’t be interrupting anything and you should definitely be there.”

I cocked my head in confusion. “You and Lizzie are talking about my sister?”

“Yes, Shannon,” Jane said with infinite patience. “You know she’ll be here in two short months, right?”

"Of course, but . . ."

"And you know she asked me to help book the hotel rooms for the crew and the production staff, right?"

"No." I picked up my toolbox. Jane slipped her arm through mine and we strolled toward Lizzie's bookshop a half block away. "I hadn't heard that."

"Well, she did and I'm thrilled to do it. But it's going to take some jockeying and planning, as you might imagine."

"I believe it." Chloe was the co-star of *Makeover Madness,* a popular rehab and design show on the Home Builders Network. I was thrilled with her success and overjoyed that the show was coming to Lighthouse Cove to feature some of our beautiful old Victorian mansions. And I was pleased to hear that my best friends were jumping in to help make the visit a success.

"But what's Lizzie doing?" I asked. "Is she helping you make reservations?"

"Oh no. I can do that on my own. But Chloe was hoping that Lizzie will stock her new book and maybe host a book signing while she's in town. So a few of us decided to get together to work out all the schedules and logistics."

"My sister, the superstar," I murmured. I still couldn't believe that Chloe had recently published her very own book on home rehab, design, and décor. She had sent me an advance copy and it was gorgeous. Her accomplishments had far exceeded everyone's expectations — including her own — and I couldn't be happier or prouder of her.

Jane squeezed my arm. "She really is a star. And besides, she's our hometown girl. We're all excited to see her again."

"Me, too." I meant it. Especially since my little sister rarely came home anymore, except for the occasional holiday. And even then, she would sneak into town for a day or two and be gone before we'd even had a chance to catch up on old times.

Chloe had left town ten years ago, the summer after she graduated from high school. It had been her dream to make it big in Hollywood, and she'd been determined to do whatever it took to make that happen.

She had started out as a lowly office gofer and in her spare time she worked for a local theater company building sets. And after a few years . . . it happened.

She was discovered in that theater, not as an actress but as a carpenter. A producer hired her for a bit part on a DIY Network show and from there she went on to hit the big time as co-host of *Makeover Madness.*

With her innovative ideas and her talent as a contractor, she helped turn that show into the highest-rated program on the network. It didn't hurt that she was smart and talented and beautiful, but viewers loved her most of all because she had the best sense of humor and absolutely loved her job.

And now, besides being a TV star, Chloe would soon be a bestselling author. Did I mention how ridiculously proud of her I was? Who would've thought that hanging out on construction sites with our dad all those years ago would turn out to be so profitable for both of us?

I'm Shannon Hammer, a building contractor specializing in Victorian home renovation. My hometown is listed on the National Trust for Historic Preservation because of its hundreds of Victorian-era houses and buildings, so it made sense that Chloe would eventually bring her television show back home to Lighthouse Cove. She and her producers planned to shoot a series of episodes featuring major rehab jobs on Victorian homes. And the best news of all was that Chloe wanted me to work on the houses with her. Me! I was beyond excited.

But that didn't mean I was totally on board with Chloe allowing Jane to do all this heavy lifting for her staff and crew. Had my sister gone so completely Hollywood that she didn't think about the "little" people anymore? That didn't sound like Chloe at all. I wondered if maybe she was just overly stressed and pressed for time.

"I guess I'm still confused," I said to Jane. "Chloe's producers usually arrange all the travel details. Why did she ask you to do it?"

Jane smiled. "She didn't really ask. She just called to get some information on hotels and the next thing I knew, I was on the phone with her executive producer, Bree Bennett, who wanted to hear all about Hennessey House. How many rooms we have, our rates, what meals and amenities are included, you know. We worked out a few specifics and I told her I'd take care of everything else."

I frowned. "Everything else?"

"Her staff and crew are going to need a lot more rooms than I have available, so I offered to take care of booking the Inn on Main Street for them."

I nodded slowly. "That makes sense. You're kind of an expert in that regard."

"I am," she said with a confident smile. Jane had been the manager of the inn for five years before she opened her Hennessey

House, a massive Victorian mansion left to her by her grandmother. "And then Bree called back for more info and I happened to mention that Emily's catering company could provide pastries and coffee every day. And then Chloe called to ask about the book signing, so that got Lizzie involved. And then Emily reminded me that Gus has a limousine service if anyone on the show wanted to use it. And, well, here we are."

Jane and I had gone to school with gorgeous Gus Peratti, the best auto mechanic in town and the guy who had won Emily's heart.

I smiled, feeling better knowing that Chloe wasn't running our friends crazy. Not personally, anyway. And besides, nobody here seemed to mind. At least, not so far. I would have to make sure that once the production people arrived, they didn't steamroll Jane, Lizzie, Emily, and everyone else in town. "So you managed to get the whole gang involved. I'm officially impressed."

"And we're all going to get credit on the show. Isn't it wonderful?"

"That's very cool," I said. "I just hope you're not too busy to handle all this extra work. If it starts to feel like Chloe's imposing on you . . ."

"She's not." Jane laughed. "It just feels that way to you because she's your sister. I, on the other hand, am totally psyched. It's sort of like I'm working in showbiz, you know?"

I chuckled. "Showbiz-adjacent, anyway."

"Close enough," she said breezily. "Besides, Chloe is so sweet."

Sweet? Chloe? I loved my sister, but that was not a word I would normally apply to her. Smart, savvy, a little snarky, sure. But sweet? I wondered just how thickly she'd laid on the sweetness. On the other hand, my friends weren't exactly naïve. Especially Jane, who had known Chloe her whole life. If she and the others didn't want to do the work, they wouldn't have volunteered. Still . . .

I glanced up at Jane, who was two inches taller than me — and had been since first grade when we were the two tallest kids in class, a fact that had bonded us for life. "If you feel like you're about to freak out from all the demands, just call Chloe and tell her to get the producers to take over. They're used to doing this kind of stuff. And I can help, too. With . . . whatever."

"No way would I dump my work on you," she said adamantly. "First of all, you've got your own arrangements to take care of, right?"

True, I thought. I was supposed to scout out three or four run-down Victorian houses ripe for rehab. The producers would come to town in the next week or so and choose a few of them to be featured on the show. Chloe also wanted me to line up four or five other smaller interior jobs that the two of us would tackle for the show's website. And in the meantime, I had a bunch of ongoing jobs that would start to get backed up as I spent more time working on the TV show projects.

"And second," Jane continued, "I've got a ton of people offering to help me. This is going to go off without a hitch."

Famous last words, I thought. "We'd better knock on wood."

"Very funny," she said, lightly elbowing me in the side.

"Yeah, I'm just kidding. It's going to be great." But as we passed one of the many sycamore trees that grew along Main Street, I reached out and knocked on the thick brown wood trunk. Because why tempt fate?

Two weeks later

I met with Wade Chambers, my head foreman, at the site of one of the first houses on my Chloe list. I was already waiting by the tailgate when he climbed out of his truck, and together we pulled the extension ladder out of the back.

"They picked the Bloom house for the show?" he asked.

"It's one of the four they're going to decide on," I said as we lugged the ladder up the walkway. "I really hope they choose it because it's got great bones. The final result would be beautiful."

"You're right," he said, gazing up at the three-story tower. "It's got all the Victorian elements and it would be perfect for the show. As long as it doesn't crumble and fall down between now and the time Chloe gets here."

"It could happen." In its heyday, this Queen Anne Victorian had surely been one of the more stately jewels of Lighthouse Cove. With its traditionally asymmetrical roofline, multiple gables, rounded front tower, and wraparound veranda, not to mention the overabundance of gingerbread trim, the home was a true classic. But it had been deserted for at least twenty years and, like Wade said, I wouldn't be surprised to see the place collapse at any moment.

"I ran into Margaret Bloom at the market," I said. "She begged me to put in a good word. She told me she's spending every day in church, lighting candles and praying that the house gets chosen for *Makeover Madness.*"

Wade chuckled. "I'm not sure it works that way."

Margaret still owned the house that had been in her family for six generations, but when she got married, she moved into her husband's home, a beautiful Eastlake-style Victorian over on Ivy Hill north of the town square. She had kept her maiden name of Bloom just as her three sisters had done since the Blooms had long been one of the most prominent families in Lighthouse Cove.

"She told me they can't spare the money to refurbish both of their houses and according to the terms of her father's will, she can't sell this one. She'll have to pass it on to her kids eventually, but meanwhile, it's falling apart. She'd be thrilled if Chloe and the producers choose it. That way, she can get the work done for free."

"It definitely needs help," Wade said, glancing at the veranda. "It's kind of a disaster and that's a damn shame."

"Disasters are exactly what Chloe asked me to find for the show," I said with a grin. "She told me to come up with some real stinkers."

He chuckled. "Then she'll be very happy with this place. So what are we doing here?"

"I'll show you." I lifted the front of the ladder up. "Let's go around to the side."

Wade grabbed the far end and we carried the heavy ladder around the side of the house to the point where the wraparound veranda ended. "Let's set it up right here."

"I guess I shouldn't complain that so many of the old houses are falling apart," Wade reasoned as he helped lean the ladder up against the side of the house. "It keeps us gainfully employed."

I grinned at him over my shoulder. "You got that right."

"Okay, I assume you're the one climbing up there." He grabbed hold of the railings. "I'll keep it steady for you."

"Thanks." I stared at the ladder, looking all the way to the top. I wasn't afraid of heights but this thing stretched up thirty-two feet. Even my most macho crew guys were a little daunted by the climb. My throat was suddenly dry. "That's a long way up."

"And it still won't reach the peak of the gable," Wade said, pointing up at the decorative wood pieces tucked under the peak of the roof. "We'll have to get the boom lift out here if Chloe wants to restore those gable carvings."

My construction company owned a two-man boom lift with a basketlike platform and a fifty-two-foot articulated arm, the kind of thing the telephone company used to reach the highest electrical poles. It was an expensive piece of heavy equipment that my father had won in a poker game a few years back from the owner of our local hardware store. True story. Because of Dad's good fortune, we were happy to rent it out to other contractors when we weren't using it ourselves.

"For now," I said, "I just want to get close enough to check out the dentils along the eaves." Taking a fortifying breath, I slowly climbed thirty-some feet until I could reach out and examine the closest square of wooden molding. But as soon as I touched the first one, my fingertips went right through the rotted wood. I tested a few more spots along the eave and found them all as badly damaged.

"I was afraid of this," I shouted down to Wade. "We've got to get these repaired before Chloe shows up."

"Why?"

"Because the wood is rotten."

"But that's part of the deal, isn't it? It

actually looks kind of cool in a disturbing sort of way."

Was he smoking something? "No, it doesn't. It looks plain old creepy. Decrepit, faded, and sad."

"Exactly," Wade shouted cheerfully. "Chloe will love it. She'll want to get some close-up shots of the rot first before we get to work making it beautiful."

I sighed. He had a point. "But I hate to think that people watching the show will believe that the houses in Lighthouse Cove are dilapidated and mangy."

Wade snorted a laugh. "Why would they think that? Lighthouse Cove is famous for the hundreds of beautiful Victorians we have here."

"Right, so why would we want to show off all the ugly parts?"

"Because if they see all this rotting wood and peeling paint, they'll think we're freaking geniuses when we make it all shiny and pretty again."

I gazed down at him and nodded reluctantly. "You're right. Guess I'm just nervous about the whole television thing." I stared up at the offending dentil and sighed again. "Okay, we'll leave them for now."

"Good. Ready to come down?"

"Not yet." I pointed up at the main gable

rising thirty more feet above me. "Look at those gable brackets. I can see the worm holes from here. And the carvings are falling apart. They'll need to be filled and sanded and then painted."

"Yup," Wade agreed. "But *after* the film crew gets here. Chloe loves stuff like that."

I frowned because he was right. "How is it that everyone knows my own sister better than I do?"

"I watch her show," he said with a shrug, clutching the ladder as I studied the weathered wood siding. "It's really interesting and Chloe's great. I always learn something new."

I didn't respond, just made a point of scratching off a bit of peeling paint.

Wade started to laugh. "Do you even watch your sister's show?"

"Of course I watch it," I said, properly outraged. "I mean, usually." I huffed out a breath. "Okay, fine. I *record* them so I can watch them anytime I want."

"Uh-huh. Better watch a few episodes before she gets here."

"I will," I groused. I would never admit out loud that watching my sister's TV show made me feel a bit inadequate. I mean, we were both contractors and basically had the same job, only she did hers on national television. It was weird. Despite being proud of her, I guess I was a little jealous, too, which was just plain silly.

I took another minute to check out some water damage I noticed under the eaves of the veranda, then began the climb down. "I would love the chance to restore this house to its former glory."

Wade scraped at a patch of peeling paint. "You and me both."

We retracted the extension ladder and carried it back to Wade's truck. Once it was secured, he took his tablet out of his backpack. "Do we have a schedule yet of the work we'll be doing with Chloe while she's here?"

"I'm expecting the producer to come to town this weekend. I'll show her each of the houses and she'll make the decisions on which houses we'll work on and in what order. And once we've nailed down those details, I'll get together with you and Carla and finalize a schedule for the crew. According to Chloe, they plan on using some of our guys."

"I hope so. That would be a kick."

"At the very least, I'll see if they'll let our guys work on the smaller projects we've got lined up."

"Do you know what those are?"

"Yeah. Chloe's been in touch with one of her high school friends to expand a closet. Freddie Baxter wanted to add on a new bathroom and Mac wants to build a deck on the side of his house."

"Off the kitchen?"

"Yes. The northern exposure will be perfect in the summer. I was going to do the work anyway, but if Chloe wants us to do it for the show, that would be great."

"Oh, yeah. Right by the ocean, they'll be able to get lots of great shots of the waves and the beach."

"And the lighthouse."

"Awesome," he said, and climbed into his truck. "Keep me in the loop."

I grinned. "Always."

Present day

After arriving home from work tired, drywall-mud-caked, and downright grungy, I jumped into the shower. I hadn't even dried my hair when my dog, Robbie, began to bark frantically and made a beeline down the stairs and straight for the front door.

"All right, all right," I said. Throwing on a T-shirt and sweatpants, I followed him down and opened the door in time to see a sleek black limousine come to a stop in the driveway. "Looks like the queen has arrived."

I walked down the front steps just as my sister stepped regally out from the backseat of the limousine. She wore jeans and a bejeweled denim jacket, and her long blond hair was pulled back in a ponytail, making her look like a teenager.

At first glance, the two of us didn't look related at all. But if you looked beyond our hair color, you'd see that we were obviously sisters. When Chloe turned sixteen she decided to become a blonde and never looked back. I had always been happy with my wavy red hair, despite its occasional similarity to an unruly mop.

I grinned and felt my heart stutter in my chest. It had been too long since she'd been home.

Hurrying down the walkway, I grabbed her in a hug. "Come here, you. Gosh, you look so great! I can't believe you're finally here."

"I can't, either. We're going to have so much fun." She held me at arm's length. "How do you keep getting more beautiful?" And then she pulled me close again.

"In case you hadn't noticed, my hair is a wet mess."

"And yet you still look fabulous. I should

hate you."

I laughed. "We're definitely related. I was just thinking the same thing about you."

She smiled. "Aren't we lucky?"

"And just a little full of it."

Still laughing, we both turned as Gus Peratti jumped from the driver's seat. "Hey, Shannon."

"Hi, Gus. Haven't seen you in forever." I gave him a quick smooch on the cheek. "Thanks so much for taking care of Chloe."

"Not a problem." He jogged around to the open trunk and began pulling out at least a dozen various suitcases, a hanging wardrobe bag, and several large duffel bags.

"Did you bring enough stuff?" I asked.

She smoothed her hair back. "In case you haven't noticed, I'm very important."

I chuckled and pulled her close. "God, I've missed you."

Chloe wrapped her arm around my waist and rested her head on my shoulder while Gus loaded up on suitcases and traipsed up the steps and into the house.

"Is everything okay with you?" I asked her.

"Wonderful," she said a little too emphatically. "I'm just so glad to be here."

Chloe stared up at the house we had grown up in. Like so many of the homes in town, it was a Queen Anne Victorian with the usual charming affectations. I had painted the entire house white with touches of sky blue trim a few years ago, which was a big change from the previous multiple-color style of dark browns and blues with forest green trim and a splash of beige here and there. I had also replaced the clamshell shingles covering the top half of the house with horizontal wood siding that matched the rest of the exterior. It gave the house a clean, tidy look that I loved.

"It looks so peaceful," Chloe whispered.

She couldn't have given me a better compliment. "I hope you like it."

"I love it." Her eyes narrowed. "Wait, did you replace the bay windows?"

"I did." Originally there were three narrow sash windows that I replaced with a gracefully bowed, single piece of glass.

"Wow. That's a showstopper." She climbed the ten steps up to the front porch and walked over to study the bay window up close. "The glass itself is curved. How did you do that?"

"It was tricky but I found a glazier in Eureka who rose to the challenge." *Tricky* was one way to put it, I thought. *Pain in the rear* would be more accurate.

"Gorgeous."

"Thanks. That means a lot." And it reminded me that Chloe hadn't been home to visit in over five years. Oh, we talked on the phone or Skyped every other week or so, and Dad and I had traveled south to see her a few times. To this day, I still didn't know why she didn't come home more often. Maybe she would finally open up to me on this trip. I could only hope.

Gus came back out, grabbed two more large bags plus two smaller bags, and easily walked back up the front stairs to the door.

"We'd better help," I said.

"Good idea."

We jogged down the steps to the car. I grabbed a duffel bag and a couple of the smaller totes. Chloe picked up the last three shopping bags and we followed Gus into the house.

"Where would you like these?" he asked.

"Oh, just leave them here and we'll take them upstairs eventually."

"A couple of these bags are really heavy," Gus said. "Let me take them upstairs for you while you two get reacquainted."

He was going above and beyond the call of duty, but that was what friends were for. "Thank you, Gus. Chloe's room is down the hall, the third door on the left."

"My old room?" Chloe said.

"Do you mind?"

"Absolutely not." She clapped her hands together. "It'll really feel like I'm back home. Actually, I'm getting a little emotional just thinking about it."

I grinned. "That's only fair since I've been freaking out for weeks in anticipation of your arrival."

"Why?" Chloe looked surprised. "The show is going to be a blast. I'm so excited you're doing it with me."

"I'm pretty excited, too. Also scared to death, but I'll snap out of it."

She gave a light shrug. "If we screw it up, we'll just do another take."

"You make it sound so easy," I said with a laugh.

"It will be."

Gus made two more trips upstairs and then took off, but not before Chloe tried to tip him.

He politely refused. "Your company made us a very generous deal while you're in town, so tips are not necessary."

"Then how about if we take you and Emily out to dinner later this week?" I said.

"That sounds perfect. Good to meet you, Chloe." He winked and strolled out the door.

Chloe waved, then sighed. "God, he is a beautiful man."

"That's the consensus. And Emily sure thinks so."

"He told me he went to school with you, but I don't remember him."

I laughed. "How could you forget him?"

"I have no idea." She shook her head and stared at the door where Gus had just departed. "I guess I was a little self-absorbed in high school."

"Weren't we all?" I led the way into the kitchen and while feeding Robbie and my pretty orange-striped cat, Tiger, and cleaning their water bowls, I told Chloe the story of Gus and Emily and how the ghost of Mrs. Rawley brought them closer together.

"That is so amazing," she said, taking a seat at the kitchen table. "So the ghost led you to the wall where she'd hidden her diary?"

"Yes. It was pretty bizarre to see paint cans flying through the air and the chandelier swinging all on its own."

"Oh my God, you're giving me goose bumps." She rubbed her arms briskly. "Will you tell that story on the air?"

"You really want me to?"

"I do. That's exactly the sort of thing that viewers love to hear, especially when it's connected to an old home like this story is."

I took a breath to fortify myself. This

whole showbiz thing was new to me. "Okay, I'll do it."

"Great." She pulled out her phone and began to type. "I'm just making myself a note."

Robbie finished his nibbling and scurried over to the table, where Chloe patted her knees in invitation. The friendly Westie immediately jumped onto her lap and settled in for some petting, scratching, and stroking. Not to be outdone, Tiger curled herself around Chloe's ankles and made herself at home on top of her shoes.

"I love your little creatures," Chloe murmured.

"They love you, too. Do you have any pets?"

"No. My old boyfriend was allergic, or at least that's what he always told me. Now that's he's gone, maybe I'll get a cat."

"You should. It's nice to come home to someone who's absolutely thrilled to see you."

She laughed. "It probably helps that you're the one feeding them."

"That's the bargain we've struck. I feed them and they love me."

She put her elbow on the table and rested her cheek in her hand. "I could use some unconditional love."

As if on cue, Robbie turned and licked her chin.

Chloe laughed and gave Robbie's ear a soft scratch. "Thank you, Robbie. See, that's what I'm talking about."

"So, speaking of your old boyfriend . . . what ever happened to Joe? You never really said."

She gazed at me. "He turned out not to be the dreamboat I described when I first met him."

"I'm sorry."

"It's my own fault."

"But you lived with him for two years."

"We had fun for a while. I thought we would get married. I love his parents. I still miss them. But you know, when the guy you're living with turns around and gets another girl pregnant, it's usually a sign."

"Ugh. A really big sign. What an idiot."

"It's okay. I'm too busy to have a relationship."

I sat down across from her, anxious to change the subject to something a little less upsetting. "So, it's almost five o'clock. Do you want to unpack?"

"Not really. Do you mind if we just chill out for a little while?"

"Do you want to take a nap?"

"God, no. But I would love a glass of wine."

"We are definitely related." I opened a bottle of Pinot Noir and poured two glasses, and then we walked back to the living room to relax. Tiger and Robbie followed, naturally, and we all settled down on the big comfy couch.

"So tell me about your life," I said, after waiting for her to swallow her first sip of wine. "The show is going well, I know. And you always look so smart and beautiful, even when you've got paint on your hair."

She groaned. "You saw that episode, did you?"

"Yes." I had finally managed to binge-watch three seasons of the show and while I would never admit that little fact, I was prouder than ever that Chloe was my sister. She was truly talented. "That same thing happened to me a few years ago and it took weeks to get the paint out. Now I never paint a ceiling without wearing a hat. Which isn't easy with this head of hair."

She waved her hand at me. "That's another thing you should mention on the show. Any little details or stories or advice. The viewers love it."

"Speaking of viewers, you know you've got a lot of fans in town. I hope you're ready for the adulation."

She laughed. "It never gets old."

I scrunched a pillow and leaned back into the cushions. "It feels like forever since I saw you last. So tell me everything. The show is incredibly popular and your book is selling like crazy, that has to feel good."

"The book." She shook her head in wonder. "I'm in shock over how well it's doing."

"I'm so proud of you." I smiled at her for a long moment. "Never mind that I'm consumed with jealousy."

She laughed again as I'd hoped she would, but then she sobered. "I feel bad for not calling more often, but it has been sort of a whirlwind. My head still spins at the thought of all those personal appearances. I just got back to the show last week and now we're on the road again."

"Was your crew happy to see you? I hope everyone is treating you well."

"They are the best. Everyone's so supportive."

"Good. I remember when you first started on the show, you said that Blake Bennett was really nice and helpful to you. Is he still? Was he happy about your book?" Blake was Chloe's co-star and one of the producers of *Makeover Madness.* He was married to Bree, the executive producer.

"Oh, yeah, Blake has been totally supportive. I asked if he wanted to help with the book and he said no way." She chuckled. "He figures I can do all the work and if the book is a hit, it means more people will watch the show."

"I guess he's right." I swirled my wineglass. "Oh, speaking of Blake, I met his wife, Bree, last month when she was up here scouting for locations. She was, um, nice. A very interesting woman."

Chloe's smile tightened. "Seriously? Nice?"

The last thing I'd wanted to do was diss Chloe's boss, but Chloe obviously knew me too well. "I guess she was a little full of herself."

"That's more like it." She gave Robbie an absent scratch. "Don't get me wrong, Bree can be nice when she wants to be. Unfortunately, that doesn't happen very often."

My gaze narrowed. Okay, I might not see my sister often, but I could still read her expressions and emotions fairly easily. "What do you mean?"

"Nothing really." Chloe shrugged and reached for her wineglass. "Except that right before I left the studio this morning, she fired me."

CHAPTER TWO

"What?" I jumped to my feet and waved my arms in the air like a ranting monkey. "What do you mean, she *fired* you?"

Chloe was uncharacteristically calm. It was spooky. My sister was not known for her Zen-like personality.

"Just what I said."

I, on the other hand, was going nutso on her behalf. "How dare she fire you! You're the star of the show!"

"Yeah, I know." Her expression darkened. "And so does she."

"Are you all right?"

The mask fell back into place as she composed herself. "Of course."

"Why aren't you furious? Who are you and what have you done with my sister?" I slapped both fists on my hips and stared at her. "So what're you going to do about it? But wait, this doesn't make sense. You're here. You're starting to film tomorrow." I stared at her, shaking my head. "What's going on?"

Chloe stood and grabbed my arms. "It's okay, Shannon. Don't flip out. She fires me every other week. She fires people all the time. She's even fired Blake, and he's her husband."

Well, this explained why Chloe wasn't half-crazed and it helped throw cold water on the flames lighting me up. "She fires her own husband? All the time? But you and he are the stars of the show. I don't get it. Is she insane?"

My sister shrugged. "A little. In the last two years the show has become ultrapopular. The network loves it and has put a lot of extra money into it. I think all that power has gone to her head. She likes to have things her way and if you don't comply, she will punish you. We call her the dominatrix now."

It made me grateful that I ran my own business and didn't have to take orders from anyone else. It also made me wonder how Chloe was keeping so calm.

"So let me get this straight. You still have your job, right?"

"Yes, because I just ignore her when she does stuff like this." Chloe sighed again. "But honestly, I'm getting so tired of her shenanigans."

"Shenanigans? Don't you think that's a little mild? She sounds like a whacked-out bully."

She beamed at me. "I like that description better."

"You should because it's true. What's confusing is why you're not thinking of her like that. Come on, Chloe. This is beyond weird."

She pushed a strand of hair back from her face on another sigh. "Yeah, I know, but it's not like she's deranged. She's just . . . weird."

"You're making light of it, but I'm worried about you. I hate her for threatening you. It's got to be really stressful. And it's not fair. You've worked so hard to get where you are and you deserve to be happy."

"I am happy. Really. Well, most of the time." She sat down, grabbed her wineglass, and took a healthy sip. "Look, to be honest, I don't have a lot of interaction with Bree. Mostly she deals with Blake, who absolutely loves her."

Was love really that blind? "Why? She sounds awful."

She shrugged. "The two of them seem to click together. And let's not forget that she's very beautiful, so he's willing to put up with a lot."

I sat back down. "Seriously? You're so much prettier than she is."

"You're my sister," she said with a wry smile. "Your opinion doesn't count. But I love you for saying so."

"Well, if you want an objective opinion, you can ask Mac. He saw Bree while she was here."

"Mac saw her? That's interesting."

"The whole town saw her. As you must know, she is no shrinking violet."

"Hardly." Chloe snorted and sipped her wine.

"She made sure that everyone knew she was a big-time Hollywood producer." I took a drink of mine, too. "She threw her weight around wherever she went."

Chloe raised one eyebrow. "I wish I were shocked. She's a real piece of work."

"It was a bizarre day for me." I took another sip of wine as I reflected on Bree's visit last month. "I spent the whole morning with her, showed her four houses I thought would be good for the makeovers. Fabulous homes, really, but in disrepair, obviously. She was kind of dismissive, but since she's your boss, I decided I would be nice to her, no matter what.

"And it wasn't easy. I even offered to take her to dinner that night, but she told me she needed to spread the joy, as she put it. Told me she was meeting with several real estate agents who also had houses in mind for the show."

"Spread the joy," Chloe muttered. "That's so Bree." She stretched her legs out and rested her feet on the coffee table. "Sorry she was dismissive with you."

"I wouldn't care, except that I did notice her behaving differently around the men she met."

"Yeah, she cranks up the charm around the guys. So how did Mac meet her?"

"I took her out to the lighthouse mansion to show her where I want to build the deck. She loved the location right on the beach and agreed that it would be a good segment to use online."

"I'm glad. So was she civil to Mac?"

"Civil? Hmm."

Chloe sighed and shook her head. "She flirted mercilessly, right?"

I gritted my teeth. "With all the subtlety of a jackhammer. She's formidable, I'll give her that. Mac handled it fine, but I caught him making faces behind her back."

"Good for him." Chloe laughed. "I've done it myself and hey, it's better than shoving her off a cliff."

I laughed, too. "I guess so. If you want honesty, I'll tell you that the time I spent with her was the longest few hours of my life. I don't know how you deal with her every day."

"I love my job, Shan," she said. "And she doesn't actually spend that much time on the set with us, so it's usually easygoing and fun. But speaking of Mac, when do I get to meet your famous mystery man?"

"How about tonight?" I really wanted my sister and Mac to meet and become friends. "I'd like to invite him to dinner if it's okay with you."

"I would love that." She grabbed her phone to check the time. "It's almost six now. What time do you want to eat?"

"I wanted to make sure you were up for socializing before I made any plans. We can eat anytime you're ready. I thought we'd walk to Bella Rossa. I made a reservation for seven o'clock, just in case. I'll call Mac and see if he can meet us there."

"Can you believe I've never been to Bella Rossa?" she said. "I can't wait."

"You'll love it. It's got Uncle Pete's vibe all over it."

She smiled. Our uncle Pete owned the popular Italian restaurant and wine bar on the town square and he was often there to greet customers. The place was an offshoot of Pete's winery and vineyard east of town. It was a shock to realize Chloe had never been there.

"I can't wait to see Uncle Pete," she said.

I frowned. "You know he's out of town fishing with Dad, right?"

"Yeah. Dad texted me earlier to say they're halfway through Oregon and should be back by tomorrow afternoon."

"Good. We'll have them over for dinner."

"Wonderful."

"You'll probably see a bunch of familiar faces tonight. It's a happening spot. Well, as happening as we get around here."

"Then that's where we need to be."

"I know, right? Okay. I need a minute to dry my hair and change clothes."

"I'll need more than a minute."

"Yeah, I might need *two* minutes. But first let's go check out your room."

"Good idea."

I followed Chloe upstairs and down the hall. When she got to the door of her room, she stopped. "Oh. It's all so . . . different."

"Just some paint and new drapes," I said self-consciously, having no idea if she would hate me for updating everything.

"You've really changed things." Her voice

was wistful, but I couldn't tell if she was pleased or disappointed.

I spoke up, to fill the silence that stretched out as Chloe looked around the room where she'd grown up. "I added a few doodads here and there. I hope you don't mind. I took down your NSYNC posters, but I didn't throw them away. They're still in the closet."

She nodded absently as she strolled around the room picking up or tweaking every little tchotchke and doohickey I'd placed here and there in my attempt at décor. I had replaced her rickety old bookshelf with floating blond wood shelves, but I'd kept all of her favorite childhood books and added some fun romances as well as my favorite mysteries and thrillers. A modern blond wood desk and comfy chair were placed under the shelves and another wall held a flat-screen television. The brightly colored handmade quilt covering the queen-sized bed was from my friend Marigold's Crafts and Quilts shop.

"Well?" I said, a little nervous that she hadn't commented. Especially since she was now considered the queen of design with her new book on the market. Not that I was intimidated or anything. "You're making me really tense here, Chloe . . ."

She turned and I could see that her eyes were a little watery, but she was smiling. "You did a great job. It's so pretty. Really cheerful."

I let go of the breath I'd been holding. "I'm so glad you like it."

"I love it."

Wow. Funny how nervous I'd been and what a relief it was to know that my sister approved of what I'd done. Chloe was amazing at what she did. And yes, in my own defense, I was darn good at my job, too. But she was the designer. I'm the builder. "Good. That's good. So, do you need some help unpacking?"

"Let's do that later. I'm starving."

"Okay, I'll just go fix my hair and we can meet downstairs in ten minutes. Okay?"

"Sounds like a plan."

I dashed down the hall to my bathroom, where I dried my hair into a semblance of a style. Then I reached for my phone and called Mac.

"Hey, Irish," he said warmly. "I was hoping you'd call. Did your sister arrive?"

"Yes, she's here and she would love to meet you if you're up for dinner." I gave him the details and we agreed to meet at the restaurant as soon as he could get there.

After I hung up, I applied moisturizer and

dabbed on some lip gloss, then changed out of my T-shirt and sweatpants and into a slightly more tasteful outfit of black skinny jeans, soft cashmere sweater, and short black boots.

"That will have to do on short notice." I checked myself out in the mirror and began to think about introducing Chloe to Mac. Would they like each other? Would he like her more than me?

"Oh my God, shut up," I said to my reflection. Why was I suddenly feeling so insecure?

"Because you're a knucklehead," I muttered in response. Grabbing my leather jacket, I jogged downstairs and was surprised to see Chloe waiting by the front door.

"You were fast," she said.

I smiled. "You were faster."

"I was already dressed so I just brushed my teeth, combed my hair, and here I am." She slid her phone into her pocket. "I just texted Dad to let him know about dinner tomorrow night."

"Good. I'm sorry he wasn't here to greet you today."

"No worries," she said, waving off my concern. "I know he had this fishing trip planned for over a year."

"It's their annual trip to Pemberton. They've gone up there for the past six or seven years."

"Oh, I've heard all about it," she said with a smile. "And I've been to that area. Some friends and I went skiing in Whistler a few years ago. It's beautiful up there."

Dad and Uncle Pete and two of their buddies drove Dad's RV up to British Columbia every year to go fly fishing on the Birkenhead River when the salmon were running.

I grinned. "I'm sure he'll have a thousand pictures to show us. Along with plenty of salmon to cook." I pulled my house keys from my purse and opened the door. "Okay if we walk?"

"Sure. It'll give me a chance to check out the old neighborhood."

"It hasn't changed too much." I locked the door and we chatted as we walked north toward the town square.

She looked back over her shoulder at our family home. "You've really done a lot of work on the house."

"I like to stay busy."

She chuckled. "I remember."

I groaned. "That's right. You were still here when I went through that mess with Tommy. I was afraid I would drive my car off the pier if I didn't keep busy, so I revived the vegetable garden and started working on the house."

"Tommy was such a jerk."

"Yes, he was," I admitted. "But I don't really blame him. It was mostly Whitney's fault. She was determined to prove that she could steal him away from me . . . and hey, she did it."

"What a great basis for a marriage," Chloe said, scowling. "Just to prove she could get him to sleep with her before you."

I shrugged. "It worked for her."

"She got pregnant and set Tommy up just to hurt you." Chloe threw one arm around my shoulders and gave me a quick hug in solidarity. "She was a horrible person."

"She still is," I said lightly. "But look, these days Tommy and I are good friends again and it drives Whitney crazy."

Chloe laughed. "The best revenge."

"Yup."

"Something tells me you made out better than she did."

I liked to think so. "Well, she's got three cute kids and a darling husband. But then, her father recently lost all his money so she's probably suffering in her own special way."

"I hope so." She scowled. "I'm sorry to be so cold about it, but that's what happens when all you care about is money and status. It was that way with all those girls in the Mean Girls clique."

"They were pretty awful."

"I hated them so much."

I wrapped my arm around her waist. "I know."

Back in school, we both hated the "townies versus rich kids" attitude. Many of those rich kids had moved to town because their parents loved the lifestyle the town afforded them. After all, we had the beach, the marina, the rolling hills, the beautiful homes, and the nearby wine country. But some of the kids were unhappy with the move and took it out on those of us who were born and raised here.

Chloe had truly loathed the class structure that the wealthier kids tried to impose on us. The *townies.* Her anger blossomed and grew until things got ugly. During her freshman year in high school, Chloe's best friend, Madison, died of cancer. Chloe was bereft and some of the newer kids in her class mocked her for taking it so hard. There were fights. Chloe kicked the crap out of two of the girls and even one boy. After she was threatened with expulsion, Chloe resisted making new friends and even cut off some of her oldest friends when she saw them hanging out with any of the new kids.

And then an expensive plaque disappeared from the school trophy case. One of the mean girls falsely accused Chloe and she was actually arrested by the old police chief — until the real culprit was discovered.

Chloe figured that this was the way things were going to be for as long as she remained in Lighthouse Cove. No wonder she felt as if she had to leave.

Once she got to Hollywood, she realized that everyone she met was from somewhere else, which meant that they were all starting out on an even playing field. Chloe found it easier to make friends there and be happy again. Dad and I missed her, but we both knew she was better off where she was. As long as she was happy, that was all I cared about.

"Honestly, Shannon," Chloe said as we turned on Main Street. "I don't know how you survived high school, with all that nonstop drama. And then you actually stayed here. I couldn't wait to get out."

"I know and I understand. But I've always loved it here." I looked around my neighborhood and liked knowing everyone who lived in those tidy homes. I'd worked on many of them and being an important part of our town meant a lot to me. "I never wanted to move away. Of course, after Tommy, I was pretty miserable, but that had nothing to do with where I lived — although it wasn't easy having Whitney in my face every day at school. But I still had Dad and you and Uncle Pete and all my friends. And I had my job, which I loved. So I stayed. And I'm glad I did. I'm happy here."

Chloe gave me a long look, then smiled. "I'm so glad to hear it."

"I want you to be happy, too, kiddo. Don't get me wrong, I know you're a superstar so I can't feel too sorry for you."

She laughed and swatted my arm. "Very funny."

"I'd like you to come home more often . . ."

"I always mean to, Shan," she said. "But then I get busy — not really an excuse, though, is it?"

"No, but that's okay. I really do hope Bree backs off and leaves you alone."

She took a deep breath and exhaled. "You and me both, sis."

We were a few doors down from the restaurant when I saw a tall man standing in the shadows. "There's Mac."

Chloe whispered, "Are you sure? That guy looks dangerous."

I smiled. "He is."

MacKintyre Sullivan was a former Navy SEAL turned award-winning, bestselling thriller author. He had moved here about a year ago and had bought the famous lighthouse mansion on the beach just north of town. We met when I lost control of my bike out on Old Lighthouse Road, rode into a cow pasture, and flew over the handlebars. Mac witnessed the crash and carried me and my sad, mangled bike back home in his SUV. It wasn't a cute first meeting but it was memorable for sure.

As we walked closer, Mac stepped out from the shadows and smiled. "Hello there."

"Whoa," Chloe murmured.

"Hi, Mac," I said, chuckling at Chloe's reaction. I could relate. Mac was tall, dark, and gorgeous and had an air of danger simmering just beneath the surface. Like a modern-day pirate or something. I almost giggled, knowing he would love that description.

"Hey, Shannon," he said, pulling me in close for a kiss.

It took me a few seconds to come back to the moment, but then I turned to Chloe. "Chloe, this is Mac Sullivan. Mac, this is my sister, Chloe."

Mac beamed at her. "Hi, Chloe."

She mumbled a greeting and they shook hands.

"She's usually more expressive," I explained, "but she's had a long day." *And she doesn't often meet gorgeous ex–Navy SEAL guys on the sidewalk,* I thought, chuckling.

"Then let's go eat," Mac said jovially. He walked to the door and held it open for us.

I started to walk forward and Chloe yanked me back to hiss in my ear, "Why didn't you warn me? He doesn't look anything like his book cover."

"It wouldn't have done any good," I said. "He has to be seen to be believed."

It was true. His book cover photos showed a handsome, serious man, but in person Mac was much more striking and intriguing and, well, gorgeous. His hair was dark and short-cropped and his blue eyes could pierce right through you in the best possible way — unless you were a bad guy. He was muscular, tanned, funny, and smart. And when he smiled at you, the world lit up like a sunrise over the redwood forest.

At least, that was how it had always been for me. Best of all, Mac seemed to think I was pretty special, too, and that realization never got old.

We were shown to our table and within seconds the waitress brought us a basket of bread and a cruet of rich olive oil for dipping. We ordered a bottle of Uncle Pete's estate-bottled Pinot Noir and the busboy brought us glasses of water.

When the waitress walked away, Mac asked about Chloe's flight and the drive into town from Mendocino. We continued the small talk for another minute until the waitress brought the wine, opened it, and poured us each a glass. Then she took our meal orders, collected our menus, and promised to return with an order of fresh garlic toast. Because who didn't need more bread in their diet?

"So you start filming tomorrow?" Mac asked.

"We won't start filming the actual show," Chloe said. "But our second unit will start filming establishing shots around town. You know, for editing purposes and also to give an idea of where we are. They don't need me for that, so I'm going to spend part of the day checking out all the locations Bree lined up." Chloe looked at me. "You'll come with me, right? I'd like to grab a cameraman and you and I can record some stuff."

"Sure." Although I had a sudden neurotic moment wondering what I would wear. I figured Chloe would help me out with all those details later.

"Good," Chloe said. "It'll be fun. Oh, I know. We can start out by sitting on your front porch. I'll introduce you and we'll talk about Dad and how we grew up on construction sites, and then the camera can widen out and show your house. We can walk around and I can point out some of the highlights of the work you've done over the past few years."

"That sounds neat," I said. "Have you seen any of the houses you'll be working on? Bree kept it a mystery so I have no idea which ones she chose."

Chloe rolled her eyes. "Yeah, Bree likes to jack up the suspense and keep at least two homeowners guessing."

"So you don't even know what the work will entail?"

"Nope. She likes to wait until the owners are actually on camera and Blake announces which house we're going to rehab."

"Really?" I felt like I'd missed something. "I've never seen you do that on the show."

She grimaced. "They only play that segment of the show on the website. It's because the network hates it, too. They think it looks too much like a bad game show. And it rarely turns out happily."

"I can imagine," I said. "It sounds mean-spirited."

Chloe nodded. "It is, but that's Bree in a nutshell. The homeowners have no idea that they're in competition with each other. But Bree loves the drama and Blake's willing to play along because he loves Bree."

"If you've promised a home makeover to two different owners and only one of them gets it?" Mac shook his head. "It sounds like it could get ugly."

"I stay out of it. Like, *way* out of it." Chloe took a quick sip of wine. "Blake handles that part of the show. The cameras record the owners' reactions and there's usually some tears and some choice words. And then one of the PAs takes the loser away and we reset cameras and I'm there to start the real show. I introduce the house and take a little tour around, and then we move right into the demolition work."

"That's the fun part," I said.

"I agree," Chloe said. "So you can come with me tomorrow?"

"I'm all yours."

She gave me a thumbs-up. "Great. Mac, would you like to come to the set this week?"

"Me?" He was clearly taken aback, which didn't happen often. But he quickly recovered and grinned. "Absolutely."

"I'll give your name to Bree's assistant.

She'll get you a badge and you'll be all official."

"Cool. Thanks." He wiggled his eyebrows at me.

Chloe laughed. "And if you need any . . ." Her voice faded and she stopped talking.

"Need any what?" Mac asked.

But she was staring over my shoulder, apparently distracted by something happening near the front door of the restaurant. Her eyes were wide and her face had gone pale.

"What's going on?" I said, turning in my chair to see what had frightened her. I got a quick glimpse of a man talking to the hostess.

She grabbed my arm. "Don't turn around."

"Don't be silly. Why not?" I sneaked another look at the guy. He wore a pale blue polo shirt, had sandy blond hair, and wasn't very tall. I couldn't see his face, but there was something familiar about him. When I turned back to my sister I recoiled. "Chloe, you're white as a sheet."

"It's just . . ." She huddled down in her chair, hiding from whomever she'd seen. "I can't believe he's here."

"Who is he?"

Mac glanced over his shoulder, but then turned and leaned closer to Chloe. "Can I go after him for you?"

"No," she whispered. "I mean, thanks, Mac, but I can handle it."

"Handle what?" I demanded. "How can you handle anything when you're scared to death? Who's got you freaking out like this?"

She glanced past me and after a moment, she exhaled in relief. "I think he's gone."

"Who?"

"It's not important. Sorry. Got caught by surprise."

"Not important? Really?" I grabbed my wine and slugged it back. "Okay, drama queen, let's just forget that you looked ready to pass out. And never mind that you almost gave us a heart attack."

"I'm not a drama queen," she said, sounding wounded.

"No, you're a nutball." But I felt bad for raising my voice. Chloe's color was better but her eyes were still wide enough to have me concerned. I reached over and gave her hand a quick squeeze. "But you're *my* nutball, so I forgive you." I peeked back at the doorway. "Seriously, who was that? I couldn't see his face."

"He's . . . nobody. Really, it's nothing." She took her own big gulp of wine and grabbed a piece of bread. Her breathing finally calmed down. "Sorry I made a scene."

I leaned in. "If you don't want to tell me, just say so. But don't sit there and lie to me. Something's going on. We all know it." I scowled at her. "Besides, you scared Mac."

Mac flashed her a crooked grin. "And I don't scare easily."

She studied him for a long moment. "No, I don't guess you do." She took another deep breath and let it out. "Okay, I just saw a guy I never thought I'd see again. Especially after the last time."

"Who?" I demanded.

"What happened last time?" Mac asked.

She pressed her lips together in frustration. "He tried to blackmail me. I promised if I ever saw him again I would kill him."

Chapter Three

"What?" I might've shrieked the word.

Chloe slapped her hand over her mouth. "You did not just hear me say that."

"Yes, I did," I countered brusquely. And I wanted to hear a lot more. "What did he do to you? And who is he? Why was he trying to blackmail you? Why is he here? Tell me right now. What happened?"

"Okay, okay, calm down."

I think my eyeballs actually bulged right out of my head at that ridiculous statement. Someone tries to blackmail my sister, she threatens to kill him, and I'm supposed to keep calm? Impossible. "Calm down? You're driving me crazy. I can't —"

"Stop!" She hissed the word, then smiled cheerily at the waitress who walked up just then.

Mac put one hand on my arm and I felt that steady pressure as a sign of solidarity. I appreciated it. A lot.

"How are we doing?" The woman took her time, checking on the bread, pouring each of us more wine, letting us know our dinners were almost ready. Meanwhile, I was about to go bonkers. Maybe it was a good thing she was taking forever to leave.

When the waitress finally walked off, I disregarded Mac's steadying hand and jumped on Chloe. "Tell me everything before we're interrupted again."

"All right, all right. But first I need some fortification." She swirled the wine and then slowly sipped it.

"Seriously?" I leaned in closer. "*I'm* going to kill you."

Mac was no help. He'd given up trying to hold me down and instead, he now held up his napkin thinking he could hide the fact that he was laughing as I went bat-crap crazy.

Chloe swallowed carefully, then finally spoke. "Will you dial it down if I start talking?"

"No promises. But I can promise to go completely whackadoodle if you don't."

"Fine." It took her another moment. "Okay, do you remember Richard Stoddard?"

I blinked. "Sure. He's Whitney's cousin. How could I forget?" I turned to Mac. "We used to call him Richie Rich because he thought he was too good for all of us."

Mac nodded. "Similar to Whitney."

"Exactly." See? This was why I was crazy about Mac.

Chloe grabbed her head in agony. "I forgot he and Whitney are related. That just figures. They're equally horrible people."

"The difference is, Whitney is horrible, but she's smart. Richie is just plain slimy. And horrible."

"I think you've nailed it," she said.

"I don't remember meeting anyone named Richie," Mac said.

"He goes by Richard, and you would remember this guy," I said. "He's a pompous prig who looks down on everyone he considers beneath him. Which is almost the entire town."

"Why does he stay?" he wondered.

"My guess is," I said, "no other place will take him."

Chloe shrugged. "I thought most of his family lived here, but I really have no idea anymore."

I frowned. "I can't imagine they like him much, either."

The waitress rushed over with our salads, then offered ground pepper to each of us. She was an excellent waitress, but she was getting on my last nerve.

"So tell us what happened," I said when she finally walked away.

"Okay," Chloe said with a heavy sigh. "But it's a really long story."

"We've got all the time in the world," Mac said sensibly. "I mean, we just got our salads."

I smiled. "Mac is really good at solving problems. After all, he's a world-class plotter and he deals with serious issues in his books. Really, whatever happened to you, he can help. And so can I."

She grabbed a bite of salad slathered in blue cheese dressing, chewed and swallowed, then began. "I don't know if you remember, but the summer after high school, I was working with Dad on my friend Peggy's house. Her parents wanted to make some of the bedrooms bigger."

"Oh, sure, the Connolly house. Aren't we scheduled to expand one of her closets for your show?"

"Yes. And that's part of the long story."

I speared a lettuce leaf. "I remember that summer. You were partying a lot."

"I lacked direction," she said stiffly.

I chuckled. "One way to put it. I recall Dad trying to curtail your use of power tools."

"I was just kind of miserable." She sighed in memory. "It was time to move out."

I patted her hand. "I know." Chloe's restless spirit had really fought against all of Dad's attempts to rein her in. As much as they loved each other, they just couldn't communicate then. And I was no help at the time.

"You're distracting me."

"Sorry. Go ahead."

"So going way back to the fifties, Peggy's great-grandfather Joe owned the movie theater in town. He loved old movies and I guess he used to bring home his favorite film reels for safekeeping. He kept them hidden in an old closet upstairs." Chloe paused for another big sip of her wine and then pushed her salad around the plate. "And then he died. And apparently he didn't tell anyone in the family about these films, so they stayed hidden for like, sixty or seventy years or more."

"Wow," Mac mused. "They must be worth a lot by now."

"Wait for it." She took another quick sip of wine. "Now we detour back to Richie Rich. That same summer after high school, Richie decided he liked me. I don't know why, since he'd spent three years taunting me for being a townie. I guess maybe he was slumming."

"You were the prettiest girl in school," I said defensively. "Of course he was interested in you."

She smiled. "Yeah. Whatever. Anyway, he kept hanging around the Connolly house, begging Dad to give him a job so he could get close to me."

"Creepy."

"I know, right?" She gulped down a bite of salad. "Dad wouldn't hire him because he didn't like the guy, either. So one day Dad asked me to sweep out old Joe's closet because Peggy's parents wanted us to knock down a wall and expand the master bedroom. So I was sweeping and Richie was hanging around, not actually working because he's really just a lazy-ass jerk. Did I mention that before?"

Mac grinned. "Words to that effect."

Chloe smiled back and I was relieved to see it. Mac had that effect on people.

"It's true," she said. "So while I was cleaning out the closet, my broom accidentally snagged part of the old paneling and a strip of wood came loose. And that's when I found a false panel in the wall. And behind the panel were all these old movie reels. There were sixteen reels and they were amazing. Old films from the twenties and thirties and forties. Classic movies you've actually heard of. So Richie sees them and says, 'Let's take them and sell them.' "

"Did you?"

"Of course not." She looked at me as if she couldn't believe I'd even suggested it. Heck, I couldn't believe it, either.

"They didn't belong to me," Chloe said tightly. "I might've been a little flaky back then but I wasn't a thief."

The busboy arrived and cleared our salad plates. As soon as they were gone, the waitress showed up with our dinners. I took a moment to savor the amazing aromas. After we got all the extra parmesan cheese we wanted, plus more wine, the waitress said, "Enjoy your meal," and left us to chow down.

And we did. I swirled my pasta around my fork, dredged it through the Bolognese sauce, and took a bite. "This is heaven."

"Okay," I added, waving my fork at Chloe. "A small break to eat this amazing dinner, then it's right back to the story. Agreed?"

She nodded, since she was too busy chewing to talk.

"Good idea." Mac grinned. "And I'll need a bite of that."

I gave him a generous portion and Chloe and I traded bites, too. Mac fed me some of his rich, tangy Braciole.

"Oh, that's delicious."

"Yeah," he said.

"This is so good," Chloe said, twirling the capellini Pomodoro that she'd ordered with a side of meatballs. "I can't wait to see Uncle Pete and ask where he found his chef."

"You can ask him when he and Dad get home." I swirled my wineglass. "I thought we could grill steaks when they come for dinner tomorrow night."

"Or salmon," Chloe said. "You know they'll bring back tons of fresh fish."

"True." I glanced at Mac. "Either way, you're invited."

"Thanks, Irish." He smiled as he squeezed my hand. "I'd love to join you."

"Good." He looked at me with so much intensity that I forgot where I was for a moment. Finally he grinned at me and I remembered I was still on planet earth. Oh, boy. With a self-conscious laugh, I turned to Chloe. "Okay, so Richie wanted to take the film rolls, but you said no. So what happened then?"

Chloe winced. "Richie stole them."

Mac set down his fork. "What? He stole the films?"

"Yes. I left them neatly stacked in the

closet when I finished that afternoon. I knew they'd be perfectly safe there overnight, you know? And I was going to tell Dad about them and also explain to the Connollys where I'd found them. But when I got back the next day they were gone. I asked Dad if he had moved anything and he said no. All he said was that I did a real good job cleaning out the closet, but he didn't say a word about the film cans."

"So how did you know Richie took them?"

"He told me." She scowled and stared at her plate. "He bragged about it."

I shook my head in disgust. "What a crook."

"Yeah, and I was in a total panic. What if the Connollys were looking for those film reels?"

"Apparently they weren't," I said. "I've never heard a word about them, and you know how gossip spreads around here."

"Yes, but back then I didn't stick around long enough to find out. By then I had already made plans to move to Hollywood. I had a job lined up and an apartment."

"I remember." I nodded as the years rolled back. "We packed up your car and then Dad and I followed you in our truck and moved you into that first apartment in Burbank."

"Right. And I started my job at the talent

agency the next week." She smiled briefly. "So imagine my surprise when Richie walks into my office a few days later. He had driven down to Hollywood because he knew that would be the best place to unload the films."

"He should be in jail," I muttered.

"If only," Chloe said, winding several strands of capellini around her fork. "He told me he'd made a boatload of money selling them and I was a sucker for not going in on the deal with him."

"What deal?" I said. "There was no deal. He stole someone else's property and pocketed the money."

"That's what I said," Chloe assured me. "Not that it did any good. He was so sickening. He said that if I ever told anyone about this, he would make sure that Dad got blamed. And I believed him."

"But Dad wouldn't."

She waved the words away. "I couldn't be sure. I was young and stupid. And I was so mortified and worried about Dad. So I decided to track down the films and try to buy them back. In my mind, I figured that if the news got out that something so valuable had been stolen from one of Dad's clients, his reputation would be ruined forever. After all, I wasn't just on his crew, I was his daughter, his flesh and blood, and this was entirely my fault."

"But you didn't do anything," I insisted.

She gave me a look. "You know that wouldn't matter to the wealthy people who used to hire him to rehab their homes. And Richie was part of that crowd. He would've messed with the story enough to make it look like Dad had given me permission to steal the Connollys' property."

I shook my head and reached for my wineglass. "This is horrible."

"Yeah, it was pretty bad." She chewed her lip for a moment, then confessed, "I thought that if Dad couldn't work, he would spiral into some kind of deep depression. I mean, Mom was gone, so Dad would be left with nothing."

"Oh, Chloe. Did you really think that?"

She blinked away tears. "I didn't know what to think. It was a pretty crazy time. I was consumed with guilt."

I vowed to talk more about this someday, but for now I wanted to get back to her story. "Did you find the films?"

"Yes." She shook away the sadness by taking a quick bite of a meatball. "I finally found the auction house that had bought the reels from Richie, but by then the local film buffs had swooped them up. So now I didn't know what to do. If I told the auction house that the films were stolen, the truth would come out and Dad's reputation would suffer."

"Don't you think your father could've dealt with this?" Mac asked quietly.

"I was just a kid," she said. "I didn't know what to do. The one thing I did know was that it was my fault. If I had just told Dad about the films right away when I found them, none of this would have been happening. But I was always getting in trouble in school and I figured everyone would believe that I'd stolen the films." She shook her head and reached for her wineglass. "I was so guilt-ridden. I knew I couldn't come back to Lighthouse Cove until I found those films and returned them to the Connolly family."

"Oh, honey." I jumped up and gave her a hug. "Is that why you never came back?"

"Pretty much." She hugged me back hard enough to convince me that this had been haunting her for years and that it was a relief to get it all out.

"I'm so sorry you had to go through this all by yourself."

"It's crazy, isn't it? All these years. I was driven to recover them all. And I did, one film at a time."

I sat back down. "Wait, didn't you work at an auction house for a while?"

"Yes, I got a job at the same place Richie took those films. I was able to download a list of all the films and all of the buyers. I knew which reels they'd bought and how much they paid for them."

"You really went to a lot of trouble."

"I did. I felt like I owed the Connollys that much." She sighed. "It was only because of me that Richie was at their house to find the films in the first place. Now if I were Richie, I would've tried to steal them back from the people who bought them, but I couldn't do that."

"Of course not."

"So I saved my money in order to buy back as many of them as I could."

Chloe had been going through all of this for years and never shared it with any of us. Instantly, I was furious with myself. I'd known that something was wrong with my sister, but I'd never pushed for answers. I'd wanted her to come home. To trust me. I should have gone to her a long time ago and demanded she tell me what was going on with her.

I stared at Mac, feeling miserable. "I just can't believe she went through this."

He gazed at Chloe. "The story you're telling sounds like a plot for a movie."

She nodded. "Pretty intriguing, right? Sadly, though, the ending is a major disappointment."

"Why?" I asked. "What happened?"

"I actually managed to buy back a number of the films, but I was still missing a few. Then just last year I met the buyer who owned the rest of them. I knew I could get him to sell them to me, so I concocted a plan for *Makeover Madness* to come to Lighthouse Cove to do a special on Victorian houses. I called Peggy to see if she would like us to do a touch of rehab on her family home, for free, of course. She jumped at the possibility and I suggested expanding the closets. She loved that idea."

"So . . . what? You were going to sneak the film cans back into the house and leave them in the closet?"

"That's right. And I would miraculously unearth them and they could do what they wanted with them."

"Wow," I murmured. "Pretty elaborate plan."

She shrugged. "That's what happens when you've been living with a lie for so long. You tend to dwell on it constantly and build it up until you've got this great big crazy quilt of plots and possibilities."

I shook my head. Her story was exhausting as well as amazing. "So you met with the owner of the films?"

"Yeah. And he told me something kind of important."

"What's that?"

She exhaled heavily. "He said that those old celluloid film reels are very fragile and they disintegrate eventually."

"Oh my God," I whispered.

Absently, she waved her fork. "Well, I should've known it from the start. I mean, I worked in the movie business. Everything's digitized these days. I just never, well, I never considered that." She flashed us a weak smile. "But at least I'm pretty."

I laughed. "Stop it. You're smart and you're brave. You took action and you found out a lot of stuff that not too many people know. Anyway, keep going. I'm on the edge of my seat."

"Okay, this guy told me that the films would ultimately turn to dust and that the best thing I could do with the ones I'd already bought was to donate them to this nonprofit foundation that protects and preserves old motion pictures. Some big-name Hollywood directors started it and it's housed at the UCLA campus. It's kind of a big deal."

"Did they give you money for the films?"

"No." Her lips twisted in a wry smile. "Did you miss the part where I said 'donate'? It was considered a charitable donation."

"Oh, yeah." I frowned. "Well, I guess that's something to feel good about."

"It is. And I do. I feel good about it. It didn't help the Connollys any, but I'm determined to tell Peggy and her family everything that happened. I could've had the production company cancel the Lighthouse Cove trip, but I wanted to do this. I wanted to face the Connollys." She took a breath and shuddered it out. "I'm going to tell them that Richie Rich stole their great-grandfather's property. After that, it'll be up to them whether they want to try to get money from him."

"Good luck with that," I said. "I think I mentioned he's a slimy critter."

"The worst." She took a bite of her pasta. "So that's it."

I glanced at Mac, who looked slightly shell-shocked. I'm sure I had the same look on my face. "So that's why you rarely came back to visit. And the few times you have come back, you practically sneak into town so nobody will see you."

"Yeah." She shook her head, a little bemused. "I couldn't risk running into Richie, for one. And facing you and Dad was always hard because I felt so ashamed of myself. I mean, now I can admit I might've blown things out of proportion, but back then I was kind of a mess. If you combine my guilt over the stolen film cans with my bad attitude in high school, you end up with me feeling like the black sheep of the family."

"No way."

She smiled. "Yeah. And the longer I stayed away, the easier it was to just make up excuses for why I couldn't come home."

Some big sister I was, I thought. I reached over and rubbed her arm. "My poor little sis."

"Hey, I'm not poor," she said lightly. "I'm a superstar."

Smiling, I said, "I love you, Chloe. I wish I could've helped you get through this."

"I love you, too, sis. Thanks." She twirled more pasta, then glanced up at me. "Just so you know, I called Peggy Connolly on the ride into town earlier. I plan to tell her the whole story, too."

"That's pretty brave."

She gave a light shrug. "It's necessary."

We ate in silence for a minute, and then Mac spoke up. "I'm sorry you had to go through that, Chloe."

"Thanks, Mac. I know it sounds like a sloppy melodrama, but I learned a lot about myself in the process. And I'm not quite as guilt-ridden as I was, which is a good thing, right?"

"Yeah, since you were never guilty of anything in the first place." After a long moment, he continued, "Would you mind if we set up some time to talk more about this? It's a good story, Chloe. Fear. Survival. Redemption. Good stuff. I'd like to use it as backstory in my new book if that's okay with you. And if you'd rather not, I'll understand."

"Are you kidding?" Chloe said, her eyes lighting up. "I would love it."

Thrilled by Chloe's positive reaction, I reached over and squeezed Mac's hand. "Thank you."

"Nothing to thank me for. I'm glad you brought me along tonight."

"And we haven't even finished dinner," I said. "See? Not such a long story."

"Well, I can fill you in on the other six years of pain and anguish if you'd like." She slapped one hand to her chest, threw her head back, and said, "I was poor, but proud, walking through the heavy snows of Los Angeles to my rat-infested shack . . ." She paused, looked at us both, and then grinned.

We all laughed and finally settled down to enjoy the rest of our dinner. I had to admit I'd been nervous the whole time Chloe was talking. I had no idea what her story would entail, but it seemed to have come to a satisfactory ending. Yes, she had lost money buying back the film cans, but she had gained some pretty amazing insight.

But there was one loose end that worried me.

"What do we do about Richie Rich?" I asked.

"Tie him to an anthill?" Chloe said hopefully.

I nodded. "Medieval but effective."

"Hey, I've got friends . . ." Mac let the rest of that sentence die off, but since he had been a Navy SEAL, I appreciated the thought.

Chloe frowned. "Maybe I'll get lucky and never see him again."

"I wouldn't count on that," I said. "This is a small town and you're a superstar, remember?"

She made a face. "In that case, maybe I'll threaten him with a lawsuit."

"Or a restraining order," I suggested.

"There's your happy ending," Mac said with a grin.

■ ■ ■ ■

The next morning Robbie woke me up when Chloe let a camera crew into my kitchen. It was a small crew, just two guys, but it was a shock nonetheless. I gave Robbie a grateful scratching, happy that he had alerted me to throw on my sweats instead of my usual undershirt and shorts.

"I made coffee," Chloe said brightly.

I stumbled toward the coffeemaker. "And that's why I've allowed you to live."

She chuckled. "Good one. The guys got here a little early so they could set up some shots. I invited them in for coffee."

"Great." I turned to the two men sitting at the kitchen table. "Hi, guys. I'm Shannon. Welcome to Lighthouse Cove."

"Thanks, Shannon. I'm Gary." Thin, short, and nerdy, he was completely adorable. He held up his coffee mug. "Fantastic coffee."

"I'm Bob," the other guy said. He had to be over six feet tall and muscular and I wondered if he'd been a linebacker in a previous life. "Sorry to intrude."

"You're not intruding," I said weakly. "You just . . . caught me off guard. I'll get dressed and be down in about half an hour, okay?"

"While you get ready," Chloe said, "we'll finish our coffee and set up those outside shots we talked about last night."

"Sounds good. I'll meet you out there. Wait." I was awake enough now to realize that her hair was expertly coiffed and her face was beautifully made up. Her clothes were deceptively casual but now I noticed how perfectly they accentuated her figure and how the colors and fabrics seemed to bring out the blue in her eyes and the glow of her cheeks. I was going to look totally tacky next to my baby sister.

"Dang, Chloe," I whined. "You look like Contractor Barbie. Did someone come over to do your hair and makeup?"

Her eyes narrowed and she lifted her chin. "We have a makeup person on staff, but I'm perfectly capable of doing it myself. I know how to make myself look good on camera."

"Well, I don't." I wasn't sure if that was just a statement or a warning. "Maybe you'll give me some pointers."

The clouds in her eyes disappeared and she smiled. "You bet. I'll come upstairs in a few minutes."

"Thanks." Once upstairs, I managed to shower and dry my hair in fifteen minutes.

I pulled out my meager cosmetic bag of tricks and stared at the items inside. Except for mascara and lip gloss I rarely wore makeup, but now I was determined to give it my best shot. I used a little sponge to apply liquid foundation, then tried to fiddle with a highlighter under my eyes. I brushed on a touch of blusher and added a subtle application of eye shadow. I used a lip brush to add some color and finished up by carefully applying mascara. I didn't want to look like a raccoon. I just wanted to look fabulous.

"Not bad," I said to the mirror. But I was still missing that glow that Chloe had achieved.

Seconds later, she walked into the room carrying a small suitcase. "Okay, let's do this." She studied my face for a moment and frowned. "You don't need much help. Which makes me want to hate you."

"Oh, please. I look like a big-haired freckle-faced farm girl. Not that there's anything wrong with that. But you look chic and gorgeous. It's not fair."

"Give me a minute." She set the case on the counter and opened it to reveal more makeup than I'd ever seen outside of a department store cosmetics counter. First she wiped off as much as she could of the stuff I'd already applied. Then she used my small sponge to add her own industrial-strength foundation, blending it in with a lighter shade in the corners of my eyes and underneath my lashes. She added a pale whoosh of shadow under my eyebrows and redid my lipstick with something so gooey, I was afraid to speak for fear of my lips sticking together.

"That is serious stuff," I murmured, unwilling to open my mouth too much.

"That's how we superstars roll." Finally she grabbed a long-handled brush and stroked a perfectly angled layer of blusher onto my cheeks.

"There. You're perfect."

"Wow." I laughed when I looked in the mirror. It looked like me, but . . . glam. "I like it. How's my hair?"

"It's stupendous."

"Don't make fun. Shouldn't I pull it back so it's not so wild?"

"Maybe when we start doing demo, but for now it's curly and sexy and everyone will love it."

"Really?"

She gave me a look. "Yes, really. Now let's check out your wardrobe."

I led the way into my bedroom and slid my closet doors open. "It's, you know, pretty basic."

"Oh, I know," she muttered. "But hopefully we can find something that doesn't make you look like a truck driver."

"But that's my signature style."

"And it works for you," she said, laughing as she riffled through my shirts. "But we're going for something more along the lines of, well, hmm."

"Contractor Barbie?" I suggested dryly.

"Exactly." She pulled out several work shirts. "Which of these fits best?"

I pointed to my favorite shirt, a thin denim that looked good on me, if I did say so myself. "This one."

"Okay." She also reached for a navy blue henley and a pink tank top, then grabbed a pair of slim jeans, one black and one blue, and handed the stack of clothes to me. "Any combination of these colors should work for the camera. And layers are always good, so pick what you like best and meet me outside."

Somehow I made it out to the front porch ten minutes later and joined Chloe, who was sitting at the top of the steps. Bob the camera guy and Gary the sound man were standing on the walkway surrounded by a bunch of equipment. Bob had the camera pointed up at Chloe and Gary held a boom mic that stretched out and above her.

I sat down next to her. "How do I look?"

"Perfect," she cried, hugging me. "I love the pink tank under the denim shirt. Feminine and professional."

"Okay. Good." I was nervous. Why was I nervous? This was my house. My sister. My work. But I was doing it all in front of a camera that looked very intimidating.

"I'm so excited." Chloe grinned at me and gave me two thumbs up. "We're going to rock this show."

"I hope so." I didn't often have time enough to sit on the porch, so I took a moment to gaze around, enjoying the view. Our house had been built on a small rise, so from this vantage point I could watch sailboats bobbing in the marina, then turn the other way and gaze over the multitude of Victorian rooflines across town to the rolling green hills beyond.

I ran my hand over the smooth wood planks, pleased that my crew had done such a good job refinishing the porch. No splinters would find their way into our butts, thank goodness. And why that thought occurred to me at that moment, I had no idea. Still, I was grateful.

Bob adjusted the viewfinder on the camera

and stared into it. "Looking good, Shannon."

"Thanks, Bob," I said, absurdly pleased.

Chloe harrumphed. "What am I, chopped liver?"

"You always look ravishing, princess."

I elbowed her. "Seriously? Ravishing? Princess?"

"We have to call her that," Bob said. "It's in her contract."

"Oh, stop," she said, waving her hand at him. "I'm perfectly happy with 'Your Highness.' "

Bob and Gary both guffawed.

"I love these guys," I whispered.

Chloe smiled. "Me, too."

"I love you back," Gary said with a wink, and I realized he could hear every word we said. Duh, he was the sound man.

"Let's do a quick rehearsal," Bob said. "Chloe, you'll introduce Shannon and you two will chat for about a minute, right?"

"That's right," Chloe said with authority, starting to sound more like a director than a star. "Then we'll both stand up and walk over to the bay window. And as we're talking you can zoom in to get a close two-shot."

"Got it." He stared at the bay window for a moment. "You two should both stand on the far side of the window so I can get in there and show the details."

"Let's rehearse the move," Chloe said. "Are you ready?"

My heart began to beat faster. For heaven's sake. I was going to take a few steps on my own porch. I took a breath to steady myself and said, "Sure."

"Okay. We're talking, we're talking, I'll mention the window, maybe a few other style details, and then I'll say something like, 'Let's go look at that window.' And then we'll both stand up and walk across the porch."

"I can do that." It sounded easy enough.

"Let's see it."

We both stood and walked across the porch, ending up at the far side of the window.

"Okay right here, Bob?" she asked. "Can you move the camera in close enough?"

"That's perfect," Bob said. "It's like you've done this before."

Chloe shrugged. "Maybe once or twice."

Bob turned. "Gary, you okay with the boom?"

"Yeah, but I'm going to mic them both, too, just to cover my bases."

"Good idea."

"We're going to wear microphones?" I

asked. We walked back to the steps and sat down again.

"Yeah," Chloe said. "Little lavalier mics that clip to your collar. They'll pick up our conversation more clearly and the boom will be available to pick up ambient sounds. You know, birds chirping, the ocean waves in the background, the sounds of our footsteps, stuff like that."

"Huh. Interesting." I might be the older sister, but here, she was the expert.

Chloe gave me a shoulder bump. "Yeah. You don't really notice it, but those kinds of sounds add to the sense of place."

"You're pretty smart about this stuff."

She leaned close and whispered, "Superstar."

I laughed and smacked her arm.

She flashed me a wicked grin. "That's never going to get old."

I was grateful we were all joking around because if I wasn't laughing, I was afraid I would be fainting. What made me think I could ever do what Chloe did every day? I should've been slapping drywall mud on walls or replacing lead pipes in an old bathroom. That was my comfort zone. But this? Showbiz? When Chloe asked me to do the show with her, I should've refused politely. Now I was stuck. What if I tripped?

What if I flubbed my lines? What if I —

"Counting down," Bob shouted.

"Yay!" Chloe grabbed my arm. "Here we go."

Oh God, I thought. *I can do this.* I took a few more deep breaths. It felt like I was perched at the top of a roller coaster, staring down at a really long dip.

"Nine. Eight. Seven."

"I can hear you breathing, Shannon." Gary grinned. "Everything cool?"

Chloe chuckled. "You look like you're about to hurl. It's not a good look for television."

"I'll be fine." But I was still breathing heavily, still shaking, still wondering what in the world I was doing here.

"Five. Four."

Chloe grabbed my hand and whispered, "Just picture Whitney. You want her to see you floundering?"

My eyes widened. There was no way in hell I would ever allow Whitney Reid Gallagher to see me wilting like a chicken-hearted scaredy cat. I glared at her. "Well played, sis."

"Whatever works."

I gave her a determined thumbs-up. "Let's do this."

Chapter Four

Hours later I was still basking in the glory of my three brilliant minutes on camera. Despite having two men staring at me and recording my every breath and word, it had only taken a few seconds for me to feel completely natural talking to Chloe about construction and design. I held my own with her and even managed to toss in a few semiclever lines here and there. I could already see the headlines in my mind.

A Makeover Madness *Tour de Force.*

Shannon Hammer Nails It. Yeah, that was a good one.

"Okay, see you soon," Chloe said, interrupting my reverie by wrapping up her phone call. "Bree and Blake finally made it to town. I've got to go meet them and pick up the shooting schedule. And I can introduce you to everyone."

I couldn't help but notice her pressing her hands together. Was she nervous about introducing me to her co-workers? Then I got it. "Let me guess. You'd like me to be the buffer between you and Bree."

"Yes, please. I know I sound like a wimp, but if you're there with me, she's more likely to behave herself. Plus I won't have to stay and hang out with them all evening. I'll tell them we've got to go check out the work sites."

I was bummed that Chloe thought she needed backup. She should've been on top of the world with her job and happy to be around her co-workers, but Bree seemed to be poisoning the whole experience. "Of course I'll be with you. And you don't sound like a wimp."

She gave me a sideways glance. "Oh, sure. I'm cowering behind my big sister so the mean lady won't attack me."

I smiled. "When you put it like that, you do sound like a wimp, but I'm still going to stick close by you. And besides, you handle her just fine all on your own back in Hollywood, so don't be so hard on yourself. And to tell you the truth, I really want to meet Blake. And I'd like to see Bree again now that you've confirmed that she's a crank."

"I really appreciate it," she said, clearly relieved.

"I'm happy to be your buffer anytime. But

don't expect me to be too friendly with Bree after what she did to you." I considered taking one of my hammers with me as a defensive weapon, just in case. Probably not a good idea.

Chloe waved off my concerns about Bree. "She probably doesn't even remember firing me."

"If that's true, then she really is psycho."

My sister gave it some thought. "I've always figured she was just too self-involved, but psycho might apply, too."

We had finished filming our front porch segments an hour ago and Gary and Bob had taken off. They planned to drive around town to film various shots of Lighthouse Cove, then grab some lunch. I'd given them a list of the best places to shoot, including our pretty town square, the old fishing pier, the beach, some of the pastureland outside of town, the old wooden water towers that dotted the landscape, the breathtaking Alisal Cliffs south of the marina, and the myriad of beautiful Victorian homes everywhere in town. And if they still had time, I suggested they might want to drive three miles north and check out the lighthouse.

Once the guys had left, I'd fixed sandwiches for me and Chloe and then we ran to the grocery store to pick up something special for dinner.

Earlier that morning, we had heard from Dad, who gratefully accepted our invitation to come for dinner. He admitted that they'd had their fill of salmon for a while and put in a request for steaks, which always sounded good to me. At the market I found five beautiful rib eye steaks, plus a bunch of asparagus, baking potatoes, a tub of sour cream, and ice cream for dessert. I already had all the makings for a big salad in my backyard vegetable garden.

Now I set our dishes in the sink and turned on the hot water. "I'll be ready to go in five minutes."

She was staring at her phone. "Dad just texted me again. They're two hours away and will definitely make it for dinner."

"Good," I said, chuckling, "since we already went shopping for steaks."

"I just sent him that message," she said. "He sent back a happy-face emoji and a heart."

"Aww, sweet." When the lunch dishes were stacked in the drainer, I dried my hands and hung the towel over the edge of the sink. Then I texted Mac to let him know that dinner was on tonight and when to show up. When I finished texting, I turned to Chloe. “Okay, I’m ready whenever you are.”

“Just have to run upstairs for one minute and then I’ll be good to go.”

Five minutes later we left through the back gate. I was about to climb into my truck when I realized I had no idea where we were going. “Is your boss staying at Jane’s B and B?”

Chloe stopped, too. “That’s where she’s sleeping, but we’re using a couple of suites at the Inn on Main Street as production offices while we’re here.”

“So we’re headed to Main Street?”

“Right,” she said. “The production assistants came to town a few days ago to set up the office equipment and arrange work spaces and stuff.”

“Then we should probably just walk.”

She gave me a crooked grin. “I live in LA, so walking rarely occurs to me. But it’s barely two blocks away, right?”

“Yup. Let’s hoof it.” I looped my arm through hers and started down the driveway to the sidewalk. But then I stopped. “We talked about driving around and checking out the work sites after you finish playing nice with Bree. You still want to do that?”

“Sure.”

“Then we should drive.”

She patted my hand. "I'm glad we had this little chat."

I laughed as I dragged her back to the truck.

The production office was buzzing with activity when we arrived. I waited near the door as Chloe grabbed Blake Bennett and pulled him toward me. "Blake, this is my sister, Shannon Hammer. Shannon, this is my co-host and partner in crime, Blake Bennett."

He pulled a toothpick out of his mouth and grinned as we shook hands. "Shannon, I've heard great things about you."

"Hi, Blake. Thanks." I gave Chloe a quick smile. "That's nice to hear."

Blake Bennett was very good-looking in a rugged-cowboy kind of way. I supposed it was a good look for a manly guy who worked on a show where he was hauling tools around and swinging sledgehammers for fun.

But I was frankly shocked to see how much older he looked in person. Blake was probably somewhere in his late forties. I wondered how much makeup he would have to wear to look so much younger. A lot, I guessed.

I had to admit that personality-wise, he and Chloe made a good pair — even if

Chloe did most of the heavy lifting on the show.

Blake glanced from me to Chloe and back. "You guys don't look much alike."

That was something we'd heard our entire lives. The truth was that Chloe had been born with straight, light strawberry-blond hair and when she was old enough, she started coloring it to make herself a "real" blonde. The look suited her.

And my big wavy red hair suited me, too.

"I look more like my dad, and Chloe takes after our mom," I explained briefly. It wasn't exactly true, but that kind of stuff was nobody's business, was it?

He smiled and I noticed he had fabulous white teeth. "Well, you're both beautiful," he said. "And talented. I meant it when I said that Chloe's said good things about you."

"Has she?" I glanced again at my sister. It was great to know that even though we didn't spend much time together anymore, Chloe still thought of me as much as I did about her.

"Of course." Chloe smiled. "I wanted to feature you on this set of shows, so I talked you up. Told them how you run the family company and how generally awesome you are."

"Yup," Blake said. "We're all looking forward to working with you."

"Thanks, Blake. I'm really excited about it."

"We are, too." He gave a little salute.

"Here's your coffee, Blake," a girl said from behind me.

I turned and realized she was a woman, not a girl. But she was so petite and her voice was so high that I'd mistaken her for someone much younger. Probably not the first time that had happened.

"Thanks, kid," Blake said, taking the mug from her.

"Hey, Chelsea," Chloe said. "This is my sister, Shannon." She gave me a glance. "Shannon, Chelsea is Blake's assistant."

"Chelsea," I said, smiling. "Nice to meet you."

Chelsea assessed me for so long that I wondered if she thought I might be vying for her job. She had wide blue eyes and amazingly pouty lips, and I wondered for a moment if she practiced that fish-face look in the mirror. But then she smiled briefly and I felt guilty for having that snotty thought. "Hi, Shannon." She turned back to Blake. "I'm going to the store to buy your sodas and I'll put them in your trailer. Be sure to call me if you need anything else."

Blake didn't look at her, just waved. "Got it."

She frowned as she walked out of the office. It was clear that Chelsea had a crush on Blake. Did he know? He seemed oblivious of the woman.

Chloe took me around the room to introduce me to everyone else in the office. I didn't see Bree anywhere, but I met the accounting clerk, a couple of their equipment drivers, and the two production assistants, Carolee and Lorna. Carolee handed each of us a copy of the shooting schedule.

We both took a moment to read through it. "So we start shooting tomorrow morning at the Bloom house."

"I see that."

"Did you also notice our call time?"

"Uh, yeah. Ouch."

"Add two hours to that for hair and makeup and setup and rehearsal."

"Two hours?" I stared at the rundown. Yes, I was pleasantly surprised that they'd chosen the Bloom house, but if they planned to shoot the first scene at seven o'clock in the morning, it meant that we would have to be on the set by . . . five o'clock?

"Oh dear God." I was used to getting to a construction site early, but this was a lot earlier than that. If that was going to be our schedule every day, it would take some getting used to. But at least the Bloom family wasn't residing in the house, so we wouldn't have to dislodge anyone at the crack of dawn.

I decided to stick with the bright side. "I'm glad Bree chose the Bloom house. That's one of the ones I showed her. Margaret Bloom is a sweetheart and you'll love this house, Chloe. It's completely deserted and basically falling apart, but it's totally worth saving. It'll be gorgeous when you're finished with it."

"Can't wait to see it." She studied the rundown. "But, Shannon, they have another house listed here, too. The Wagner house. Do you know the family?"

I skimmed farther down the rundown to find the address of the second residence. It took me a minute to place the house in town. "If it's the house I'm thinking of, it's been bought and sold a bunch of times and the different owners have done some weird add-ons. I don't know the people living there now."

"I think their name is Wagner," Chloe said somberly.

"Wow, good guess. Is that why they call it the *Wagner house*?"

She grinned. "Yep."

I laughed, but quickly sobered as I read more details. "This says that *both* families are scheduled to show up first thing tomorrow morning." I leaned in close and whispered, "Is this where Blake announces which house they've decided to work on while the owners are standing there?"

She grimaced. "Yeah."

"And you and I won't be on camera for that, right?"

"Right. Remember I told you that Blake does that segment by himself?"

"I remember, but . . ." I read it over again. "So looking at the rundown, we don't actually know which house we're going to be working on."

"No, but Bree does. She's scheduled all the equipment and supplies for one house or the other. It's a weird way to run a show, but like I said, she loves the drama."

"I'd say she loves chaos," I muttered, already worried about having to deal with disappointed — or worse, furious — people.

Chloe glanced around. "Yes, but don't say that too loudly."

Making a quick decision, I said, "I want to be there when they film Blake making the announcement."

"Are you sure, Shannon? It's kind of depressing."

"But if they reject the Bloom house, I want to know about it. I'm the one who suggested that Bree look at the house in the first place. And Margaret Bloom is an old friend. If she's rejected, I still have to live in the same town with her and her family." Just thinking about it made my stomach churn. "If I can do anything to help ease the disappointment, I've got to try."

"I know it's rough on everyone."

I nodded, mulling something over in my mind. "If Margaret loses out on the makeover, I might offer to do some work on their house for a discount."

"That's awfully nice."

I shrugged, feeling a little down, almost as if the Bloom house had already lost the competition. I really wanted to fix that house. And the thought that Bree would deliberately set people up to have the rug pulled out from under them irritated me. "I feel sort of responsible for dragging Margaret into this."

Chloe breathed heavily. "I hate Bree for doing this to people."

I decided to take heart in the fact that the scheduled "reveal" would take place at the Bloom house. That had to mean something, right? Ready to change the subject, I glanced at the second page of the rundown. "Looks like we've got Mac's deck and Peggy's closet scheduled for next week. And the Baxters' bathroom, too. And all that while we're refurbishing the main house, right?"

"Yes. Should be a fun-filled week."

"I don't know how you do it."

"It can get crazy but we always have a good time." She sloughed it off with the attitude that she'd been doing this for so long, it was old hat to her. "Plus we always have a full crew to pick up the slack while we're filming one segment or another."

"That reminds me," I said. "We talked about it on the phone, but you never said for sure whether you wanted to use any of my crew."

She looked perplexed. "Absolutely yes. I thought I told you."

"Maybe you got busy and forgot?"

She winced. "That would figure. I'm really sorry. But yeah, even though we bring in a huge crew to do a lot of the heavy-duty demolition and rebuilding, we always hire local crew to work with us on anything we need done immediately. I hope your guys are available."

"Definitely. I've got five people I can spare. One of them is my lead foreman, Wade Chambers. Do you remember him from school?"

"I do," she said with a grin. "He's a nice guy."

"And Sean Brogan," I added. "Does that name ring a bell? He's my lead carpenter. I thought I'd ask him to work with us, too."

"Of course I remember Sean. He's my friend Amy's big brother."

I was happy that she'd remembered. "That's right." I wasn't about to mention it to the production staff, but Sean had been a murder suspect last year after I discovered his older sister Lily's remains in the dumbwaiter of Mac's house. It was a long, sad story, but happily Sean had been completely exonerated.

All of a sudden I felt the energy in the room change. Carolee and Lorna abruptly stopped talking. The others turned and stared at the door as another man strolled into the office. I looked over, too, and the phrase *hubba hubba* popped into my head.

The man was built like he'd been carved out of marble. It helped that he wore a T-shirt tight enough to see his six-pack abs and muscular arms.

Chloe waved. "Oh, Diego. Come here. I'd like you to meet someone."

The other women watched him move as he walked toward us. With an easy grin, he gave my sister a big hug. "How're you doing, Chloe?"

"I'm super. Diego, this is my sister, Shannon. And this is Diego Navarro, our head carpenter."

"Hi, Diego." I reached out to shake his hand and he simply held mine in his.

"What a pleasure to meet you, Shannon," he said, flashing me a beautiful smile. "It's a treat to work with Chloe and I'm psyched to be working with you, too."

I caught a slight accent and as we shook hands, I tried not to stare. The guy was young, maybe early twenties, and drop-dead gorgeous. In another life he would've been cast as a superhero in some megablockbuster movie. Tall and muscular with dark hair, dark eyes, and bronze skin, he seemed as genuinely sweet as he was handsome.

"Thank you, Diego," I said, finally slipping my hand from his. "I think it'll be fun."

One of the bedroom doors opened and Bree Bennett walked out wearing linen palazzo pants and a tightly fitted tank top that showed off her tanned arm muscles to perfection. Glancing around, she spotted Chloe. "Oh, good, you're here. I'm just finishing up with Suzanne, but I want to see you in my office as soon as she comes out."

Apparently they'd set up one of the bedrooms to be Bree's private office. I shot a glance at Chloe, who looked slightly queasy. I wasn't at all happy that the producer wanted to see my sister alone. So much for being a buffer between the two of them.

"Sure, Bree," Chloe said in an upbeat tone. Then as soon as the woman closed the door, she turned and faced me. "I shouldn't be too long."

"It's no problem," I said.

Less than a minute later, another woman walked out of the designated office. She was tall and thin with long blond hair braided down her back. "Chloe!"

They hugged each other like long-lost friends.

The woman glanced at me with interest. "Is this your sister?"

"Yes, this is Shannon," Chloe said. "Shannon, this is Suzanne Roberts. She's our production manager, which means she's really important and we couldn't do any of this without her."

"Shannon, wow, it's so good to meet you." She shook my hand vigorously. "Chloe is my anchor. My rock. My everything."

Chloe laughed. "Oh, shut up."

I shook hands with her. "Hi, Suzanne." I liked her immediately, mostly because she really seemed to like my sister. It also helped that she had a wicked sense of humor. Gazing up at her, I realized, *Holy moly, this woman is tall.* At five foot eight, I considered myself tall enough, but Suzanne towered over me. She had to be over six feet.

"It's true, she really is disturbingly tall," Chloe said dryly, apparently reading my mind.

"And not *model* tall," Suzanne insisted with a lopsided grin. "More like, you know . . . awkward geeky tall."

"You're beautiful," Chloe said staunchly. "Anyway. Shannon, if you need anything, you talk to Suzanne. She keeps an eye on everything from the budget to scheduling to legal snags to . . ." She stared up at Suzanne. "What in the world do you actually do?"

"As little as possible," Suzanne said.

"She's kidding."

"Yes, I am." She looked at me. "Seriously, please let me know if you need anything. I'm here to help."

I nodded. "Thanks, Suzanne."

"Chloe," Bree called from the other room. It sounded like a commander barking an order.

Suzanne winced at the sound. "Sorry I can't stick around, but call me later."

Chloe gave her arm a squeeze. "I will."

She ran out of the suite and Chloe turned

to me. "I won't be long."

"Okay." I glanced around, then whispered in her ear, "If you don't see me in here, I'll be waiting in the bar."

"Excellent idea."

She walked into the bedroom office and closed the door behind her.

Diego coughed self-consciously. "So, Shannon, you've lived here a long time?"

"I was born and raised in Lighthouse Cove."

"It's a beautiful place."

"I've always loved it."

"I can see why." He gave me another cheerful smile. "So maybe you can give us some restaurant recommendations."

"Absolutely." I listed a few of my favorites off the top of my head. "Why don't I write up a list of other places to eat and things to do while you're here?"

"That would be awesome." His slight accent made everything he said sound seductive.

"I'll have it for you tomorrow. In fact, I can make a bunch of copies for whoever wants one."

"Thanks, Shannon. Everyone will appreciate it."

"I want you all to enjoy the town." Heck, if the crew enjoyed it and the show went well, maybe they'd come back and do another few episodes at some point. "It's a pretty cool place."

"I think I'll check out that pub tonight."

I grinned. "You'll like it."

He glanced toward the bedroom/office door and frowned slightly. "I should get going," he said. "Thanks again, Shannon. I'll see you tomorrow morning."

"See you then."

He started to walk away but stopped abruptly as shouting erupted in the bedroom.

"For God's sake, Bree! You can't do that."

My shoulders stiffened. That was Chloe shouting!

"Who's going to stop me?" Bree said.

"I am."

"That's the dumbest thing I've ever heard you say."

Shocked that my sister's boss would talk to her that way, I glanced around the room, but nobody would make eye contact with me. Was it because it was *my* sister doing the shouting? Or were they trying to ignore the fact that their boss was so aggravating and stupid? And did Bree insult Chloe like this all the time? Were they all accustomed to it? And if so, why would Chloe put up with it?

Diego wisely slipped out of the room.

I caught a strong whiff of shared guilt in the room, as if they were all part of a dysfunctional family and Mama Bree's whacko behavior was being revealed to an outsider, namely me. Now they couldn't sweep their dirty little secret under the rug.

No wonder none of them would look me in the face.

Or maybe I was imagining things. But I didn't think so.

Bree was murmuring something we couldn't hear, quickly followed by Chloe yelling again. "Damn it, Bree. You'll ruin everything."

"Does this happen all the time?" I demanded of anyone in the room.

"Bree can be . . . difficult," someone muttered. I think it was Carolee.

Difficult didn't hardly cover it, I thought, still surprised that my sister was yelling at her boss and being insulted in hearing range of her co-workers.

I couldn't stand being in that room a minute longer. Frankly, I didn't trust myself not to barge in there and tell Bree to stop treating my sister so horribly.

If Bree did anything to hurt her, I wasn't sure I'd be able to hold back from smacking her upside the head with my favorite all-purpose, solid steel sledgehammer.

I had to get out of there. "See you all tomorrow," I said loudly, and walked out. The sooner I got to the bar, the better.

But as I left the suite, I happened to glance down the hall. Standing at the separate entrance to the bedroom, with one ear pressed against the door, was Richie Rich.

What was he doing here?

It helped that his back was to me, but he was clearly so caught up in his eavesdropping he didn't notice me. As he listened, he checked his watch and huffed out an impatient breath.

After hearing Bree berate my sister for the last few minutes and now watching this jackass snooping around, I hit my boiling point.

"Hey!" I shouted. "Get out of here!"

He didn't even look my way to see who was yelling at him! Instead, he pulled the hood of his sweatshirt up over his head and scurried off in the opposite direction, disappearing around a corner.

"What a weirdo." I exhaled in frustration and walked off in the direction of the bar.

I couldn't wait to see Chloe and find out what all that screaming was about. I just hoped she hadn't been fired again. It didn't sound like it. No, it sounded like Bree was trying to pull off something stupid and Chloe was angry about it. I could feel the tension through that closed door.

The vision of me swinging that sledgehammer flitted across my mind and I blinked it away. Not that I would ever resort to violence, but the fact that I was actually envisioning it was not a good sign. I was a fairly even-tempered person, but don't screw around with my family!

The bar was almost empty except for a few people lingering after lunch. I sat down at a small table in the corner and ordered a beer. It was a bit early in the day to start drinking, but it was a warm afternoon and besides, I needed something to help calm myself down. The waitress brought it right away, along with a small bowl of pretzels, and I gave her a grateful smile.

"It's five o'clock somewhere," I muttered to myself, and took a sip. Relaxing into my chair, I tried to breathe more steadily as I gazed around at the people in the bar in an effort to take my mind off the scene I'd just left.

After a moment, I pulled the shooting schedule from my purse and stared at it, hoping I could make a list of things I needed to do to prepare for tomorrow. But

I couldn't concentrate. My brain was still playing over the words I'd heard Bree shouting at my sister. Chloe shouting back didn't seem so out of line when you considered that the boss had called her "stupid" at the top of her lungs. And besides the fact that I'd overheard Bree and Chloe arguing about something obviously important to both of them, I'd also caught Richie Rich listening in on the whole discussion. Why? What was he doing here?

"I hope you ordered me one of those."

I glanced up at Chloe. Relieved that she didn't seem to be crying or red with outrage, I managed a smile. "I didn't expect to see you so soon. Sit down." I waved at the waitress and ordered a beer for Chloe.

"So I assume you were still in the office when Bree and I went at it?"

"Yeah," I said. "Everyone was. It was awkward. Even more awkward would've been me storming in there and shutting Bree up myself."

"Sorry it upset you. And I appreciate your restraint. Honestly, what you heard seems to be happening more and more often lately."

Afraid of her answer, I winced as I asked, "Did she fire you?"

"Oh no. Today she loves me."

"That's *love*?" I broke a pretzel in pieces and bit into one of them as I shook my head in disbelief. "That would be a relief except for the fact that the two of you were blaring angrily at each other. The words I heard did not fill me with a feeling of love."

Chloe bit into a pretzel with enough power to snap steel. "That's because she's insane."

Just then the waitress brought Chloe's beer. Then she dashed off to fill other orders.

"So what's she up to now?" I asked. "What were you yelling about?"

Chloe sighed deeply. "Apparently she's firing her husband."

"Excuse me," I said. "I'm not sure I heard you correctly. She told you she's going to fire Blake?"

"No, no." Chloe waved her finger at me and took a sip of beer. "I misspoke. She's already done it. She fired Blake."

"But you said she doesn't mean it when she fires someone."

"Not usually. And Blake didn't look too upset earlier, did he?"

I shook my head. "Not at all."

Frowning, my sister said, "Maybe he was just playing it cool in front of the staff."

"Maybe."

"It would be just like him to pretend everything was fine. But this time I'm not so sure she doesn't mean it."

"What's different about this time?"

She took another deep breath and let it out. Then she leaned in and said very quietly, "She told me that one of the big networks wants to mount a brand-new home improvement show. We're talking big budget, big salaries, prime-time slot. And they want me to host it."

"But, Chloe, that's fantastic," I said.

"Oh, it's great. Don't get me wrong. I'm thrilled." She took another sip of beer. "Except my co-host would be Diego Navarro. They're planning to push Blake out of the picture."

Ah. Well, hadn't I just been mentally tallying that Blake was kind of old for the job? And that Diego was hunkalicious? Still, didn't loyalty count for anything in Hollywood?

"But . . . Blake is the star," I said. "I mean, so are you, but wasn't he the one who created the show in the first place?"

"Exactly right." Chloe slumped back in her chair. "That's what I told Bree. And besides that, the viewers love him. You should see how the fans come out whenever we show up anywhere. He's got legions of followers, and not just women. Guys love him, too."

"Diego's kind of gorgeous," I said lamely.

She chuckled. "Totally. Everyone loves him, too. But I'm not sure he's a real star."

"Not yet," I said. "But I have a feeling he's going to be huge someday. He's . . . I don't know how to describe it. He's magnetic. Hypnotic. I kind of couldn't take my eyes off him."

"Yeah, I get that," she admitted wryly. "And I really like working with him, mostly because he actually *works.*"

"What do you mean?"

She turned and scanned the room to make sure we weren't being overheard. "Okay, have you ever watched the show and noticed how Blake can describe exactly what we're going to do in a room and then in the very next scene, he's gone and someone else is doing the work he just described? Usually me or Diego."

I stared at her. "I've never noticed that. Sorry. I mean, I watch the show, but . . . are you serious?"

"That's okay," she said quickly. "You're not supposed to notice. But the fact is, Bree won't let Blake do any real carpentry or construction. What he does is point and describe and lead the camera around, giving a little history of the house and architecture and stuff like that. He searches out old fixtures and he talks about the dangers of lead pipes, anything that involves speaking to the camera. And basically, he looks good doing it."

"But you can't be serious about him not working. I saw him start a demolition project just the other night. He had a sledgehammer and . . ." I tried to recall the segment I was watching. "Okay I can't actually remember if he swung the hammer and broke through the wall. Wow. That's weird."

"You didn't miss it, because he didn't do the actual demo," Chloe said with confidence. "He talks about it. He looks at the camera and grins and tells people exactly what he's going to do, and he kind of goes through the motions, picking up the hammer or the power drill or whatever. And then we always cut away."

Hollywood was starting to sound even more bizarre than I'd believed. "But why? He seems perfectly capable of breaking down a wall or hanging drywall or whatever it is you're doing."

"*Seems* being the operative word. He's a klutz. The last time he used a ball peen hammer he came close to shattering his knee. Walked with a limp for weeks."

"Oh, come on."

"And he almost poked his eye out with a screwdriver." Laughing a little to herself, Chloe went on. "I'm not making this up. I've seen it for myself. Seriously, the man is a menace around tools."

I felt like someone had just told me the Easter Bunny wasn't real. "But that's crazy. I can't believe it."

Chloe took another sip of beer. She reached for the cocktail napkin and absently began to shred it. "When he was younger, Blake was on top of everything. And yeah, he did create the show himself, and when he met and fell in love with Bree, he made her the executive producer. But over the years, he's lost his touch." She shrugged as if she'd gone over this with herself time and time again. "I don't know, maybe he's been doing it too long? Maybe he doesn't really care? Don't get me wrong, he's still a great businessman, but just not much of a tool man. Not anymore. Except he *looks* the part of a brawny contractor type, so people believe what they want to believe."

I shook my head, feeling a little dazed. "I'm blown away."

"That was my reaction, too." She nodded sagely. "And to tell you the truth, I didn't even see it for the first few months I was working with him. The director and Bree would go over the series of shots with me and Blake, and they would act like it was all perfectly normal. Blake's job was to explain what was about to happen and then the crew and I would step in and actually *do* the work."

"Weird."

"And it's gotten even worse since he hired Chelsea. If Bree suggests that he do the smallest thing that isn't scripted, Chelsea whisks him away before Bree can finish the sentence. Poor Chelsea. She's in love with the wrong man. No matter how toxic we all think Bree is, Blake has blinders on. He really loves her."

"I don't get it." I sat silent for a long moment, biting off bits of a pretzel. "So tell me about this new show."

She took a breath, had a sip of beer, and set the glass down again. "It's major, Shannon. They've got these huge sponsors backing the show and it's going to premier right after the Super Bowl next year."

"Holy moly. That's huge."

"I know! The head of the network is flying up here sometime next week to meet with me and Diego." She slapped one hand to her belly. "God, I just realized I'm nervous."

"Who wouldn't be? But it sounds like an

incredible opportunity. And nobody deserves it more than you."

"Aw, thanks. I hope it works out because I really hate the idea of leaving a show I love to start something completely new."

I munched on yet another pretzel for another moment. "So why, exactly, were you yelling at Bree?"

Her shoulders drooped. "You couldn't hear what she was saying in the beginning, but it was pretty bad. She just kept ranting, saying awful things about Blake. I don't like that she's going along with what the network wants and not protecting Blake. So I defended him. For all the good it did. The thing is, maybe he doesn't do the construction work anymore, but he's really good at the chatter. He's funny and charming and like I said, the audience loves him. And that's as important to me as having someone who can swing a hammer, you know?"

I shook my head at the thought. That might've worked on her show, but it didn't apply to real life. On a real construction site, if someone couldn't do the work, I would have to fire them, plain and simple. It didn't matter if they were charming and funny. But then, *Makeover Madness* wasn't real life; it was showbiz. And despite the fact that my sister and I both worked as building contractors, I was beginning to see how very different Chloe's job was from mine.

"By the way," I said, "just for the record, you're funny and charming on the show, too. But I understand what you're saying. Blake is your friend and he was responsible for getting you the job. You feel you owe him."

"I do," Chloe said. "I owe him a lot more than I owe Bree."

"But she seems to hold the power."

"Yeah. It made me so sad to hear her say all that stuff about her own husband. And my friend."

"You didn't sound sad. You sounded angry as heck."

"I was. Still am." She rolled all the little bits of napkin into a ball. "So now I'm torn. I can't turn down the network job, but I feel horrible about Blake."

"But won't he keep working on *Makeover Madness*?"

She stared at me, looking floored. "Dang, that's a good question. I didn't even ask. Bree bulldozed right past all of my protests and told me to shut up and be ready to meet the network honchos next week."

"So no room for discussion with that one." I thought about it for a minute. "But she did say that the network wants you. Does that necessarily mean they'll hire her to produce the show?"

Chloe pondered that. "Honestly? I have no idea. I was so discombobulated, I didn't even ask the right questions. I'm not sure she would've answered me, though. She likes to withhold information sometimes. It's a power play. Anyway, for this network show, she's acting like it's a done deal. No more discussion."

"Maybe you could ask Suzanne about it."

"Good idea. I'll do that." She finished her beer and reached for her tote bag. "Are you ready to go?"

"No. Wait." I waved her back into her seat. "Sit. I haven't mentioned a very important detail."

She sat back in her chair. "What is it?"

"As I left the suite, I happened to notice someone standing in the hall outside the bedroom door, listening to your loud conversation with Bree."

She made a face. "Who was it?"

"It was Richie Rich."

"What?" she shrieked.

"Shh!" I glanced around to make sure the whole room wasn't watching us. But nobody was paying us any attention, a good thing.

"What in the world was he doing there?"

she wondered. "What a creepy little snoop."

"He totally is. He checked his watch at one point, like maybe he was late for something. I confess I was so angry after listening to your stupid boss yelling at you that when I saw Richie, I shouted at him."

"You did?" Her eyes lit up. "What did he do?"

"He didn't even look at me. He knew he was caught, though. He threw his hoodie over his head and scurried off in the opposite direction."

"Coward. He's so icky." She pondered it for a moment. "Do you think he was following us?"

"I wouldn't have thought so, but after the story you told us last night, I wouldn't put anything past him."

"Me, either." She grabbed one last pretzel and finished it off.

"Maybe he knows Bree," I said. "She was visiting here for a few days last month."

"Oh, yeah. They might've met during that visit."

"He's a real estate agent now, so it makes sense." I thought about it for a moment. "Remember how I told you she wanted to 'spread the joy?' She was planning to meet with a number of real estate agents while she was here."

"She does that. When we're about to go on location, she'll line up a few meetings with local agents to look at a whole variety of houses. So one of those agents could've been Richie."

"Seems logical."

"And she's such a flirt," Chloe added, her lip curling in distaste. "Anything could've happened between them. Can you picture it?"

"Those two together?" I squeezed my eyes shut and waved her words away. "I don't want that image in my head."

"I don't blame you. I'd like to think that Bree is more discriminating than that. Richie is way too slimy for her taste."

"I hope you're right."

"Me, too." She grabbed her bag and stood. "Let's get out of here before one or both of them walk in and ruin the rest of our day."

Chapter Five

On the drive over to the Bloom house, I remembered to call Wade to find out how our newest crew member was getting along with the rest of the guys.

"It's a regular love fest out here," Wade said. "No worries."

I frowned. "Is it really going well or are you just trying to get me to stop worrying?"

"Is it working?"

I had to think about it for a few seconds. "I guess so."

"Good." He chuckled. "Seriously, it's going great. In fact, we're all going to the pub tonight and Niall's buying the first round. Care to join us?"

"I would love to, but my dad and uncle are coming over for dinner tonight."

"Ah. They're back from their fishing trip?"

"Yes, and he announced that they're officially sick of salmon so we're grilling steaks."

"Steaks, huh? Well, have fun. I'll keep you posted on how it goes at the pub."

"Thanks, Wade. Text me if anything wild happens."

"You bet. Talk to you later."

I disconnected the call and turned right on Shorebird Street.

"So who's Niall?" Chloe asked. "And why are you so anxious to make sure everyone gets along?"

"Niall is my friend Emily's brother. He just moved here from Scotland. He plays rugby and he used to be a history professor and Emily informs me that he's quite a good drinker." I glanced at Chloe and grinned. "He's also an artist with brick and stone, so I was excited when she told me he was moving here and looking for a job. I hired him to build a retaining wall at one of my job sites and I just wanted to make sure everyone was getting along. I mean, first of all, he's Emily's brother. And second, it's good to get along with the people you work with."

"I agree."

I shrugged. "I've got a great crew and it always makes me nervous to add someone new to the mix. You know, upset the balance or whatever."

"So true. He sounds interesting."

"Doesn't he?" I grinned at her again. "I haven't officially met him, but Wade said that he's been playing well with the others, so they're all going out to the pub tonight."

"And Wade's going to keep you posted?"

"Knowing Wade, he'll text me a minute-to-minute breakdown."

She smiled. "It's nice that you and the guys on your crew are so close."

"We're all friends. You know a lot of them, since most of them go all the way back to grammar school with me. I've got a couple of women on the crew now, too. It's fun having them around."

"I love working with other women. It's such a rare treat."

"I agree." I turned left on Bayberry Lane and was shocked to see a long row of large trailers and huge semi trucks parked on the opposite side of the street from the Bloom house.

I wouldn't normally leave my pickup in a client's driveway, but there was no room on the street so I pulled in and parked. "Are all of those trucks here for the show?"

"Yes. Most of the crew got here yesterday so they're probably still setting things up."

We got out of the truck and I scanned the lineup across the street. "What do you use them for? Are they all dressing rooms?"

Chloe pointed. "Those first three are dressing rooms and the one behind that is our mobile production office. Then comes the wardrobe, hair, and makeup truck. And that big honkin' semi down there is filled with film and lighting and sound equipment. And that last one on the end, the one that looks like a horse trailer? Those are actually the portable bathrooms. The truck goes by many other names, but we'll keep it clean for now."

"Are there a bunch of trucks over at the Wagners' house, too?"

She shrugged. "We'll have to go over there and find out."

I couldn't imagine they would go to the trouble of parking a bunch of trailers and trucks at both houses, so I hoped this meant that the Bloom house was the one chosen for the makeover. But I kept quiet for now. Gazing up and down the street, I shook my head. "The neighbors must love this."

"Believe it or not, they're usually pretty cool about it," she said. "I mean, it's a little hectic and congested for a few days, but the production company sends out letters to everyone on all the adjacent streets giving them the dates we're filming and warning them about the traffic. We also offer to let them come and watch the filming and meet the 'stars.' And they're welcome to visit the catering tables for coffee and donuts. Most people are excited about it and don't get too riled. And we're usually only here for a few days. A week at the most."

"You finish a whole house in a week?" That was way impressive, even for Hollywood.

She laughed. "No. It takes a few months. But we shoot the main intros and the big demolition work in those first few days and then we've got a crew that stays on to finish the rooms and paint the exterior. After that we bring in a landscaping company to make the whole thing look pretty. And then our film crew and Blake and I come back for a day or two to take the beauty shots for the results show."

"It's showbiz magic."

She grinned. "You got it."

"So," I said, turning and spreading my arms wide. "Here's the Bloom house. Do you love it?"

It was after two o'clock and the surrounding trees were beginning to cast shadows against the walls, lending the home a spooky quality that gave me shivers.

From the street the front lawn stretched for almost fifty yards, leading to a wide set of stairs running up to a veranda that covered the front of the house and curved around one entire side.

"It's fantastic," she said, gazing up at the three-story Victorian. "You're right. This is going to be magnificent when we finish with it."

"I'm glad you see what I see." I frowned as my doubts took over. "But it's so run-down, I worry that Bree will think it's too much work for you guys."

"No, it's perfect," Chloe said, approaching the veranda. "Look at how that beam above the veranda is sagging."

"I know. Bree might not want you to do this much work."

"But that's the whole premise of the show. We can turn this into a palace." She looked at me and winked. "Hollywood or not, I'm still our dad's daughter. We can work wonders on this old beauty."

"I know we can. I just hope Bree makes the right choice."

We walked around the outside of the house. Chloe stopped to test the strength of one of the railing balusters that lined the raised porch and gasped when it came off in her hand. She gave a rueful laugh. "Yeah, definitely needs work."

"Every aspect of the place is just sad."

"But that's a good thing. *Makeover Mad-*

ness, baby."

I smiled. "Okay, I'll hold on to that thought." I took the baluster from her and scrutinized it. "These balusters are classically Victorian. We should try to save as many as we can. They can be stripped and filled, and then sanded and repainted, but it'll take a while."

"Yeah. And those posts will have to be replaced."

"Along with the wood plank flooring."

"Definitely." We came back around to the front and Chloe decided to test the steps leading up to the porch. She made it all the way up without falling through a hole, but I thought she just got lucky. "We'll have to check these steps more closely when we have time."

"At the very least they'll need sanding and painting."

After spending another fifteen minutes examining the clapboard wood siding — which would have to be replaced — and the windowsills and shutters at the front of the house — which needed new hardware and paint — Chloe turned to me. "I guess I've seen enough for now. Should we go check out the competition?"

"Good idea. Let's make it quick, though. We still have to get home and start dinner."

Back in the truck, I pulled out the show rundown and checked the address for the Wagner house. "It's just a few miles away."

Ten minutes later we pulled up in front of the place. There were cars parked in the driveway so we didn't get out of the truck.

"It's a good paint job anyway," Chloe allowed.

I glanced around. "I imagine each new owner did a little something when they moved in. It still needs a lot of help, a new roof for one thing, but it's in much better shape than the Bloom house."

"Looks like some of those owners added a few modern touches." She pointed toward the front porch. "Those fan brackets look plastic."

"They seem more western hoedown than Victorian. They don't even go with the look of the columns." I frowned up at them and then realized that my sister and I had the same expression on our faces. Dad would be proud.

"And all that rickrack and fake gingerbread along the eaves? It looks a little frantic."

"We could tone it down, I guess, but I really hope Bree runs away from this one."

"Me, too."

I peered up and down the street. "Have

you noticed there are no film trucks parked anywhere?"

"I hadn't noticed."

I laughed. "Oh, sure." My spirits rose slightly. "I've got to think it's a good omen for the Bloom house."

"It is, but you didn't hear that from me."

"I won't say a word," I promised, but happily clapped my hands. "I'm cautiously optimistic."

"I am, too. The Bloom house is a much better fit for the show. It's such a classic style and it's in the worst shape, so we can make a real difference there. I can't wait to get started."

As I pulled away from the Wagner house, I frowned. "I just hope the Wagner family doesn't get too angry when they find out their house isn't getting a makeover."

Twenty minutes later, we were home and Chloe was picking out her wardrobe for the next day while I went out to the garden to pick veggies for our dinner salad.

The basket was already full with leaves of romaine and butter lettuce, two carrots, a bunch of radishes, and clumps of various green herbs, when Chloe walked out followed by Robbie.

She sat down on the side of the raised bed.

"You've done an amazing job with Mom's garden."

"Thanks. You know how important it was to me during my senior year. I can't ever see myself letting it go to seed again."

Our mother had been a horticulturist and a botany professor at Lighthouse College. She loved this garden, but after she died, none of us had the emotional wherewithal to keep it going. It wasn't until I broke up with Tommy in my last year of high school that I decided to dive back into the garden. It kept me busy and relatively sane through a really bad time and I still enjoyed working it.

Chloe's phone rang and she checked to see who the caller was. "It's Diego."

"Oh, say hello for me."

With a nod, she pushed the speaker button so I could hear what he was saying. "Hi, Diego, what's up?"

"Hey, Chloe. Thought I'd better give you a heads-up."

I watched Chloe's forehead furrow in concern. Did Diego always call with bad news? He seemed too sweet for that.

I rolled my eyes at the thought. I didn't even know the man, for Pete's sake. But Chloe was looking worried, so it couldn't be a happy call. Who knew?

His tone was almost mesmerizing, deep and powerful. Given his natural charisma and Chloe's bright optimism, it was no wonder the network seemed to think they were a winning pair.

"The owners of one of the houses got wind that they're not getting the makeover," he said. "Bree wants us on the set early so we can schmooze them out of their misery."

Chloe stood and paced up and down the walkway in front of the lettuce. "How did they find out?"

"One of the PAs called this afternoon to give them directions to the shoot tomorrow morning. They decided to drive over to the address to make sure they knew where they were going. They saw all the trailers and activity and made an educated guess."

"That was pretty smart of them," Chloe reasoned.

He snorted. "Yeah, unfortunately for us. Anyway, Carolee said that they called Bree and gave her an earful. Threatened to sue the show and Bree personally for breach of something-or-other."

I didn't want to take joy in the news that Bree might be sued. I should've tried to feel some sympathy for her, but I wasn't that noble. Honestly, she was really an awful human. I couldn't help but think that she was getting exactly what she deserved.

I just didn't want Chloe to suffer by proximity.

"We know that won't happen," Chloe said, looking slightly more upbeat than a moment ago. "Bree always has the homeowners sign a contract that stipulates that the producers have the final say on whether a house gets the makeover."

So much for getting sued, I thought. But hopefully the angry couple's threats would at least cause Bree to lose a good night's sleep.

"I'm just wondering if they'll even show up tomorrow," Diego said. "Carolee overheard the conversation and said they were really pissed off."

"But still, they're contractually obligated." Chloe shrugged. "Bree covers her bases."

"I'll say," he muttered. "Well, I just wanted you to know the latest scoop. I always hate walking into a situation that's about to detonate with no forewarning."

"You and me both," she said. "I really appreciate the call."

"You bet. See you tomorrow."

"Bye, Diego." She disconnected the call and gazed at me. "You heard all that?"

"Of course. Has that happened before? Where the owners find out ahead of time?"

"It's happened a few times, but as I told Diego, Bree's usually a few steps ahead of everyone when it comes to playing the game."

"It's a crummy game," I groused. "I was hoping she might get sued. Or at least threatened."

Chloe shrugged and set her phone down on the kitchen porch step so she wouldn't forget it. "Oh, she's been threatened plenty of times. It just never sticks."

"Knock-knock. Anybody home?"

The gate swung open and my father and Uncle Pete strolled into the backyard.

"Dad," Chloe cried. She launched herself at him and clung to him like a koala bear to a eucalyptus tree. Luckily he wasn't carrying anything breakable or he would've dropped it to grab her. And thanks to my father working in construction most of his life, he was strong enough to remain standing upright.

"Hi, honey," he said, hugging her tightly.

I laughed as I moved around them to give my uncle a hug. "Hi, Uncle Pete. Welcome home. How was your trip?"

"It was a great trip, but it's always nice to get back home."

"How many fish did you catch?"

"Oh, honey." A satisfied smile curved his

mouth. "We've got a cooler full of beauties in the truck. We'll bring it inside in a minute."

"Wonderful. We had dinner at Bella Rossa last night. It was fabulous as usual."

"I hope they gave you the family discount."

I grinned. "They sure did."

"Good." He gave me another hug. "You're looking happy and healthy."

"Thanks. I'm both."

"Glad to hear it."

Chloe finally let go of Dad, and I noticed both of them had weepy eyes. I felt a little sniffly myself. After all, we hadn't seen Chloe up here in years. I hoped that would change now that her past secrets were out in the open. Well, partially, anyway. I wondered when or if she would tell Dad what had happened.

Chloe grabbed Uncle Pete, and Dad stepped around them to give me a warm hug. "It's good to see you, sweetheart."

"You, too, Dad." After a moment, I said, "How about we move inside and I get you a beer?"

"You're speaking my language."

"Come on." I led the way into the kitchen and found two beers in the refrigerator. Handing him one, I said, "Isn't it nice to have Chloe here?"

"I tell you, it's a sight for these sore eyes." He ran his hand along his lower spine. "Of course, she nearly broke my back."

"I heard that," Chloe said, walking inside with Uncle Pete.

We all laughed again and I poured two glasses of wine for Chloe and me.

"Let's have a toast," Dad said. "To Chloe."

"Hear, hear," Uncle Pete said.

"And to your safe return home," Chloe added.

We raised our glasses — and cans — and clinked them all together. Then while Chloe filled them in on all of her latest adventures, I put the potatoes in the oven to bake. A moment later I realized I hadn't finished harvesting our salad, so I walked back outside to complete the task. Robbie followed me out to keep me company.

A few minutes later the gate opened again and Mac walked into the yard.

"Mac." I didn't quite hurl myself at him, Chloe style, but I did run over and wrap my arms around his neck.

"Hi, baby," he whispered, and kissed me. After a long moment, he said, "You take my breath away."

I smiled and kissed him again. "I'm so glad you're here."

He pressed his forehead to mine. "I wouldn't want to be anywhere else."

"Me, either."

Robbie barked, destroying the mood, and we both smiled. Mac bent over to give the little white dog a scratch behind his ears.

"Would you like a glass of wine?" I asked.

He lifted a brown bag. "I brought a bottle."

"Oh, that's so nice." I took the bottle and checked out the label. "One of my favorites."

He grinned. "I know."

"Thank you. Dad and Uncle Pete are already here and working on their first beers. Chloe and I already poured ourselves some wine, so help yourself to what's left of that bottle. I'll put this on the table for dinner."

"Sounds good. I'll take it inside and you can finish what you're doing out here."

"Perfect. I'm almost done."

I watched him walk inside, followed by Robbie, who was rapturous now that another attentive human had arrived.

With a blissful sigh, I finished snipping chives and then cut a few leaves of kale to blend with the other lettuces I'd picked earlier. My last stop was the tomato plant growing in a huge pot at the end of the row. I spotted three medium red beauties, plucked them off the vine, and placed them in my basket.

Back inside the kitchen, Dad and Pete were telling tales about their wild fishing party and all the salmon they'd caught.

"I don't know how we'll ever eat all that fish."

"I'm happy to help," Mac said jovially.

Dad chuckled. "I'm going to hold you to that."

"Speaking of fish." I glanced at Uncle Pete. "Did you want to bring the cooler into the house?"

"Oh, yeah." He set down his beer. "Jack, let's get that thing inside."

"As long as I'm helping to eat them," Mac said, setting down his wineglass, "I can help carry them."

"We'll take you up on that offer," Dad said, and the three men walked out of the room.

I filled the sink with water and soaked the lettuce and other veggies. Then I turned to Chloe. "I can't stop thinking about tomorrow morning. I hope the Wagners don't cause too big a scene."

"Don't worry. Bree will explain everything and then Diego and Blake and I will fawn all over them."

"Blake? But I thought he was fired. Was

he reinstated?"

"All I know is that his name is on the call sheet for tomorrow morning, so I'm assuming he'll be there." She sighed. "It's probably just as well that the Wagners found out before the fact because now there won't be any emotional explosions while we're filming them."

"I've said it before, but Bree really ought to rethink this whole situation." With a wave of my hands, I added, "Not that it's any of my business, right. Maybe I should just shut up about it, but I worry about you having to work with her every day. She sounds so toxic."

"Don't worry." Chloe grabbed my shoulders and gave me a ten-second back massage. "It's been a weird couple of weeks, but usually we get along well enough. Basically, she leaves us alone to do our work."

"Unless she's being psychotic?"

"Right," she said with a short laugh. "Well, nobody's perfect. And when it's time to negotiate for more money or perks or whatever, my agent handles it. And happily, I usually get whatever I ask for."

"As you should."

"Yes. Because I'm a superstar."

"True, you are."

"I know!" She reached into the sink,

pulled out a carrot, and held it like a microphone. "I'd like to thank the Academy . . ."

I laughed. "It's so good to have you home, Chloe. Come back more often, okay? Dad misses you and so do I."

She dropped the carrot into the water, reached out, and hugged me. "I miss you guys, too. And I promise. I'll come home so often you'll get sick of me."

"Not going to happen," I said. "You know I'll still worry about you, but as long as you promise you're happy, I can try to chill out a little."

"Thank you." She gave me another hug. "Oh, I've got to get the asparagus ready."

"You go ahead and use that side of the sink and I'll make the salad over here."

The three men stumbled into the house carrying a huge cooler that looked like it weighed a few hundred pounds. They set it down carefully in front of the refrigerator.

"How much salmon is in there?" I asked.

Pete looked a little sheepish. "Ten big ones."

I felt my jaw drop. "Are you kidding? You'll take some home, right?"

"We both have plenty for ourselves."

"Mac? Can you take some home?"

"I have a better idea. Why don't you keep

them here and I'll come over for dinner every night for the next six months."

I smiled at him. "You're invited anytime." Then I shot a look at Uncle Pete. "Can't you take some into the restaurant?"

He rubbed his chin thoughtfully, then admitted, "I've already put quite a few aside for the restaurant."

"I hadn't realized we'd caught that much," Dad said with a wince. "But when we packed everything up, there was quite a lot."

Yeah, like enough to feed thousands.

"I hope you left some for the other fishermen."

"Everyone caught their limit. It was a good month for salmon."

"I can see that." I gazed at the cooler, then back at Dad. "Did you clean them?"

Dad grinned. "You know I wouldn't bring them over here without cleaning them first."

I gave him a wry smile. "Right, because I would've sent them home with you."

That had always been our deal. Ever since I was a little girl, I had refused to clean fish. I would cook them and I would do the dishes and a lot of other things, but I drew the line at cleaning fish.

"Okay," I said, opening the cooler. "Wow, these are big. I can probably fit two fish in this freezer. The rest will have to go in the garage freezer. Oh, hey, maybe Wade and the rest of my crew would like to take a few."

"Sounds like a plan," Dad said with a wink, and finished his beer before dividing the salmon between my kitchen fridge and the deep freeze out in the garage.

Once the steaks were grilled to perfection, the asparagus was sautéed, the potatoes were baked, and the salad was tossed, we sat down at the dining room table and feasted.

Chloe regaled everyone with stories of her life in Hollywood. Mac mentioned that the latest big-budget movie based on his Jake Slater thriller series was in preproduction. Finally I told everyone about the Bloom house. Chloe jumped in to describe the dilapidated old place, the rehab plans, and the shooting schedule, and I somehow slipped and mentioned that there might be some histrionics tomorrow morning with the owners of the rejected house.

"What does that mean?" Dad asked.

I looked at Chloe and winced. "I probably shouldn't have said anything."

"Too late," she said, chuckling. After a sip of wine, she explained, "It's something the producer likes to do to stoke up the drama." She told them what usually happened on the first day of shooting and how the Wagners had already discovered the truth. "So, they might be in a pretty bad mood tomorrow morning. But we'll all be there to try to calm them down."

"I've met Rolly Wagner," Mac said. "He's a humorless stickler for following the rules and his wife is worse. Good luck with them."

Chloe's eyes widened and I was pretty sure mine did the same. "Oh no. They sound awful."

I grimaced. "This could get ugly real fast. I'm almost afraid to show up."

"Are you kidding?" Mac grinned. "Sounds like a hoot. I'll be there first thing tomorrow morning. I wouldn't miss this spectacle for the world."

It was barely four thirty the next morning when I walked into the kitchen. I hadn't slept well, knowing we might have an angry couple to deal with, so Chloe and I had agreed to be ready in plenty of time to have an extra cup of coffee and a hearty breakfast before we left for the day.

Robbie had been beside himself with excitement that I was up so early to play with him. He circled around me over and over as I tried to walk into the kitchen. My cat, Tiger, more intelligent than either of us, was still in her bed. "Easy there, Rob. You're going to make me trip and then I won't be able to feed you."

I was saved when Chloe came in, once again perfectly coiffed and clothed. "Hey, Robbie, come play with me."

He scooted across the room and danced at her feet.

"He's so adorable," she said, pouring a cup of coffee.

"He's in heaven," I said. "Breakfast is almost ready so you can sit down and take it easy."

"Wow, okay. It smells really good."

"I made an omelet with cheese and onions and tomatoes."

"Yum." She carried her coffee mug to the table and sat. Robbie stood at attention by her chair and Chloe leaned over to pet him. "Good boy, Robbie."

"He knows something is up," I said. "I was in the shower at four o'clock. I'm never awake this early."

"Where's Tiger?"

"She's the smart one. Still in bed upstairs."

"Well, Robbie," she said, rubbing his chin. "You're very handsome even if you're not as smart as the cat."

I laughed. "He makes up for it in heart and enthusiasm."

I used a spatula to flip the omelet over and covered the pan to cook it another minute. Meanwhile I pulled toast from the oven and put a piece on each plate along with a slice of turkey bacon for each of us. Slicing the omelet evenly down the middle, I put one half on Chloe's plate and the other on mine, and brought them both to the table.

"This looks so good," Chloe said, taking her first bite. "I'll make pancakes tomorrow."

"That's a deal."

Still sleepy, we chitchatted about nothing important and fifteen minutes later, we were finished with breakfast. I put the dishes in the dishwasher, checked that Robbie hadn't slurped up all of his water, and then we left for the shoot.

I drove around the corner and found a parking place on the side street.

"I've got our parking pass," Chloe said, and handed me a yellow flyer to leave on my dashboard.

We climbed out of the truck with our bags. Chloe had suggested that I bring two extra changes of clothing along with all my cosmetics and any hair product I used.

"Our hair and makeup girl will help you out with anything you're missing."

"I hope so. My goal is to stand next to you and *not* look like a hag."

"Ooh, honey," she said, cringing. "I'm not sure that's possible."

"Very funny. You're a laugh riot first thing in the morning."

She grinned. "I know."

I lifted the smallest of my three toolboxes out of the bed of the truck. This one held all of my pink tools, which were good to have around since no male crew members would walk off with them. Chloe had suggested that I talk about my pink tools on camera and I had reluctantly agreed. Pink or not, these tools could cause some damage if one wasn't careful.

"Is anybody here?" I asked as we walked down the driveway of the Blooms' house.

She pointed to the equipment truck. "There's light coming from Bob and Gary's truck. They're probably in there with their guys, getting their stuff together." She glanced around the spacious front yard. "Looks like the gaffer and his assistant have already rigged the cables and lights for the outside shots."

"Okay, I see a light on in the wardrobe trailer."

Chloe checked her watch. "We've still got an hour before they even start setting up for the first segment."

"What about our hair and makeup?"

"She won't be ready for another half hour."

"So much for getting here early." I stared at the house and the surrounding trees. Except for the tops of the chimneys, the rest of the house was still in shadow. "How about if we check out the house? Margaret gave me a key."

"I'd love to."

We strolled up the walkway to the front steps and gingerly climbed up to the porch. Even though Chloe had checked the steps out yesterday, I was careful where I put my feet. You never knew when the final straw would occur and your foot would go right through a rotted piece of wood. I'd been there, done that, and had the scars to prove it.

We made it to the front door without a mishap and set our bags and toolboxes down.

I unlocked the door and turned the knob. The door creaked open, giving me shivers across my shoulders.

"What a sound," Chloe whispered with a nervous laugh. "It's like the Addams Family lives here."

"Definitely spooky." I walked into the

house, rubbing my arms to get rid of the chill.

The sun was rising in the east, but the room was still dark. There was barely enough light pouring through the double bay windows, but we could still see some of the splendid features of the front room.

"Look at that crown molding," Chloe said, gazing up where the walls and ceiling met. "It's got to be eighteen inches wide."

"And that's real mahogany," I said.

"Thank God they didn't paint over it."

"Don't you hate that?"

"Ooh, Shannon. Look at the archway in front of the bay windows. It makes it feel like a little alcove, perfect for a cozy reading nook."

"I love it." I turned and saw the fireplace on the opposite side of the room. "Wow, that mirror over the mantel looks like the original."

"And the mantel and header look like Persian marble."

"These floors are the original hardwood," I said. "But they'll have to be sanded down and polished because they're scratched up pretty badly." I crouched down to run my fingers over one particularly bad scratch. "It looks like someone dragged something all the way across the room."

Chloe walked slowly toward the fireplace, glancing up at the marble columns on either side that went all the way up to the ceiling. When she got closer, she said, "This hearth is so elegant. These tiles are . . ." She gasped loudly. "No!"

"What did you find?"

"Oh God. No, no. Sh-Sh-Shannon. We . . . we've got to get out of here."

"Oh no. Are there spiders?" I hated spiders. Crossing the room, I almost collided with her as she was backing away.

I grabbed her shoulders to stop her. "What's wrong?"

She pointed ahead. "There's a . . . it's a . . ." Her whole body trembled.

"You're being weird." I took another step closer and finally understood. My breath came out in stuttering waves as I forced myself to take in exactly what I was seeing.

In the darkness I had thought that a large pile of firewood was scattered in front of the fireplace. But no. It was a woman's body draped across the cold tile hearth. She was dressed in flowing linen pants and a tank top. One of her fancy gold heels was hanging off her foot, held on by a single strap around her ankle.

"Wait here," I said.

"Shannon, no. Let's get out."

"Just a sec." Watching where I stepped, I moved close enough to check for a pulse. There was nothing. The woman was dead. Her hair was matted with blood and some of it trickled down the side of her cheek to pool on the marble surface.

I stared down at her lifeless form, marveling that Bree Bennett was as beautiful in death as she had been in life. Just maybe a few degrees colder.

"You're right," I said, grabbing Chloe's arm. "Let's get out of here."

Chapter Six

Back outside, I called 911 to report the death. The dispatcher was Ginny Malone, another high school buddy, so I said hello.

"Hey," Ginny said. "That you, Shannon?"

"Yeah, it's me." I paced on the walkway in front of the steps, wondering if she knew the phone number of everyone in town.

"Snagged another one, did you?"

I was pretty sure she meant another *body,* and that just wasn't fair. Sure, I'd come across a few dead bodies over the last year or so, but who hadn't?

I rolled my eyes. Outside of a funeral service, nobody I knew had ever even seen a dead body, let alone stumbled across one in their daily travels. But I didn't want to think about that glaring fact just now, so I ignored Ginny's comment. "Besides the general dispatch, would you mind giving Chief Jensen a separate call to let him know?"

"You bet, hon," she said. "Hang in there, Shannon."

"Thanks, Ginny."

When I finished the call, I turned to Chloe, who was sitting on the top step. "I'm going to go tell Bob and Gary what's happening." The two men were the only crew people I knew well enough to talk to. There had to be other people inside the various trailers and trucks or sitting in their cars finishing their coffee, but they would all find out eventually.

"I should go with you." But she didn't stand up, and when she gazed at me, her eyes were damp. She pushed her bangs back from her forehead, a clear sign that she was rattled. "And I should probably make a few calls, but I'm not ready."

"Then just sit here and try to stay calm. Take some deep breaths. Don't worry about anything for a few minutes."

"Easy for you to say."

I gave her a sympathetic half smile. "I'm so sorry, sis."

"I'll be okay. Hurry back."

I jogged across the street and down to the equipment truck, where I found Bob and Gary arguing over a scene in *The Big Lebowski.*

"Sorry to interrupt," I said, "but I've got

some bad news." I told them about Bree and watched their mouths fall open. They both looked gobsmacked.

"Are you serious?" Bob said. "Bree?"

"Holy cow," Gary whispered. "That's . . . oh, crap."

"I know," I said. "It's horrible."

"How did you . . . ?"

"Chloe and I found her just a few minutes ago."

"Whoa, that's a bummer," Gary said. "Are you guys okay?"

"I'll be fine. Chloe's rattled, but she'll be fine, too. Anyway, there's not much anyone can do until the police arrive, so if you want to hang out here . . ."

Bob glanced at Gary. "Think we should wait in the truck?"

"I don't know, man. It might make us look suspicious."

Bob frowned. "Like we're hiding or something?"

"I know the local police pretty well," I assured them. "They won't think you're hiding."

"Because we're not," Bob insisted. "But man, I just don't want to go out there right now. I mean, what can you say to anyone? It's a freaking tragedy. I still don't believe it."

"It's like some kind of a bad dream." He looked at me. "Yeah, I think we'll hang here for a little while."

"Sounds good," I said with a nod. "Might as well hunker down until the police come looking for you."

"I don't like the sound of that," Gary said, his gaze darting left and right. "Police come looking for us? That's never a good thing."

"I didn't mean it like that," I said, unsurprised by the reaction. For some reason, people freaked out more over the police than a dead body.

Bob waved me away. "Don't mind Gary. He's an old hippie who likes to think he was kept down by the man."

"Dude, I'm not that old."

I bit back a smile. "See you guys later."

Obviously, people processed sorrow in a lot of different ways. I figured those two would get over their shock and wander out in a few minutes to commiserate with their friends on the crew.

Meanwhile, I was more concerned about Chloe.

But as I approached the Bloom house, I saw a catering truck parked in the driveway. The workers were moving fast. Already, two long utility tables were covered in white tablecloths and held four huge coffee urns, along with cups and spoons and napkins and all the other necessary coffee-and-tea accoutrements. Trays of pastries, donuts, and muffins took up the rest of the space and a few people were already starting to help themselves to the goodies.

And there in the middle of everything, looking as calm and pretty as a summer day, was Emily Rose. I was giddy with relief to see a good friend in the midst of this weird circus and ran over to give her a hug.

"Darling Shannon," she said, and I had to smile. Her lovely Scottish brogue was a joy to hear.

"I'm so glad to see you," I said.

"And look at you, so glamorous! I can't wait to watch you make your television debut."

I changed the subject. "By the way, according to Wade, Niall had a great first day on the job."

"It warms my heart to hear it. Thank you for giving my brother a job." She looked a little closer and frowned. "What's going on? Is something bothering you, Shannon?"

Figured a good friend would notice my stress.

"Yes." I leaned in to whisper, "The producer of the show was murdered sometime during the night. The police should be here any second."

"Oh, dear. Oh no." She had to shake her head a few times to let the words sink in. "And you found her, yes? My poor Shannon at the center of it all again. Well, this is going to cause a stir. But never mind. What can I do to help?"

I couldn't have wished for a better response. "Just keep it quiet for now. I'll check with you in a while, but right now I have to get back to Chloe. I'm worried about her."

"Go to your sister," she said. "I'll bring around a cup of tea in a moment."

I gave her a grateful smile. "Thanks, Emily."

Chloe was still sitting on the steps and I joined her while we waited for the police to arrive. I could tell she was shaken to the core and I knew that feeling. Strangely, I seemed to be handling this sort of thing much better than I used to. And I wondered if I should worry about that.

"The police will be here any minute," I said. "They'll get everything sorted out."

"I don't know how I'll explain it," she whispered.

"Explain what?"

"How she died."

I wrapped my arm around her shoulders. "Honey, you weren't here. You can't explain it. So don't worry."

"But I argued with her, Shannon. And then I was the first one to find her. Just, you know, lying there."

"Everyone argued with her." I patted her knee. "Chloe, this isn't your fault."

"I'm not so sure," she said, and broke down, burying her face in her hands as she sobbed and sobbed.

I held her tighter and worried. Was there something here I didn't know about? Was she actually feeling guilty about Bree's death? Of course she was. But none of this was her fault!

After another minute, her shoulders stopped shaking and I could feel them rise and fall as she breathed in and out, in and out.

Finally I said, "I'm pretty sure the police will want to shut down the shoot for a day or two. Will you be okay with that?"

"It's fine with me. I want them to do whatever it takes to find out what happened."

"Okay, good." I thought it was a good sign that she was starting to think beyond this traumatic moment.

It was still early, but every few minutes one more production person or crew member would show up to grab a cup of coffee and a donut. If the police didn't get here soon, I would have to say something to all of them.

And that was when it occurred to me that I hadn't seen Blake Bennett show up yet. Had he been fired after all? I glanced around, searching the faces of the people scattered down by the trucks. "Chloe, when does Blake get to the set?"

She checked her watch. "He's usually here by now. Sometimes he sleeps in one of the dressing room trailers, just to be close by."

"So you don't think he actually was fired?"

"No, I really don't." She suddenly went rigid. "Wait. Do you think he's hurt, too?"

That hadn't occurred to me, but now I wondered. And worried. "I'll go look for him. Which trailer is his?"

"I'm not sure. He doesn't have a personal private one he uses. He just takes what's available. It's pretty relaxed around here."

"I'll check them all. Stay here."

I started to clatter down the steps, but stopped abruptly when one of the wood planks began to give way.

"Great," I muttered. All I needed today was a broken leg. I carefully negotiated around the weak spot and continued down to the walkway. I gave myself a mental reminder to fix that step before someone got hurt.

Near the sidewalk I was almost mowed down by a tall, burly man marching directly toward the walkway, ignoring me completely.

"Hey!" I said, stopping barely in time to avoid a collision. He acted as though I were invisible, and all I could do was glower at him. I'd never seen him before and wondered if he was part of the crew. Jerk.

Then I saw Mac a block away, strolling up the sidewalk toward us, and felt instantly calmer.

"Rolly!" a woman bellowed as she came bustling down the sidewalk toward the rude man who'd almost run me down. "I told you to wait for me."

The burly man turned, scowling. "You were lollygagging."

"You're such a jerk," she muttered, shaking her head as she joined him.

I couldn't agree more, I thought, and ignored the angry couple in favor of watching Mac walk closer. But something occurred to me and I turned around to watch the jerk and the lollygagger walking across the wide grassy lawn, their heads close together as they whispered to each other and avoided everyone else.

Were those the Wagners? I wondered. It

had to be them. Mac had called the guy Rolly. He had also claimed that both of them were difficult. As usual, he was right.

"Hey, Red," Mac said when he got close enough.

"Hi, Mac," I said and gave him a fierce hug.

When I finally let him go, he stared into my eyes. "What's wrong?"

So much for my poker face, but that was okay. My friends sure knew me. I wrapped my arms around him to feel his warmth and to avoid anyone overhearing what I had to say. "Bree Bennett was murdered. We found her body this morning inside the house."

"What the —" He held me at arm's length. "Are you all right?"

I was feeling a lot better now that he was here. "I'm fine. Really. I was about to go look for Blake. He hasn't shown up yet and it's getting late. Chloe thinks he might've slept in one of the dressing room trailers. Will you come with me?"

"Let's go." We waited for a car to pass and then ran across the street. The doors to the first two trailers were unlocked and a quick peek inside showed us that they were empty, but the third one was locked. I pounded on the door, but no one answered.

A woman came running up to us. She was

clutching a clipboard and looked irritated with us. "What's going on? Who are you?"

"I'm Chloe's sister and we're looking for Blake Bennett. Do you know if he's using this trailer?"

"I saw him go in here late last night."

"Do you work on the show?"

She seemed affronted by the question. "I'm Marisa, the wardrobe mistress."

I smiled. "It's so nice to meet you, Marisa. Chloe has said so many wonderful things about you."

Somewhat mollified by my obsequious response, Marisa started talking. "I slept in my trailer last night, too. I had a lot of work to do."

Later I would have to ask her what kind of wardrobe work she did on a location shoot for people who basically wore jeans and work shirts, but for now I let it go.

"I have keys to all the trailers," she said, and pulled a heavy key ring from her pocket. Flipping through the myriad keys, she found one and tried it on the trailer door. Then she tried another one. The third key worked and the door swung out.

I climbed up the steps and stared at the mess. There were blankets and pillows tossed around the small space and piles of papers everywhere. In the wild clutter, I almost missed seeing Blake buried beneath the blankets.

"Blake!" I shouted. Was he . . . dead?

Mac moved right over to the sofa bed and shook his shoulder. "Hey, Blake. Wake up."

"Urrrgh."

I felt a rush of relief. "So he's not dead."

"He's just waking up."

"But he should've been on the set thirty minutes ago."

"Blake," Mac said loudly, and shook him again.

"Whaa —" Blake stirred and grumbled, "Haaaaay, whaz go on?"

"Is he drunk?" I wondered.

"That's impossible," Marisa said. "He doesn't drink." I hadn't realized she was still here, but she stood in the doorway, staring in horror at Blake.

Mac knelt down next to the bed and sniffed around, then easily rolled the man onto his back. "I don't smell alcohol." Blake groaned but didn't fight back. Mac lifted Blake's eyelid to check his eye.

He glanced up at me. "Pretty sure he's on drugs."

"No," Marisa cried. "He doesn't do drugs."

I ignored her and asked Mac, "How can you tell?"

"He's extremely groggy, but it's not from alcohol. His pupils aren't reacting quickly enough to the light. His speech is slurred and there's a loss of muscle control. I'm betting it's drug-related." He frowned again. "The real question is whether it was self-inflicted or not." He glanced at the wardrobe mistress. "Does he often miss his call time?"

"Never," she insisted, and stomped out of the trailer.

As I paced around the tiny space, I wondered again if Blake had been fired. "Should we get him out of bed or let him sleep? There's no real urgency since they won't be doing any filming today. But the police will be here any minute. And we should probably tell him about Bree as soon as possible."

"I'm not sure he's able to comprehend anything right now." Mac made an executive decision. "I'm going to call an ambulance. Meanwhile I think it'll be okay to let him sleep until the police arrive."

Just then, a siren sounded from a few blocks away.

"It's about time the police got here," I grumbled.

Mac called 911 to request an ambulance while I kept an eye on Blake. He didn't move, but he was snoring loudly so I knew he was still alive. Which was more than I could say about his wife.

Mac and I walked out and saw Marisa waiting at the bottom of the steps.

"Thank you for your help," Mac said. "I know the police will be grateful if you would keep this door locked until they get here."

"You bet I will," she said, with a resolute nod.

"Come on," Mac said, grabbing my hand. "We should be out there to meet Eric when he shows up."

Oh, I wasn't looking forward to that. Eric was a nice guy, and we were friends now, but whenever I found a dead body, the police chief behaved as though I were doing it on purpose just to make his life harder.

I clutched Mac's hand. "Let's get out of here."

Police Chief Eric Jensen climbed out of the police-issue SUV looking for all the world like Thor, the hammer-wielding god of thunder and lightning. Whereas my old boyfriend Tommy was tall and blond and adorable in a "surf's up" kind of way, Eric Jensen was even taller. He was blond, too, and rugged with muscles on his muscles and a strictly no-nonsense attitude when it came to playing by the rules, upholding the law, and keeping his town safe.

Mac and I made it halfway down the walkway in time to watch the police chief somberly scan the film set, silently taking in everything from the catering crew to the decrepit Bloom mansion to the row of big trucks along the road.

Finally Chief Jensen approached us. With a gentlemanly nod, he said, "Good morning, Mac, Shannon. Thank you for calling this in."

"It's what I do," I said.

"So once again you're first on the scene," Eric said dryly, pulling out his notepad and pen. "Can you tell me what happened?" And knowing me, he added, "Briefly?"

"I'll be happy to. First thing you should know is that we called an ambulance for the victim's husband. That's Blake Bennett, and he's sleeping in that trailer over there. Mac thinks he's on drugs but they should wear off eventually. We wanted to make sure the EMTs checked him out first."

"That was good thinking," Eric said with a quick nod. "So please go ahead."

"Well, in a nutshell, my sister and I arrived early and the whole area was deserted. We decided to go inside the house to get a jump on things and that's when we found the body of Bree Bennett. Mac arrived a little while ago and he and I tracked down Blake Bennett, Bree's husband, asleep in that trailer, possibly drugged, as I mentioned." I looked up at Eric. "Tell me when to stop. I can go into more detail on anything you want."

I was disconcerted by his frown so I had to ask, "What is it? What's wrong?"

"You have a sister?"

My mouth opened but I had no words. After everything I'd just told him, that was the one thing he picked up on? "Yes, I have a sister. She's sitting right up there on the porch steps. Would you like to meet her?"

He stared at my sister in the distance. "She's on the show."

"She's the *star* of the show." I took a deep breath. "She actually saw Bree before I did. She's a little freaked out."

"Understandable," he said. "Yes, I'd like to meet her. I'll need to ask her some questions."

"Of course." I gave Mac a quick glance. "But don't you want to see if Blake Bennett is okay first? Not that I'm telling you what to do, but we're not absolutely sure if he was drugged or not. You and the EMTs would know better. And if he was drugged, it might've been the killer's way of keeping him from discovering that his wife was about to be . . . hmm." I stopped talking when I realized that Eric was regarding me intently. Was he mentally willing me to shut up? Maybe. So I did.

"Introduce me to your sister," Eric said.

"Right. Sure. Priorities." I sneaked a peek at Mac, who wore an unabashed grin on his face. Was he laughing *with* me? I doubted it. Glancing up at Eric, I smiled tightly. "Let's go."

He started to follow me, but stopped when Tommy Gallagher drove up and parked in the driveway behind Eric's SUV. Tommy jumped out of the car and glanced around, too, but as soon as he saw the three of us, he burst into a happy grin and strolled over to say hello. He was truly the only cop I knew who could have a jolly good time at a crime scene.

"Hi, Tommy," I said.

"Hey, Shannon." He gave me a sweet little peck on the cheek. Call me shallow, but I loved when Tommy did that because invariably there would be someone watching who would report it to his snooty wife, Whitney, and ruin her day.

"How're you doing, Tom?" Mac said.

"Mac, buddy," Tommy said, and shook Mac's hand. "How's my favorite writer?"

I smiled. Tommy was such a dude.

Tommy sobered as he turned to Eric. "Chief, where do you need me?"

Eric looked at Mac. "Mac, can you show Tommy the trailer where you found Blake Bennett?"

"Absolutely."

"Tom, just keep an eye on Bennett. The EMTs should be here shortly."

Mac nudged his chin in the direction of the street. "Over here, Tom."

Once they walked away, Eric and I traipsed across the grass to the walkway. I noticed that the Wagners — if that was who they were — were watching everything with great interest. Were they aware that Bree's body was inside the house? Were they the ones who had lured her over here last night and then killed her? How angry were they when they found out that their house had lost out to the Bloom house? Angry enough to kill?

And there went my speculative mind, spinning tales of murder and revenge. You can't really blame me. This wasn't my first murder scene and I'd learned long ago that supposedly normal, everyday people were capable of truly awful things when pushed too far. And seriously, there was certainly no love lost between the two Wagners and Bree. Were they angry enough to do her in?

Maybe not, but I was definitely going to mention their names to Eric when I got the chance.

"I completely forgot that you had a sister," Eric murmured as the two of us approached the front steps. "You've managed to surprise me again."

"Good to know I'm still capable of that."

"I was out of town for a few weeks," he explained quietly, "taking care of some family business. Just got back last night."

I glanced up at him. "I hope everything's okay."

"Yes, it's all fine. But unfortunately, the details of the filming slipped my mind until Ginny called me a few minutes ago."

"That's a rough way to start your first day back at work." I climbed the steps and sat down next to my sister.

Eric remained standing at the bottom of the steps, undoubtedly aware of his intimidation factor. He gazed up at Chloe and me as if he might be appraising us. I wondered if he would mention that we didn't look alike. I hoped not. After so many years, that line had turned into a cliché and Eric Jensen wasn't the cliché type.

"Think these steps are safe?" he asked finally.

"I would tread very carefully," I said.

He nodded. "Good advice." When he reached the top step safely, he surprised me by sitting down on the other side of Chloe. It was such a friendly move, I was instantly suspicious.

"Chloe, this is my friend Chief Jensen," I said. "Eric, this is Chloe Hammer, my sister."

"Hello," she said as they shook hands.

He managed a smile. "Nice to meet you, Chloe."

"You, too." She glanced at me and then back to Eric. "Do I call you Chief Jensen or Eric?"

"It depends on whether you're a suspect or not," I said helpfully.

She chewed on her lip a moment, then nodded. "In that case, it's nice to meet you, Chief Jensen."

I wrapped my arm around Chloe's shoulder and tugged her closer. "You are not a suspect, Chloe. You have an alibi and a witness to everything you did last night."

"I do?"

"Yeah. Me. It's going to be okay." *Easy for me to say,* I thought, and I started to worry all over again.

I knew Chloe was uncomfortable around authority figures. It stemmed from her time in high school when she was wrongfully arrested by the former police chief. Because of that, I planned to stay close by, especially if Eric started interrogating her.

"I'm fine, don't worry," she murmured, giving my hand a squeeze. Was she trying to comfort *me* now? It just figured. And for some reason, I had a strong urge to break down and cry. But I wouldn't. The Hammer sisters were tougher than that.

"Of course you're fine," Eric said amiably. "Now, I'm going to check inside the house for a few minutes and then I'll probably have some questions for you afterward, okay?"

Chloe nodded. "Sure."

He glanced across at me. "Shannon, will you come with me?"

Chloe's eyes were wide as she watched me stand. I was pretty surprised, too, but I patted her shoulder as though I did this all the time. "I'll be right back."

"Garcia, Payton," Eric called, and two officers came running up to the house.

"Yes, sir," they said in unison.

"Payton, please keep Ms. Hammer company so she doesn't think we're neglecting her."

Chloe met my gaze in time for me to shoot her an encouraging smile. Mindy Payton was an old friend of mine from high school so I knew she would be nice to my sister.

"Garcia, you're with me." The two climbed up to the porch without falling through any rotten planks. Mindy hovered near Chloe while Carlos Garcia silently followed us to the front door.

At the door, I stopped them. "I should warn you that it's very dusty in there and Chloe and I probably disturbed any good footprints you might've found. Sorry."

"That's a good point. Garcia, can you go get some booties for us to wear?"

"You got it, Chief."

He ran to the truck and was back in less than a minute. We all slipped the protective disposable booties on over our shoes.

"Everybody ready?" Eric said. "Do you have a key?"

"I do," I said, "but the door's unlocked."

He scowled. "Was it like that when you first arrived?"

"No, it was locked. I had to use the key."

"So you touched the doorknob."

"Yes." My shoulders slumped. "Sorry."

"Don't worry about it. You probably weren't expecting this place to turn into a crime scene."

"Not in a million years." But that didn't stop it from happening on a regular basis.

Even though I might've obliterated the

killer's handprints, there was a possibility that they could still get something off the doorknob, so Eric pulled out a handkerchief and used it to open the door. I tried to ignore the shivers from the creaking door because there were much more sinister things going on inside this house.

Eric glanced around the large foyer. "What did you do when you got inside?"

"We walked into the foyer and right into the front parlor to start checking things out." I pointed to the wide archway that led to the living room — or front parlor, in Victorian parlance — and we all walked inside.

"First I noted the amazing crown moldings and Chloe commented on the archway over by the bay windows. We were basically discussing what sort of rehab would be needed in this room. She was standing right about where you are when she noticed the beautiful marble fireplace and at the same time I was checking out the hardwood floors. I pointed out some scratches and said that the floors would have to be refinished."

"Anything else?"

"Yes. I took a closer look at the floor and saw that at least one scratch had only just occurred. I could tell because the dust had been disturbed. The scratches start over there." I pointed toward the archway leading into the dining room. I'm thinking she was dragged from somewhere in that room all the way over to the fireplace." I pointed out the path to Eric. "Can you see it?"

He crouched down. "Yeah. You could be right. Those are some serious scratches."

"I know. Her sharp heels might've made them. They've got hard metal on the tips. And one of her shoes is dangling off her foot. It could've have been snagged by a rough patch of wood."

"It's possible," he murmured.

"So anyway, Chloe wanted to see the tiles on the fireplace, so she walked over to the mantel and that's when she saw the body." I sighed a little, remembering. "I ran over and checked for a pulse but didn't find one. Chloe was pretty freaked so I got her out of here as quickly as possible and called 911."

Eric stayed in one spot and glanced around for another minute or two. Finally he approached the hearth where Bree's body was splayed and knelt down to feel for a pulse. He lifted her hair carefully to check out the head wound.

"Carlos," he said. "Call CSI and get them over here. And as soon as we've interviewed the production people, I want you to get Tommy, Dan, and Mindy in here to search this house top to bottom." He turned and gazed at me as he continued to give Carlos more orders. "I don't want anyone except our people inside this house until I clear it."

"Yes, sir, Chief," Carlos said.

Eric used his pen to carefully lift Bree's hanging stiletto and studied it for a moment. I noticed that the tiny spike heel was dented and scraped. From being dragged? I thought so.

"I'll ask Ginny to call the sheriff over in Ukiah. We'll need an official declaration of death at some point today. Just remind me if I forget, will you?"

Carlos nodded. "Got it. And CSI is already here, sir."

"Thanks." Eric glanced at me and shrugged. "Carlos's mind is a steel trap."

"Ah." I was wondering why he was using the poor guy as a secretary to relay everything he wanted to get done. "Good to know."

Carlos leaned into the small two-way radio mounted near his collarbone and spoke quietly. He walked into the foyer to talk and returned a minute later. "The other officers will await your signal to start searching the house. Meanwhile, they are watching the crowd outside, which has apparently grown in size. And some of those gathered are starting to ask questions. CSI is already on the porch waiting for the okay from you to get started."

Lighthouse Cove's CSI unit consisted of one guy, Leo Stringer. But Leo was as good as it got and if necessary, he could always call the Ukiah sheriff's department for reinforcements. I wondered if that would be necessary in the case of Bree Bennett's death.

"Leo's always right where I need him," Eric murmured. I noticed his jaw was clenched as he stood and stared down at the body for one more moment. "Let's move out of here so he can get to work."

Chapter Seven

Tommy met Chief Jensen at the top of the steps. "Blake Bennett is awake, Chief. He's still groggy and appears to have been drugged. He insists that someone else did it to him. Said he never takes drugs. Doesn't drink, either."

I nodded. "Marisa the wardrobe mistress said the same thing."

I saw that Chloe was listening to every word. She still looked shaky, but she spoke up. "That's true. Blake would never take drugs. He wears his sobriety like a badge of honor and he's always preaching drug abstinence to everyone on the staff."

Eric nodded. "Thanks, Chloe." His eyes narrowed as his mind worked the problem. Turning to Tommy, he asked, "Who's watching Bennett right now?"

"The EMTs arrived a few minutes ago," Tommy explained. "And Mac is still in there with him."

Eric gave a brief nod and seemed satisfied with things for now. "I'll give Mac a call in a minute."

Mac wasn't a cop but his reputation and character were beyond reproach. He might actually be able to get information from Bennett, I thought. It might not be admissible if it came directly from Mac, but Eric could always go over the same ground later during an interrogation, if necessary.

Leo Stringer and Officer Lilah O'Neil stood by the front door. They were already wearing gloves and waiting for Chief Jensen's okay to go inside. Lilah was the cop assigned to work with Leo on the rare occasions when we had a real crime scene.

I pasted a smile on my face. "Hi, Leo. Hi, Lilah." I had met Lilah a few times and knew that she had been a pre-med student in college. I assumed her science background was the reason she had been assigned to Leo. Or maybe they just got along well together.

"Go ahead, Leo," Eric said. "I'll join you in a few minutes."

"Sounds good," Leo said, and walked into the house followed by Lilah.

"Garcia, do me a favor and go check on the EMTs in trailer number three." He turned to Mindy Payton. "Officer, start interviewing the people who were here earliest. Find out what they saw and who they noticed when they first arrived."

He glanced across the lawn toward the driveway, where many of the crew were hanging around the coffeepot munching on donuts or sitting in the chairs provided for anyone working on the show.

He glanced back at me. "Is that Emily Rose over there?"

"Yes, she's in charge of catering."

He nodded and looked at Mindy. "You might want to start with the catering group."

"Yes, sir."

Pointing toward Chloe, Eric said to Tommy, "Tommy, this is Shannon's sister, Chloe."

"Oh, I know Tommy Gallagher," Chloe said with all the warmth of a polar ice cap.

"Ah," Eric said, feeling the chill. "Shannon, walk with me. Tommy, stay with Chloe. And make sure nobody goes in the house."

"Yes, sir." But Tommy didn't look happy with what he probably considered a babysitting assignment.

I almost laughed. Would Tommy have any skin left after Chloe gave him a piece of her mind?

Eric and I remained on the porch but strolled around the side of the house and all the way to the backyard. I assumed he wanted to avoid being overheard so I went along, trying all the while to steer Eric around any badly weathered wooden planks that looked dangerous. The porch ended at a set of steps that led down to a brick patio surrounded by overgrown grass and weeds. We remained on the porch and stood at the railing, gazing out at the small forest of trees lining the perimeter of the Bloom land.

"Beautiful property," Eric murmured.

"Yes. Or it will be when we get finished with it." I sighed a little. Because really, with what had happened to Bree, I didn't know if the show would go on, as they said. "By the way, this railing is ready to fall off the porch. Please don't lean against it."

He pulled his hands away and brushed them together to get rid of the old paint flakes that had come off so easily. "Thanks for the warning."

I really liked Eric Jensen. We first met when I reported a murder in the basement of a house I was rehabbing. Since he was new in town at the time, he immediately considered me the prime suspect. It took a while to convince him I was one of the good guys, but eventually we became friends. Now, though, I wondered if he would always look at me with a touch of suspicion in his eyes. Of course, who could blame him? We always seemed to run into each other at the scene of another murder.

"Should I be worried about Tommy?" he asked.

I chuckled. "No. Chloe will just give him an earful and then they'll be new best friends all over again."

He tilted his head and looked at me. "I still don't know if I've heard the whole story on this. Care to enlighten me?"

"You know Tommy was my high school boyfriend, right?"

"I'd heard that."

"He cheated on me with Whitney, got her pregnant, and broke my heart." I shrugged, then chuckled. "I'm over it, but Chloe still harbors some resentment on my behalf."

"Okay. Got it."

"I'm glad you forced him to stay with her. Yelling at Tommy will take her mind off the fact that she just discovered a dead body for the first time."

"So Tommy's providing a public service."

"And learning an important lesson, I think," I added. "You don't want to piss off a sister."

"Words to live by," Eric said.

Privately I figured Tommy had been paying for cheating on me for years, since he'd been married to Whitney all this time.

Eric and I smiled at each other. I tended to forget that the man had a killer smile. *The better to lure you in and make you spill your guts,* I thought, and tried to prepare myself for the interrogation to come.

With a sigh I asked, "So what did you want to talk about?"

He pulled out his notepad and pen. "Let's start at the beginning. What were the two of you doing here so early?"

"Well, you know that Chloe is the star of *Makeover Madness,*" I said. "And that this is the house they're making over this week."

"Yeah, I got that." He smiled patiently. "We issued the permits so I'm aware that they're filming here this week. I'm mainly curious as to why *you* are here."

I smiled back brightly. "I get to be on the show. I'm helping my little sis with the rehab."

"Makes sense." He nodded thoughtfully, and stared at the landscaping. That was going to need a lot of work, too, I thought. "So you got here early because . . . you were starting the rehab? You couldn't sleep? Why?"

I reached into my shoulder bag and pulled out the show rundown. "First, you might want to hold on to this." I pointed out various items on the six-page stapled document. "It's got the call times and the schedule of the shots they plan to take and who's involved in each setup along with the location where each shot will take place and what equipment will be necessary. The last few pages have the names and titles and phone numbers of the entire staff and crew."

"That'll be helpful. Thanks."

"Sure." I pointed to the first page. "So here's what time everyone was supposed to be here, but Chloe and I decided to arrive even earlier because Bree was afraid that the Wagners would show up and make a stink." I explained that, unbeknownst to the homeowners, Bree had chosen two houses and planned to eliminate one of them on camera. "The Wagners found out accidentally that they were the losers. They didn't take it well."

"Were the Wagners here when you arrived?"

"Not that I could see. Almost nobody was here except for a few of the crew. But they weren't milling around. Mostly they were in their trucks and trailers, organizing their day. Or, you know, whatever."

"So . . . you went inside the house. Why?"

"Well, since it was just the two of us, Chloe and I decided to get a look at what we were up against, rehab-wise. So I unlocked the door and we walked in. And it was just as I explained to you when we were inside a few minutes ago. Basically, we found Bree's body sprawled across the hearth."

"I'm sorry."

"I appreciate that." Shivering a little, I said, "You'd think I'd be used to it, but I'm not. It's always a painful shock. I don't know how you do it, frankly. Anyway, I'm really worried about Chloe. She's so upset and she's taking it all very personally."

"Why?"

"Why is she upset? Are you kidding?"

He held up his hand to stop me. "I understand that she'd be upset. I want to know why she's taking it personally."

I suddenly realized I needed to be more careful with my words. I wasn't about to blurt out that Chloe felt *guilty* that Bree was dead, but what was I supposed to say? Oh, well. I took a deep breath and plunged on ahead. "It's just that Chloe knows Bree so well and she was such an important part of the team. And she's worried about Blake, and the staff is going to be so upset and scared and, well, you know, all that stuff." Was I starting to blather?

"Right." He jotted down some notes, then

looked up. "I heard a rumor about an argument yesterday."

I blinked. "How did you already hear a rumor?"

"People tell me things," he said with a shrug. "Must be my charming personality."

"Yeah," I mused with a smile, "that's got to be it."

"And also, I had a meeting last night at the Inn. People there were telling tales about the showbiz folks. So what about this argument?"

Again, I had to be careful. "Um, I'm not sure what you're talking about."

"An argument was overheard yesterday between the deceased woman and your sister."

I knew that word traveled quickly in Lighthouse Cove, but this was ridiculous. It just figured that the chief of police had just happened to have been at the inn a few hours after my sister was heard yelling at her boss, who was now dead. "So who told you about the argument?"

He folded his arms across his chest and gave me his patented Sheriff Stare. "You're stalling, Shannon. Is it true? Did you know about the argument? Or did you hear it for yourself?"

I grimaced. "Hard to say."

"No it's not. You either heard the argument or you didn't."

"Okay, I heard it, but I wouldn't call it an argument per se." A fight maybe, but not an argument. "They were discussing a really good opportunity for Chloe, so it was a good thing. Not an argument."

"Was there yelling involved?"

"Okay, yes, they did raise their voices," I admitted. "But that was because Chloe was defending another person on the staff. Bree had decided to fire that person and Chloe disagreed with her decision." I didn't dare tell him the full story, did I? I thought about it for a moment, stared up at his strong jaw, and decided I would hate to have him catch me in a lie. I would have to trust him with the truth.

I glanced around to make sure we were far enough away from anyone who might overhear us. "Okay, here's the thing. Bree told Chloe that she had already fired Blake. Chloe wasn't happy about it because she and Blake make a good team. So she argued with Bree, tried to talk her out of it."

He looked incredulous. "You're saying that Bree Bennett *fired* her own husband? That's hard to believe."

"It would be if you didn't know the woman," I said, frowning. I didn't know her, either. But I'd heard her yelling at my sister and that was enough to convince me.

"She was a drama queen," I continued, "and not in a good way. She liked to stir up chaos on the show and behind the scenes. She willingly set up people to be hurt and angry just to get a good scene on camera. And apparently she enjoyed firing staff people whenever she got in a mood. The staff was used to hearing her yell at people, including the stars of the show. And weirdest of all, after she'd fired someone, they would just continue to work on the show. So it didn't mean anything — except that she had the thrill of watching them cry and go crazy for a little while. Who does that?"

I didn't mention the big new show that Bree had been so excited about because I didn't think it was my place to reveal that secret. I also didn't bring up the fact that Chloe herself had been fired only a day ago, and I never would.

Eric read back his notes. "You said she 'apparently' liked to fire people and that she had just fired her husband. But then anyone who was fired simply remained in their job. So was her husband really fired or was that something your sister told you? You couldn't have known it for a fact, could you?"

I didn't like the way he phrased that question because either way I answered him, I could be hurting Chloe. Was Eric setting me up? Was he building a cage for me or my sister to suddenly fall into? And was *I* the one being a drama queen now?

I scratched my head and pondered whether I was complicating things or not. I glanced up at him and he met my gaze directly. So okay, it was too late to turn back now. I had grown to trust Eric over the last year or so and now I just prayed that my trust wasn't misplaced.

"Both," I said finally. "I heard it for myself *and* my sister told me."

"How did you hear it for yourself?"

Once again I turned to check that we were still alone. "I was there in the office yesterday when Bree and Chloe were discussing . . . what I told you they were discussing."

As soon as I said it I remembered that I hadn't actually heard Bree mention that she'd fired Blake. I was about to take back my words, but noticed Eric studying me as though I were a particularly slimy smear under a microscope.

"What?" I demanded.

"I was thinking earlier," he said, "how tiresome it is to keep finding you at a murder scene."

That was an odd change of topic. I wasn't sure if it was an insult or simply a realization. "You think I enjoy it?"

"I think it's got to be difficult."

"Difficult?" I choked on a laugh. "I'm starting to get a complex. I mean, not only do I actually have to stare into the face of a dead person, which is no fun at all, by the way. But then I have to deal with you. I mean, you know, the police, and the suspicion, and the rumors and . . ." I ran out of steam and waved away whatever I was going to say. "Never mind. I'm sure you get what I'm saying."

"I do, and you have a valid point. But meanwhile, I have a murder to solve."

"And I'm trying to help," I said.

"I appreciate that."

"I'm glad to hear it." I took a breath. "So, do you want to hear my theories?"

"I don't know. Do I?"

I smiled. "You absolutely do."

He sighed. "Okay, go for it. But we'd better make it fast. There are a bunch of people out there waiting to find out what's going on. I'll need to speak to them."

I considered it a hopeful sign that he kept his notepad and pen at the ready.

"Okay," I began, "I got a key to the house from Margaret Bloom because we're friends and I was the one who talked her into submitting her house to the program."

"I understand."

"So naturally, Bree would've had to have a key, too. Because as the producer, she would need access to the house."

"Makes sense."

As I talked my theory became clearer. I could almost see it happening as I described. "So either Bree met her killer somewhere and let him into the house, or the killer had a key, too. Or the killer stole her key, or Bree was already inside and the killer broke in some other way."

He frowned and stopped writing. "I understand those are all possibilities. But where are you going with this?"

"I don't know," I said, frustrated as my oh-so-clear vision was suddenly draped in fog. "But there are plenty of people who had a reason to meet her here as well as a motive for killing her. For instance, there's Blake. I told you Bree fired him just before she had her meeting with my sister."

"And yet you also said that people who got fired rarely faced any real consequences. So I still have a hard time believing that Blake Bennett would kill his wife for firing him. But I intend to interview him as soon as he's back on his feet."

I really wished I could tell Eric about the big secret new network show that Bree had withheld from her husband. That would've given him a major motive for murder. But it wasn't my place to talk about the new show. Eric would have to hear it from Chloe. And I would convince her that she should tell him. I had a feeling it would make a big difference in the case. If Blake had known that his wife was keeping him from starring in a big network TV show, he might've been angry enough to kill her. But I wasn't at liberty to mention any of that.

"Well, maybe Blake didn't care about getting fired," I said lamely. "But he's still her husband and the spouse is always the most likely suspect."

He barely kept from rolling his eyes. "Okay. I've heard enough. I need to get going." He tucked his pen in his pocket.

"But wait, there's more," I said, sounding like a game show host. "The Wagners have a motive, too, so I think you should talk to them. They're very angry and volatile."

"I don't know them, but I'll speak to them. Now —"

"And there's someone else. When I left the production office yesterday, I saw Richie Rich — I mean, Richard Stoddard — standing at the office door, eavesdropping on

Bree's conversation with Chloe. Do you know him?"

"I've heard the name. What does he have to do with anything?"

"He's a real estate agent in town. We think Richie showed Bree some properties while she was visiting town last month." I winced a little, because really, this was just gossip. But I marched forward because after all, it was *good* gossip. "And then he showed up at the production office hotel room the day before she was murdered. Coincidence? I wonder."

He chuckled. "You've just taken a deep dive into conspiracy theory territory. And I've got work to do."

"All right, all right." But I wasn't quite ready to surrender. "There's also a full staff of people who might've had a bone to pick with Bree. Who knows if one of them argued with her and it escalated? Oh, and Blake has a personal assistant named Chelsea who seems suspicious of every other woman who talks to him. I'm pretty sure she's in love with him, which gives her a strong motive to kill off his wife."

"Okay, we'll talk to all of them. I plan to interview the entire staff. And the film crew, too."

"Good." We walked back to the front of

the house and I noticed that all those staff and crew people were indeed standing around, waiting for some word on when they would start shooting. The way many of them were chatting or munching on donuts, though, it looked like nobody had heard the news that Bree was dead. But I had already told Bob and Gary, so that was strange. Apparently the two men hadn't said a word about it. Or maybe no one cared. And how sad would that be?

"Chloe," I said. "What's going on? Have you told anyone about Bree yet?"

She had moved from sitting on the steps to leaning against the clapboard wall of the house. Tommy was nearby, studiously ignoring her, which made me wildly excited to hear exactly what she'd said to him.

"I wanted to tell them what happened," she said. "But Tommy thought we should wait for Chief Jensen to announce it."

"I'm glad you waited," Eric said. "I wouldn't want you to be bombarded with questions you can't answer."

She flashed him a grateful smile. "Thanks."

"I'll say a few words," he said, glancing at Tommy. "And then we need to check on the husband." He stepped to the edge of the porch.

Chloe and I moved farther away while Eric called for everyone's attention.

"Folks, I'm Police Chief Eric Jensen and I'm afraid I have some bad news. There's been a death inside the house and we're going to have to shut down your production for a day or two."

There were a few gasps and a lot of frowns.

"We'll need to collect your names and check you off the production rundown," Eric continued, "so please don't go anywhere. If you could line up along the driveway, my officers will take down your information as quickly as possible. We'll try to contact you over the next twenty-four hours. And if you have any questions, please direct them to me."

"Who died?" one of the guys shouted, and the crowd echoed his question.

Eric paused for the people to calm down. "Bree Bennett."

More gasps met shrieks of disbelief.

"No way!"

"Oh my God."

"That's impossible."

"I just saw her yesterday."

"How could this happen?"

A number of women and a few men started to cry. Everyone looked completely stunned.

But someone out there knew exactly what had happened. From my vantage point on the porch, I scanned the crowd, looking for any suspicious reactions. That was when I noticed the Wagners skirting the yard and heading for the sidewalk. I ran over to Eric and pointed. "Don't let them get away."

"You two, stop right there!" he shouted.

The Wagners froze. They obviously knew he was talking to them. It was an impressive show of dominance, I thought, and gave Eric a mental thumbs-up.

Eric waved Tommy over. "Get their information, will you, Tom? Oh, and ask them where they thought they were going in such a hurry."

"You got it." He jogged down the steps and ran across the lawn to talk to the Wagners.

Eric turned and jabbed his finger toward me and Chloe. "Don't go anywhere. I've got to talk to Blake Bennett."

Once Eric was gone and Tommy continued to talk to the Wagners, I asked Chloe to move toward the side of the porch that was the most shaded and farthest away from the crowd.

"Why?" she asked.

I moved in front of her and whispered, "Because Richie Rich just walked up to the coffee service table."

"No way." She tried to push me aside to get a look at Richie.

"I want to watch him, but I don't want him to see us. We're in the shadows now. I think we're okay."

"The last thing I want is a confrontation right now." She glowered at him. "What's he doing here?"

"I have no idea," I said. "Maybe he just wanted to see the spectacle. Or maybe he's meeting someone. Oh, maybe he was planning to meet Bree here. Or maybe he's the killer and he's returning to the scene of the crime."

She stared at me. "I never realized what a rich imagination you have."

"I wish it were all imagination. But the fact is, I keep finding myself at these crime scenes. It would be odd if I didn't pick up a few pointers, don't you think?"

"Yeah, I guess so," Chloe said, still giving me a weird look.

I huffed out a breath. "Would you put it past Richie to kill Bree?"

"I can't think of anyone who would actually kill someone. But then again, Richie's such a creep." She leaned around me to get another look at the man. "I guess I wouldn't put it past him to do something awful like that."

"I wouldn't, either." I had never liked him, and knowing the way he'd treated my sister did not improve my opinion. And then seeing him eavesdropping the day before made it even worse. "He's probably a sociopath and he's certainly corrupt, so he's pretty much the perfect suspect."

"I know you've seen your share of crime scenes, but this is my first. Maybe you have a better picture of what constitutes a killer."

"Not really. It's always a shock."

She stared at me for a long moment. "So just how many . . . I mean, hmm." She winced. "Sorry. Never mind."

"I know what you're asking and hey, even my best friends wonder." I gave a strained laugh. "A few months ago I was having dinner with Jane and Emily and some others, and they started counting up the bodies. It was gruesome and weird, especially as a dinner conversation." And it had been appalling to realize just how many murders I'd been involved in. "So don't feel bad. Anyway, I think we're up to eight. It might be more. And I've been attacked a few times myself."

"Good grief, Shannon." Chloe's eyes went

wide. "That's just terrible. I think I need to come home more often just to keep an eye on you. I hope you carry a weapon with you."

"Mostly I carry hammers and pipe wrenches. They're pretty effective weapons. And yes, it's terrible. I don't know why I'm always the one who discovers the bodies around here." I threw my hands up. "At this point I'm waiting for my friends to cut me loose. I mean, who wants to hang around someone who's got a reputation for finding murder victims?"

"That's a good point. Luckily, though, you have some very loyal friends." She hugged me. "And, you'll always have *me.*"

I held on to her for a long moment. "Thanks, Chloe, I love you, too. But as for my friends, I don't know how much longer they'll stick with me if this keeps happening."

She chuckled. "You're being silly."

I hoped she was right. I knew my friends loved me, but honestly, who wanted to be around a murder magnet? On the other hand, talking about this was at least a good way to keep our minds off the sight of Bree Bennett's body on that cold marble hearth.

Ugh.

Chloe was silent for a moment as she

gazed at the side of the house. "This corner molding is completely warped."

Relieved at the change of subject, I turned to look. Touching the wood, I managed to poke my finger right through it. "It's rotted straight through. This entire porch is shot. We'll have to redo everything." I ran over and got a hammer out of my toolbox and came back. "And it's not just the moldings. Look at this corner beam." I was so grateful to be doing something normal. Something helpful. I used the claw end to rip the beam right off the house. It didn't take much effort.

"That's not good." Chloe scanned the porch area and pointed up. "And check out that header beam. It's completely waterlogged."

"I noticed that earlier. The wood has probably turned to sponge by now."

"No doubt we're taking our lives in our hands just standing here on the porch."

I gave her a hopeful smile. "We'll probably be okay for a few more minutes."

She sighed. "I'm much happier looking at rotten wood than dead people."

"Me, too." I smiled and glanced around. "This is my happy place."

She gazed out at the lawn. "Is Richie still out there?"

I took a quick peek over my shoulder.

"Yes. He's talking to . . . um. Hmm." I moved to block her view, but she pushed me aside.

"Who? Tell me."

"He's talking to Suzanne," I whispered.

"What? No." I was surprised when she stepped behind me. "I don't want them to see me watching."

"Okay. She just handed him something. Looks like a piece of paper."

Chloe frowned. "This is weird. How would she know Richie?"

"I don't know, but they seem kind of friendly." I watched for another few seconds until Suzanne walked away. "Who knows? It may be nothing. But you might want to warn her about him."

"Good idea." She scowled. "He's got a lot of nerve showing up here at all. What's he doing now?"

"Looks like he's just staring across the yard. I'm not sure why. There's nothing to see. It's just Tommy, talking to the Wagners."

Her eyes widened. "Shannon. I wonder if the Wagners are Richie's clients."

I thought about that possibility. "Now that makes perfect sense. They all deserve one another. We should find out for sure because if it's true, I can just imagine Richie bragging to the Wagners that their house was definitely going to be used. And that might be the reason they're so angry." Something else occurred to me. "What if he was demanding a kickback from them? That would piss them off even more."

Chloe scowled. "Richie's definitely the kickback type."

I nodded slowly. "We've got to find out for sure."

She sneaked a peek at Richie, who was grabbing another donut while blathering to someone at the coffee table, trying to make a point. "I know I said that Bree would never sleep with him, but now I wonder. He's strutting around like he owns the place."

"Would Bree really cheat on Blake?"

"I guess I don't know anymore. I mean, she was really putting him down during our meeting. It's just not fair. Blake is really cool."

"Except." I held up my tool. "Blake can't swing a hammer."

She giggled. "Is that a metaphor?"

I began to laugh. "That was bad. Sorry."

"It's okay," she said. "You made me laugh. For a while there, I thought I'd never laugh again."

"I know what you mean." I looked away, distracted by more activity in the yard. "Okay, Tommy is headed toward us. And it looks like the Wagners are leaving. Oh, look. There goes Richie."

Chloe turned around. "He going after the Wagners?"

We both watched as Richie began to jog across the lawn.

"Hey, Rolly," Richie yelled.

Both Wagners turned and stopped. They glanced at each other and then at Richie. Rolly Wagner folded his arms tightly across his chest. They were not happy campers.

"They must be his clients," I murmured. "Look how angry they are. That's the only explanation."

"I don't know," Chloe said, "I have a feeling most people react like that to Richie."

Richie got closer and I couldn't hear what he was saying to the Wagners, but he looked alternately contrite and annoyed. A few seconds later it appeared that the conversation was over. Then all of a sudden, Rolly Wagner hauled off and punched Richie in the jaw.

"He just hit him!" Chloe cried.

And it was a heck of a punch. I was ashamed to admit I enjoyed it.

Richie staggered backward and spun

around. Rolly started toward him again, but his wife grabbed his arm and pulled him away. "Rolly, no! There's cops everywhere!"

"Tommy," I shouted, pointing toward the fracas. "That guy just punched that other guy."

Tommy whipped around, saw what was happening, and ran back to stop the fight.

"This day just gets better and better," I muttered. "I'm going down there."

"Shannon, wait!"

But I was tired of waiting in the shadows and took off down the steps. I wanted to hear what all those losers had to say for themselves.

As I ran across the wide lawn, I could see Tommy trying to push Rolly Wagner back from grabbing Richie. Tommy was strong, but Wagner had major weight and muscle on his side. Meanwhile, Richie was sitting on the ground, looking dizzy and sick.

I stared in disbelief as Rolly pushed Tommy back. *Big mistake,* I thought, watching Tommy reach for his handcuffs. Just when I thought Rolly might take a swing at Tommy, I saw Eric come running from across the street. Eric grabbed Rolly Wagner from behind and slapped handcuffs on him faster than I could even say the word.

"Wow," Chloe said. "Impressive. He's like

the Flash or something."

I whipped around and saw my sister right behind me. "Where'd you come from?"

"I wasn't going to be left behind." Chloe rolled her eyes at the thought.

I couldn't blame her. "Well look, we don't call Eric the Flash, but I occasionally think of him as Thor."

"Yeah," Chloe said with a slow nod of appreciation. "I can see that."

Wagner's wife started shouting. "Leave him alone! My husband isn't the bad guy here." She pointed at Richie. "That guy sold us a bill of goods. He's a liar and a cheat and you should put him in jail."

"She's got that right," Chloe murmured.

I almost laughed, but Eric had a look on his face that told me I'd better stifle it. He turned to Tommy. "You okay?"

"Yeah."

"Go check on Bennett for me, would you, Tom?"

"You bet." Tommy took off running toward Blake's trailer, but he turned to throw a dirty look at Rolly Wagner, who deserved that and more.

"Garcia! Payton!" Eric barked out the names. "Get over here."

Carlos and Mindy were already standing nearby and stepped up to help.

"Take this guy to the station and book him."

"Yes, sir." They each took hold of one of Rolly's beefy arms and led him off to a squad car.

"Noooo!" Mrs. Wagner cried. "It's not fair. We were robbed!"

Eric pierced her with a look. "You were robbed, ma'am?"

"Well, sort of." She backpedaled so fast, I expected to see sparks. "I mean, he promised we would be on the show and now we're not. So it's not fair that —"

"Let me stop you right there, ma'am," Eric said, holding up his hand. "Your husband just assaulted a police officer. We can discuss the fairness issue down at the station if you'd like to join us." Then he walked away.

"Boom. Mic drop," Chloe whispered. "I'm really getting to like your Thor."

"He's not *mine.*"

"Figure of speech."

I shook my head and went back to watching Eric's next move.

"But what about him?" Mrs. Wagner whined, waving her hand at Richie. "Aren't you going to arrest him?"

But Eric kept going. I couldn't blame him for walking away from these horrible people, but I would've loved to see him slap some cuffs on Richie Rich. No one deserved it more.

Chapter Eight

The excitement was over.

The Wagners were dragged off to the police station. Tommy had gone over to the trailer to check on Blake Bennett and to hopefully spring Mac. The entire production staff and most of the crew were at loose ends, waiting for word on what they were supposed to do next. Chloe had talked to Suzanne and the other production people to figure out whether they should take the rest of the day off to honor Bree's memory and then report back first thing tomorrow morning.

It was barely eleven o'clock in the morning when Chloe and I crossed the lawn and climbed the front steps to retrieve our tote bags and my toolbox.

"It feels as if we've spent the past twenty-four hours here," I said.

"It's because of all the drama and horror we've watched unfold. It seems to have stretched the space-time continuum."

"Gee, that's almost poetic," I said, grinning.

"Hey, I'm not just a pretty face."

"No, you're so much more." I stared at all my bags and my toolbox and wondered if I even had the energy to move everything. I glanced at Chloe. "Are you hungry? I'm hungry."

"I could eat."

I shot a glance across the lawn. "Those donuts are calling my name."

"Hmm, you may be starting to hallucinate."

"Because I'm starving." I gazed longingly at the catering table. I could easily grab one of Emily's delectable pastries, but what I really wanted was a cheeseburger.

From behind me, the front door opened with a morbidly loud creak, surprising me enough that I jolted and let out a little shriek. I managed to right myself, but it was embarrassing.

"Are you all right?" Chloe asked, alarmed.

"That stupid door freaks me out every time," I grumbled, feeling silly. "I'm going to oil those hinges as soon as Eric gives me the word."

Leo the CSI guy walked out the door, followed by Lilah.

"Hey there, Shannon," Leo said, while Lilah smiled and nodded.

I pulled one of my tote bags up to my shoulder and grabbed my toolbox. "How's it going in there?"

"We've got at least another full day's worth of work to do," Leo said, his expression grim. "It's a little stuffy so I thought we'd take a break while we wait for the guys to come and transport the body."

"Will she go to Bittermans?" I asked. That was our local funeral home, where the body would be embalmed if the family approved.

"She'll have to be autopsied first," Leo said.

"It looked to me like she'd been hit in the head."

"She was. But there may be more than one cause of death to choose from."

"Oh." I wasn't sure he should've revealed that tidbit to me, but I supposed he'd seen me with Eric on a few other murder scenes and figured I was trustworthy. Which I *was*. But I still didn't think the police chief would appreciate me getting the news. Mostly because now I was going to wonder what other causes of death Bree might've suffered.

Maybe she had been drugged like Blake. Maybe she had confronted her killer as he tried to drug her and she'd fought back, so the killer had to conk her over the head with some blunt, heavy object. Or maybe she was stabbed, although I didn't see blood anywhere else. Or she could've been strangled. I didn't notice any bruising around her neck when I checked for a pulse, but I wasn't an expert, was I?

No, I was not. And that was the very best reason to just stop thinking about all these terrifying causes of death and move along to the next topic. Maybe I couldn't help finding bodies, but that didn't mean I had to focus on murder, did I?

"Are you going to be doing any work out here?" I asked.

Leo shrugged. "Just some dusting for prints."

I pressed my lips together, concerned that I'd damaged their investigation. "Did you already take care of the front doorknob?"

"Yes, the knob and the keyhole escutcheon," Leo said, "just to be safe."

I walked over to the door to study the fixture. "It's very heavily ornamented."

"Yes, classic Victorian and beautiful, don't you think? But see? There's a flat surface just around the keyhole itself." He grinned. "You never know. Might snag ourselves a partial."

"I really hope you find something," I said. "But I should warn you, I opened the door myself this morning so you might just find my prints."

"Chief Jensen warned me of that already, so I'll watch out for you." He winked at me. "We've got your prints on file."

I smiled. "Thanks, Leo."

"We're lucky you didn't use the back door, because we got some good, clear prints there. Plus there's an aluminum screen door, so we have twice as much chance of finding something."

So they thought the killer might've come in through the back door? It made sense. I thought about the layout of the neighborhood. They could've parked on a side street and hiked through the woods to the Blooms' backyard, then sneaked in through the back door and surprised Bree waiting inside.

But who had she been waiting for? I wondered. And was the person she was waiting for the same person who killed her? Had there been a skirmish inside the house? With all the dust and cobwebs in there, I would think the forensics people would notice signs of a scuffle. Maybe the scuffle took place in the backyard and she was dragged inside and left on the fireplace hearth.

Don't look now, Shannon, I told myself, *but you're focusing on murder again.*

"Hey, Leo," Lilah said. "While you're out here taking a break, I'm going to go inside and dust for prints on the staircase."

"Good idea," Leo said. "You got your briefcase with you?"

"Never leave home without it."

He grinned and gave her a thumbs-up. I assumed he was talking about a fingerprint kit like the ones I'd seen other cops carry. It did look like a briefcase, but instead of papers and files, it held a bunch of tools and supplies, mainly several containers of fine black fiber powder, a soft dusting brush, and plenty of lifting tape to capture any prints they found.

I could speak from experience when it came to cleaning up that microfine black powder they used. It was almost impossible to get rid of it all. And how sad was it that I knew this stuff?

"Ready?" Chloe said, her arms full of the bags of clothing and supplies we'd brought with us earlier.

"We'll see you later, Leo," I said, and followed Chloe carefully down the steps. When I reached the walkway I turned back to the CSI guy. "Please be careful on these steps, Leo. The wood is old and rotted."

"Thanks for the heads-up," Leo said, and waved as we walked away.

Just then, Mac jogged up the walkway. "Good timing," he said, and took the toolbox from my hand.

"Thank you," I said, beaming a happy smile. "You've been gone awhile."

"I was in the trailer talking to Blake."

"He talked to you?"

"Yeah. He woke up right after the EMTs showed up. Refused to go to the hospital."

"I'm glad he's talking," I said. "Mainly because I'm dying to hear what he said and what happened in there."

"And I'm dying to tell you." He grinned. "Are you taking this stuff to your truck?"

"Yes. Maybe." I paused as an idea formed in my head. "Hey, Chloe, wait up."

She stopped and turned. I knew she had sped up to give Mac and me a chance to talk alone. I appreciated her thoughtfulness, but I had something else in mind.

"What is it?" she asked.

"What would you say to getting the crew together and doing some work on the outside of the house this afternoon? It might be a day or two before we can get back inside, so it'll give us something to do in the meantime." When she didn't answer right away, I cajoled a little. "The catering trucks are here. We've got the guys, the tools, and we could get a jump on things . . ."

She thought about it for a moment, stared up at the massive Victorian, and nodded. "That's not a bad idea. Let me see what Suzanne thinks. With Bree . . . gone, Suzanne will have to take over the mantle of executive producer. Much as I disliked Bree, she knew how to run the show. We'll need someone with that quality. Suzanne is certainly organized, but I'm not sure she has it in her to knock heads together when it's needed."

"Maybe it won't be needed."

"Maybe." Chloe smiled. "I'd better get some of the crew involved, too. They've got their union schedules to deal with. This might take a little while."

"We'll have to clear it with the police first," I said, "but I can give Eric a call and find out."

"Oh, right. You should talk to Eric before I tell my people." She frowned. "Frankly, Shannon, I'm not sure everyone will really want to go back to work. We might need to take at least a day off to honor Bree's memory."

I grimaced. Okay, my suggestion was tacky. But in my defense, Bree didn't have a lot of admirers around here. "Of course. I'm so sorry, I wasn't thinking."

"That's okay," she said, waving away my concern. "I'm on your side. I would love to work on that porch this afternoon. It would take my mind off everything that's happened and, hey, Bree would want the show to go on."

Another good point. "Do you think maybe your cameraman and some of the rest of the crew will feel the same way we do?"

"I can probably talk them into it. I'll have to clear it with Suzanne and our associate producer to make sure we're complying with the union rules and all that jazz."

"Okay, let me call Eric and see what he says." I glanced at Mac. "I know he's busy right now and I'm probably the last person he wants to hear from. But this is important."

"You don't have to call him, Shannon," Mac said. "Eric is still talking to Blake. He's right inside that trailer."

"Oh." That was a surprise. "He stormed off after that confrontation with the Wagners and I figured he'd gone back to headquarters."

"Nope. I get the feeling he's perfectly happy to let the Wagners stew for a while. Meanwhile, Eric and many of the other cops will probably be here for most of the day. They've still got to interview people and search the house for possible evidence."

"I knew that," I muttered.

Mac laughed and wrapped an arm around my shoulders. "Of course you did."

"What about you?" I asked. "Are you going to go home? You were stuck in that trailer for over three hours. You must be ready to hit the road."

"Not really," he said, smiling broadly. "We had a pretty interesting talk."

Oh, he was teasing me with the promise of information. "Does he know about Bree?"

Mac's smile faded a bit. "He does now. He was still groggy for a while so I didn't say anything about it. But as soon as Eric walked in, Blake straightened up. Especially when he broke the news about his wife."

"How did Blake react?" Chloe asked.

Mac hesitated, then said, "He burst into tears."

"Oh no." Chloe pressed her hand to her mouth and I was afraid her own floodwall was about to crack.

I patted her arm. "Are you okay?"

She sniffled. "I'm really worried about Blake. I know he comes across as the original rugged individualist, but he was always very devoted to Bree. What will he do now?

It tears me up inside."

I glanced at Mac. "Did they take him to police headquarters?"

"Not yet. Guess it depends on what he tells them, whether they'll take him in to be interrogated. I wish I could tell you more, but Eric asked me to leave when he and Tommy started getting into some of the more serious questions about his wife's death."

"That's a drag," I muttered, completely disappointed.

"Right?" Mac said, biting back a smile. Honestly, he knew me so well, it was both comforting and annoying. "Anyway, I'm not sure what they'll get out of him. He was still weepy when I left."

"I'd say it's been an awful day for everyone." I really wanted to get into doing some work. Swinging a hammer and doing a little demo was good for the soul, and it could keep your mind busy when you really needed it.

He reached for my hand. "To answer your earlier question, I'm not going home. I'm staying here for as long as you're here."

I smiled. "That's nice. Thank you."

"Hey, there's a killer running loose around here and I'm not taking my eyes off you until they're caught."

"Killer. Right. Good point."

I knew I was probably safe enough being surrounded by all these people, but it was a truly good feeling to have my very own knight in shining armor standing alongside me.

Still, though, it would be wise to remember there was a killer in our midst. I took in a deep breath and let it go. It always helped to get a clear picture of what we were up against. Trying to lighten the moment, I said, "Well, as long as you're staying, maybe we can put you to work."

"I'll be happy to help out. Let's go talk to Eric," he suggested. "See what he says about your crew working on the house."

I looked at Chloe. "You coming with us?"

"I'll go check the production trailer and see for sure whether anyone's up for working this afternoon. Will you come find me after you talk to Chief Jensen? It's the fourth trailer down the line."

I walked with her to the production trailer, where we stowed our bags and toolboxes. Then Mac and I headed for Blake's trailer. He knocked on the door.

Tommy opened the door and stepped outside. "What's up, guys?"

"I wanted to ask Eric if he minds if we do some work on the outside of the house this afternoon."

"Let me ask him." He walked back inside and closed the door. A minute later, he returned. "He said okay, but stay away from the area around the front door and don't go inside the house, of course."

"Got it. Thanks, Tommy."

I texted Chloe to let her know we'd received the okay from Eric.

She texted back, *Wait for me.*

"We might as well meet her at the production trailer." Mac and I walked down to the trailer just as Chloe stepped outside.

"They're rounding up the crew," she said. "We can go to work this afternoon. The guys will need an hour for the setup, plus an hour for lunch."

"That's great."

Chloe nodded, "I think you were right. Most of the guys really need something to do. Taking the day off would have given everyone too much time to think about what happened." She turned to look at the Bloom house. "Besides, this is Bree's last job. We all want to make it shine."

I reached out and gave her arm a squeeze. "You okay?"

"Yeah. I mean, not great. But okay. And still hungry."

"Me, too," I said. "Let's go eat."

■ ■ ■ ■

After arranging to meet back at the house in an hour, Mac drove Chloe and me to the Cozy Cove Diner for lunch.

Once we were seated in a booth and our orders were taken and drinks were served, I turned to Mac. "So tell us everything that Blake said."

"Does he know who drugged him?" Chloe asked.

"He doesn't know much of anything," Mac said. "He got to the house around six o'clock last night. Bree had a meeting so she told him she would meet him at the house around seven, but she didn't show up until almost eight."

I frowned. "Why would they meet at the house so late? It's so dark and spooky."

"The Wagners were the ones who insisted on meeting them there, and Bree wanted to placate them because they were so angry about the decision." Mac took a sip of water. "Blake had a feeling they would want to go through the house and point out every little downside while giving all the reasons why *their* house would be better for the show. They just didn't get that it was too late."

"Plus they were wrong," I insisted. "Their house isn't very interesting. The Bloom house has so much character and it's such a classic style. Couldn't they see that?"

"Guess not. Anyway, Bree showed up almost an hour later and Blake yelled at her for keeping him waiting." Mac paused, shook his head. "As soon as he told us that, he started bawling all over again because he felt so guilty for yelling at her."

"Oh, dear," Chloe whispered.

"That's rough," I said, frowning. "He's going to have to live with that guilt for a long time. But eventually, he'll remember that Bree knew he loved her." But even as I said it, I knew none of that would make Blake feel any better right now.

Cindy arrived with our burgers and we dug in, grateful for the break. We ate in silence for a few minutes, savoring our cheeseburgers and fries.

Finally Mac set down his burger and took up the conversation. "Blake said that Bree had set up meetings with both couples. The Blooms arrived at eight o'clock and left after about fifteen minutes."

"Did the Blooms find out that their house was chosen?"

"Bree wouldn't tell them. Even though the Wagners found out that they were the losers, Bree insisted on keeping the news from the Blooms so they could get their reaction on camera."

"That's Bree," Chloe said with a shrug. "That's how she rolls." She gulped. "Well, *rolled.*"

"The Wagners didn't show up until around nine thirty," Mac said. "According to Blake, they were really fuming and said a lot of threatening stuff. Even mentioned a possible lawsuit, but Bree played it cool. Told them they'd signed a contract and they didn't have a legal leg to stand on."

"That must've annoyed Rolly Wagner."

"Oh, yeah. He got right up in Bree's face and told her there were other ways to get even that had nothing to do with a lawsuit. Blake stepped in between them and told Wagner to stop threatening his wife."

I reached for a French fry. "Rolly Wagner is a big, mean bully, so that was pretty brave of Blake."

"Yeah," Mac said. "Blake said the guy looked like he was going to explode. Anyway, Wagner warned that they'd be sorry and then the Wagners stomped their way out of the house." He took a bite of his burger and took his time chewing.

I was anxious to hear more and was not exactly known for my patience. "So then what happened?"

"At that point, Blake was ready to call it a night, but Bree couldn't leave yet. She was supposed to meet Suzanne and go over some details about the script, but Suzanne couldn't meet her until ten p.m."

I was frowning again. "That's a little late, isn't it?"

"For Blake, yes, but not for Bree," Chloe said. "Blake always likes to get a full night's sleep before we film."

"That's what he told us," Mac said, nodding. "So he took off to sleep in his dressing room trailer like he always does the night before the first shoot. He assumed Bree would go back to the B and B when she was finished and the two of them would meet up in the morning."

"So he left the Bloom house and didn't see anything after that?" I said. "That's awfully anticlimactic."

"And how did he wind up drugged?" Chloe asked.

"He insists he has no idea," Mac said.

"Do you believe him?"

Mac frowned. "I don't know him, but he seemed sincere. One of the last things he remembers is grabbing a bottle of water when he left."

"Where'd they have water bottles?" I wondered.

"The staff had set up a utility table in the dining room for Bree to work and they'd put some office supplies and a few bottles of water there. Anyway, Blake started drinking it as he walked across the lawn to the trailer and finished it before he went to bed. He wondered if someone slipped a drug into it."

I frowned. "If that was the case, then the drug was meant for Bree."

Mac gave me a look. "Exactly. Although Blake didn't get that connection. I guess he was still too sleepy. But he remembers there were three bottles on the table. As soon as he said that, Eric texted one of his deputies to gather up the water bottles in the house. They'll have them all tested."

"Right." I took another quick bite and chewed thoughtfully. "Leo Springer told me it was possible there was more than one cause of death."

Mac raised an eyebrow. "Not sure Eric would approve of him sharing that information."

"Just what I thought. And I completely agree. But I'm not about to tell the police chief that his CSI investigator has a big mouth."

"We saw blood on Bree's head." Chloe cringed as she said it. "So now they think maybe she was also drugged?"

"Maybe." I spared them my theories about the many possible causes of death. Instead, I sat back in the booth and enjoyed the last bite of my burger. But then I thought of another question. "Did Blake suggest any suspects while you were there?"

Mac looked suddenly uncomfortable.

"What is it?" I said. "What did he say?"

"Well, he mentioned Chloe and Diego and —"

"No!" I cried, then quickly lowered my voice. "How dare he accuse Chloe?"

Mac held up both hands. "In his defense, it wasn't really an accusation. He was just going down the list of people who'd had run-ins with Bree recently."

"But that would be every person on staff," Chloe insisted. "Bree was an equal-opportunity pain in everyone's butt."

"That's right," I said, still miffed. "And didn't you say that Blake himself had run-ins with Bree?"

"Yes." Chloe gave a firm nod. "The two of them were notorious for yelling and screaming at each other."

"It's not sounding like a very happy family," I said, sipping my soda.

Chloe's shoulders slumped. "Unfortunately you're experiencing all of our worst aspects. I swear, most of the time we really are a fun group."

I glanced at Mac, who gave me a look of sympathy. Chloe was obviously so miserable, I wanted to cry. I wanted the cloud of suspicion hanging over her to go away. I hated seeing her so glum. But on a bright note, seeing her so unhappy simply renewed my determination to find the killer as quickly as possible.

Chapter Nine

Mac dropped us off in front of the Bloom house and drove off to find a parking place. I watched his car disappear around the corner and thought again what a hero he was to stay on the set with me, because except for Chloe and my own crew members, I had no idea who to trust around here.

"Look," Chloe said, pointing toward the house. "They've already started to build a scaffold around the porch." She squinted to see more clearly in the sunlight. "Those are your guys, right?"

"Yeah. That was fast." I was proud to see Wade and Sean carrying scaffold piping over from the supply truck. When Eric shut production down earlier, Wade had taken the crew to one of our other job sites. But I had made a quick call to Wade before we left for lunch and they had dropped everything to come back and help us out. Was it any wonder I trusted my crew?

I glanced at the street, hoping Mac had found a parking place and would be here soon. When I saw Blake Bennett cross the street and walk toward the construction site, I was sincerely shocked. Even though the staff and crew had decided to get some work done, I never thought Blake would join them. The man had just lost his wife.

Chloe saw him at the same time and I heard a little cry escape her. She ran to him and wrapped him in a tight hug. Blake buried his face in her shoulder and I had a feeling the two of them were shedding a few more tears. I casually walked closer to hear what they were talking about. Not that I wanted to eavesdrop on my sister, but I was beginning to see how she could be a little naïve when it came to her beloved co-workers.

After all, we were knee-deep in a murder investigation. I couldn't blame her for believing the best of them, of course. This was her Hollywood family. I, however, was suffering no delusions about any of them and considered my eavesdropping just one way of protecting my sister. Especially when I knew Eric was still half considering Chloe to be a murder suspect.

That was my story and I was sticking to it, I thought as I ambled closer. And just to make it look good, I nonchalantly pulled out my phone and pretended to check my messages.

"What are you doing here?" Chloe asked Blake. "Don't you want to take a little time away from all this?"

"No way," Blake said. "If I sit in that trailer another minute, I'll go completely insane."

"But I heard you were drugged. Shouldn't you be in the hospital?"

He made a sound of disgust. "No way. Work is the best remedy for what's ailing me."

"I was thinking the same thing," she said. "Production was going to give everyone a day off in Bree's memory, but we all decided that if we kept working it would take our minds off the horrible news."

"I'm glad to hear it," he said. "I really think Bree would've wanted us to keep going."

"Oh, Blake," Chloe said, clearly overwhelmed with emotion. She gave him another hug and he didn't protest. Why would he? Blake wasn't stupid. He might've already figured out that having a dearly departed wife was likely to get him all kinds of warm sympathy and cozy hugs from a lot of beautiful women, including my very sweet and beautiful sister, Chloe.

I knew I was being cynical, but I couldn't help it. Especially when Chloe and Blake were quickly surrounded by other staff and crew members. Mostly female. They seemed to be in awe of Blake actually showing up to work. It was almost as though he had just performed heart surgery, whipped up a chocolate cream pie, and then run out and won an Olympic gold medal.

As soon as Chloe let go of Blake, Suzanne grabbed him and held on for dear life. Even though Blake was tall, Suzanne had a few inches on him. They were whispering and I could barely hear the words, except for a few odd sentence fragments.

Blake said, ". . . take care of . . ."

". . . secret is safe . . ." Suzanne said.

Then Blake muttered something like, ". . . blow it . . ."

What was that all about?

At that moment, Marisa the wardrobe mistress snatched Blake away from Suzanne and pressed him to her bosom in a suffocating clinch. She was followed shortly thereafter by Josie, the woman who did everyone's hair and makeup.

It sure looked to me like the women of *Makeover Madness* loved them some Blake Bennett. Which made me wonder what these women really thought of Bree. If they knew that she had fired Blake to prevent him from working on the new, flashy big-time network show, would one of them be angry enough to kill her? And now I had to wonder if anyone else on the staff knew about the new show.

"I know you don't want to spend the night alone," one woman crooned. "You're welcome to stay with me in my trailer tonight."

The crowd surrounding them was now three deep, but I was pretty sure the woman who'd just offered that suggestion was the wardrobe mistress, Marisa.

Unfortunately her proposition did not play well with the others. "Marisa, what are you saying?" one woman griped. "The man just lost his wife."

"Oh no! No, no!" Marisa protested. "I don't mean it like that. You guys, I'll sleep on the couch! But I'll be there for him."

"You can stay with me, Blake," Carolee the production assistant said. "I've got a beautiful room at the Inn on Main Street. There's a view of the ocean and an amazing mini-bar."

If we were rating the offers, I would go with that, I thought. Much better than sleeping in a crummy old trailer.

"No, stay with me tonight," Josie begged.

"I'll give you a haircut."

I snorted a laugh. Now *that* was a hard one to pass up, I thought. But seriously, this was getting weird.

Chloe managed to slip out of the crowd and found me hovering on the edges. "I assume you're hearing all of this?"

"I'm hearing it, but I don't believe it. These women are all in love with that guy."

She glanced over her shoulder at the crowd of living, breathing warm blankies, all devoted to their leader. "Yeah, Blake is a real hero to many of them."

"Why?"

"Simple," she said with a light shrug. "He created a great show and hired them for some really good jobs. He's generous with his compliments and he protects them from Bree. He remembers their kids' names and celebrates their birthdays. He plans a big Christmas party every year and gives nice bonuses. It's not hard to build loyalty. You just have to treat people nicely."

"But Bree was the executive producer. Wasn't she the one who authorized all of that stuff?"

Chloe sniffed indignantly. "If she had her way we'd have no benefits and barely get paid. She was always telling us we're replaceable and should be grateful to have any job at all."

"So I take it they didn't love Bree the same way they love Blake?"

She laughed shortly. "No. Bree made it clear that employee loyalty was at the bottom of her priority list. She was always threatening to cancel our vacations and would sometimes withhold bonus checks until we jumped through hoops, just for her own amusement."

I thought about that point. "I'm seriously considering every single person in this crowd a suspect."

"Probably smart," Chloe admitted.

"Blake!" A woman shot through the crowd to get to Blake and literally jumped into his arms. "I've been so worried about you!"

"Thanks, Chelsea," he murmured into her hair. "I'm okay."

I leaned in close to Chloe. "I don't know about the others, but Chelsea truly is in love with Blake. It's painful to watch sometimes."

"You're right," Chloe murmured. "She's so young."

The other women had let him go after a few seconds, but Chelsea clung to him like a suction cup. She was petite and very cute, and Blake didn't seem to mind one bit.

Chloe and I stared at the crowd for another minute, watching all these women fawning over Blake Bennett. I liked him and could admit I'd felt sorry for him earlier, especially when we found him in his trailer, passed out from being drugged. But after seeing these women compete for the tiniest morsel of his attention, I was a little confused, to say the least.

I turned away from the women to watch the hubbub of activity taking place around the house, just for a shot of normalcy. Mac was hanging with my crew and they were all laughing together, which, oddly enough, settled me. I gave Chloe a light nudge. "Ready to go to work?"

"More than ready," she said. "Let's go."

"Chloe."

We both turned and saw Eric Jensen walk up.

"Hi, Chief," Chloe said.

"What's up, Eric?"

He looked at my sister. "I have some questions to ask you and I'd like to do it at police headquarters."

"No, no," I said. "That's crazy. Chloe isn't —"

"It's just a couple of questions, Shannon," he said through his teeth. "It'll only take an hour at the most and then she'll be back to work."

I looked at Chloe and saw the color draining from her face. "I'll go with you."

"No," she said. "You stay here. Tell Suzanne where I went. I'm sure they're questioning everyone so it's probably no big deal."

"I suppose." But that didn't mean I wouldn't worry.

"Let's go," Eric said, taking Chloe's arm.

She shrugged his hand away. "I'm perfectly capable of walking on my own."

I wasn't about to let him go without giving him a piece of my mind. I walked along with him as he escorted Chloe to his SUV. But before I could say a word, Chloe spoke up. "Really, Shannon. It's not like I didn't expect this."

"What does that mean?" Eric asked.

But I knew what she was talking about.

"Why?" she asked, shaking her head. "Why did I think it was a good idea to come back here?"

"Chloe, don't," I said, taking hold of her other arm.

"He won't believe me, Shannon," she said heatedly. "They never do. Why should he be any different from the old guy?"

"Eric *is* different," I insisted. "Please. You can trust him." Despite my words, I glared at Eric. "Don't make me a liar."

Eric stopped walking and turned to me.

"What's going on here? Who's the old guy and why wouldn't I believe your sister?"

Chloe stood with her arms wrapped tightly across her stomach. Her lips were pressed together in a stubborn pout, and my mind flashed back to an angry sixteen-year-old who hated her life and couldn't wait to leave town.

I took a deep breath. "Chloe had some run-ins with the old police chief. She was wrongly accused of stealing something from the high school trophy case and the chief arrested her without even listening to her side of the story. It turned out that some of the girls had lied to get Chloe in trouble."

"I assume you're talking about Chief Raymond." Eric's voice was full of contempt as he said the name of the old chief. Chief Raymond had been mean and lazy to boot. To this day, Eric was still making up for some of his predecessor's bad decisions.

"I'm not going to arrest you, Chloe," he said quietly. "I just want to hear what happened from your point of view and find out what you think about some of your coworkers. I'd rather not do it here where anyone might overhear us."

She gazed up at him for a long moment. "That's it?"

"That's it. And then I'll bring you back

here when we're finished."

Her eyes narrowed. "You promise?"

Eric crossed his heart. "I promise."

She twisted her lips, thinking. Finally, she nodded. "Okay. I'll go."

Not that she has a choice, I thought. But I was glad that her mood was slightly less combative as she climbed into the SUV.

"I'll expect to see you back here soon," I said to Eric.

He looked at me and nodded. "She'll be back to work in one hour."

As promised, Chloe was back about an hour later. I didn't even have a minute to stop and ask how she was feeling after being questioned by the chief of police. As soon as Eric dropped her off she ran into the makeup and hair trailer to get ready for filming. She seemed happier and more energetic and she got right back into the swing of things. I hadn't done anything on camera yet, but I'd been moving lumber and carrying tools and working with the rest of the crew. I'd tried to forget that my sister was being interrogated by the police, while trying equally hard to forget that my first segment with Blake and Diego would be coming up soon. *Deep breaths,* I thought.

It looked as if the entire town had turned

out to watch us. This was in spite of the murder that had taken place the night before, or maybe *because* of it. Both sidewalks were packed with people hoping to catch a glimpse of Blake, Chloe, and Diego. And me, for goodness' sake!

All this attention was probably old hat for Chloe, who barely seemed to notice the onlookers. But for me it was a completely new experience.

"How do you ignore them?" I asked. "They applaud and whoop it up whenever one of us walks down the steps. There were whistles when I picked up a loose nail from the grass."

"I think it's lovely that they've come to see us," Chloe said, "but the way I look at it, I'm here to do a job. And more important, I have a very limited amount of time in which to do it. I wave to them and they love that. And I love it, too. But I'm not going to spend time schmoozing with them or worrying about what they think or how they feel about the job I'm doing."

"That's such a good attitude. I'll try to be more like you."

"I've been telling you that for years," she said with a cheeky grin.

"Funny girl."

"Hey, Chloe, where do you want this?"

We both turned and saw Diego carrying an extension ladder. He wore cut-off shorts and another of his tight black T-shirts, the ones that showed off every gorgeous muscle on his arms and caused some high-pitched giggles and more than a few *woo-hoos* from the crowd.

"Over on the side of the house. Thanks, Diego."

"Now that would be a distraction," I said when he walked away.

"I suppose." She shrugged. "I guess I've known him too long to be distracted anymore."

"Maybe you should have your blood pressure checked. Or your eyesight."

She laughed. "Yeah, maybe. Oh." All of a sudden she wobbled and her eyes rolled back. "Oh."

"What's wrong?"

"I feel . . . I can't . . . uhh." Her head lolled. Then her legs gave out and she collapsed on the ground.

"Chloe!" I screamed. I patted her cheeks. They felt clammy and her lips were turning a weird shade of blue. "Wake up!" I looked up and caught Mindy Payton's glance. "Call 911! Chloe's passed out."

Tommy worked to revive my sister until the

EMTs got there. They rushed her to the hospital, where the emergency room doctor determined that she had been poisoned by some as yet undetermined substance. They pumped her stomach and released her two hours later.

We were home by six that night. I brought Chloe's pajamas downstairs so she wouldn't have to make the climb up to her room. She was tucked under a blanket in the living room, sipping warm tea and nibbling on soda crackers, when Eric showed up at the house to ask her some questions.

"How are you feeling?"

"Like I just had my stomach pumped."

"Probably a good thing since the doctor suspects you might've overdosed on Dilaudid."

She made a face. "What is that?"

"It's a narcotic," he said slowly, then added, "They call it heroin in a pill."

"Heroin?" She stared at me, her eyes wide. "Oh my God."

"Don't worry," I said, worrying plenty for both of us. "They pumped it out of you." I looked at Eric. "How did it happen? All she ate was a cheeseburger and fries at the diner. And Mac and I had the exact same thing."

He nodded, then turned to my sister.

"What else did you eat after that, Chloe?"

"Nothing," Chloe said. "After you dropped me off at the house, I went to hair and makeup and then we were about to film when I passed out."

"What happened in hair and makeup?"

"You know, I talked to the girls. Josie curled my hair a little. She redid my makeup. That's pretty much it." She frowned. "Wait. I had some coffee."

Eric glanced up from his notepad. "Who all was in the trailer with you?"

"Josie, of course. Marisa. She does wardrobe. Um, no one else — oh. Chelsea was in there for a few minutes. She and Josie are pals." Chloe's eyes widened. "She brought us all coffee."

"And you drank it?"

"Barely half a cup. I thought it would help keep me awake after I filled up on that cheeseburger."

"Did you throw the cup away?"

She squeezed her eyes shut to remember. "Yes. I put it down at the bottom of the trash can, standing up. I didn't want it to spill all over the trash. Everything gets so soggy and smelly."

I looked at Eric. "Can you find the cup?"

He stood, shut his notepad, and slipped it into his pocket. "I'll give it my best shot."

■ ■ ■ ■

Chloe was feeling so much better the next morning, she refused to skip out on the day's filming. I had to admit she looked fine, probably because she'd slept for over twelve hours. I, on the other hand, tossed and turned all night worrying about my sister.

I fixed a quick breakfast of cereal, toast, and coffee, and made it to the film set a few minutes early. Unlike the day before, with so many delays and so much trauma, today people were busy and it felt like everyone was more than ready to get back to work.

We both had our makeup checked by Josie, who was relieved to see Chloe looking good.

"Are you all right?" She studied Chloe's face. "I was scared to death when I saw you faint out there."

"I'm fine."

She nodded, frowning. "Well, you look fine, too. Might need a little more blush than usual, but otherwise, you're that same gorgeous girl we know and love."

"Aw, thanks, Josie." Chloe gave her a hug and then sat down in the chair.

"I'm using a new makeup on your face

today," Josie said.

Chloe frowned. "How come?"

"You know I have my own stash that I use just for you, right?"

"Yeah, I love that stuff."

"Something happened to the liquid foundation. It turned yellow. So I'm using a new bottle that's a slightly lighter shade. I don't think you'll notice any difference, but let's try it."

A cold chill trickled down my neck. "How did it turn yellow?"

"It must be some kind of chemical reaction," Josie said, shrugging. "Or maybe it was expired. I didn't have time to figure it out so I just decided to toss it and use this new shade."

"Do you still have the bottle?"

She looked a little put out with me, but I persisted. "I'm just curious."

"I tossed it in the trash can under the dressing table. Hold on." She fished around and pulled out a small bottle of makeup. "Here you go. Have a blast."

I gave her a brief smile. "Thanks."

I wrapped it in tissue and stuck the bottle in my purse, then watched Josie go to work on Chloe. The three of us chatted about nothing in particular while I waited for my turn in the chair. I wasn't about to leave

Chloe alone with anyone on the set until we found out exactly what had happened to her. All we knew was that someone had dumped a bunch of pills in her coffee. And right now, the most obvious suspect was Chelsea. I just wasn't sure why she'd want to hurt Chloe.

Eric had already questioned the young assistant this morning, but since she was still walking around the set — with eyes red from crying — I figured Eric hadn't found enough reason to arrest her yet.

An hour later, we were finally ready to film our first segment. Despite the early hour, an enthusiastic crowd had gathered on the sidewalk.

"Yoo hoo! Shannon!" a woman cried, waving from the audience. She came toddling up the walkway and Suzanne hurried over to stop her.

"Oh, it's Margaret Bloom," I said to Chloe. "I'll just go say hi."

"I'll come with you."

"It's okay, Suzanne," I said with a smile. "This is the owner of the house. We should be nice to her."

"Oops, my bad," Suzanne said. "Sorry. We're extra security conscious around here today."

"I appreciate that," Margaret said.

Suzanne walked away and I hurried closer to greet Margaret with a big hug. I introduced her to Chloe and then asked, "How are you, Margaret?"

"I'm fabulous. What a crowd we've got. It's all so exciting."

"Yes. Very exciting."

"I heard about the murder," she whispered. "At first I thought it was a joke, but I guess not."

"No, not a joke. It was pretty awful."

"Ready to roll!" the stage manager shouted.

"That's our cue to go to work," I said. "But I hope you'll stick around and watch for a little while."

"I wouldn't miss it for the world. Bye."

Chloe and I dashed back to the steps and once there, I paced around and took a few deep breaths. I shook my arms and did several shoulder rolls to work the tension out of my system. "Can we go over what we're going to say in this first segment?"

"Yeah, let's do a quickie rehearsal." She pointed toward the porch. "I'll be standing near the far left corner and I'll talk first. So I'll say something like . . . 'The paint is chipped off, the wood is rotted, blah blah blah, there's only one cure for this. Shannon?' And then you walk in."

"Right. I walk over and pull the corner beam off the house."

"Yes, and you'll explain what you've found and what you're doing. Just the way we talked about it yesterday morning before all hell broke loose."

"If only the cameras had been rolling then."

"I know." She patted my shoulder. "No worries. We'll do it even better this time. It'll be awesome."

"Okay, good." I took another deep breath in and out and shook my arms again to loosen up. "Ready whenever you are."

We walked up the steps and Chloe took her place on the side of the porch. Gary the sound guy attached a mini-microphone to my shirt and I clipped the transmitter onto the back of my jeans. He did the same for Chloe and then cameraman Bob moved in for the shot. A few seconds later, Suzanne signaled to the stage manager, who shouted, "Action," and Chloe went to work.

I eyed Suzanne speculatively. The woman had stepped into the role of producer without missing a beat, almost as though she wasn't surprised by the change of circumstances. Was it all part of her plan to take over the show?

And boy, did that thought come out of

left field. I shook my head and forced myself to pay attention to what we were doing.

Chloe ran her gloved hand across a length of siding. "You'll notice that the clapboard siding is relatively unscathed here," she said, turning to the camera. "This area might only require a new coat of paint."

She kept her hand on the siding as she walked toward the railing at the far end. "But as we move to the end of the porch, you can see a lot more damage." She touched a vertical beam about six inches from the outer edge of the porch. "Check out this beam holding up the porch roof. It's actually warped. Can you see how it bends?" She turned. "And the siding here is completely rotted." She looked into the camera. "Everything on this end of the house has been much more exposed to rain and wind and sun damage for years. I'm concerned that we might have to remove the entire outer shell of this wall and replace it."

She patted the wide piece of molding at the corner edge of the house. "See this corner beam? Watch what happens when Shannon tries to scrape away the paint."

I stepped into the shot and held up my crowbar. "To check how much damage has been done to this molding, I'm going to use the flat end of my crowbar to scrape the wood." I began to scrape along the surface and watched it crumble and fall apart.

Chloe shook her head. "It's disintegrating before our eyes."

"This entire corner molding will have to be replaced along with the siding." I turned the crowbar around. "There's a loose nail in here that I want to remove." I used the claw end to remove the nail, but instead of just the nail, the entire piece of molding, from the roof to the porch floor, was ripped off the corner of the house. Which was exactly how we'd planned it. I had to admit that it made a heck of a show.

"Whoa." Chloe smiled at the camera. "That's going to leave a mark."

I laughed. "No kidding."

"Shannon," she said. "If this were your house, where would you start making repairs?"

I clutched the crowbar. "With a job like this, it's almost like working triage. In an emergency room, the first rule, always, is *stop the bleeding.*"

"Good rule to follow."

"Right," I said, nodding. "So in the case of an old house like this where some things are dangerously close to falling down around you, the first thing you need to do is check and reinforce the main beams. I usually start in the basement because if the wood beams are damaged down there, the whole house could literally collapse. In the case of this porch, that roof up there" — I pointed upward — "is not going to make it through another winter."

The camera then followed Chloe as she walked back to the center of the porch. "Shannon's right. Look at this." She pointed to the peaked roof above the porch steps. "This header beam has sustained so much water damage, it's turned to sponge."

I walked over with a stepladder, set it down, and climbed up. "Not only that, but look. The pitch of the roof itself has been warped. So when it does rain, the water soaks right into the wood instead of draining into the gutters." Taking my crowbar again, I barely scraped the surface of the header beam and watched as flakes and chunks of wood fell to the ground.

Chloe covered her head. "Hardhats are essential with work like this."

I climbed down from the stepladder and walked a few feet out of camera range to grab the two hardhats waiting there. Stepping back into the shot, I handed Chloe one of the hardhats. "Here you go."

We both grinned as we put them on and

then I said, "So yes, the corner beams and clapboard siding are clearly a mess. They look bad and they have to be replaced. But this porch roof is actually hazardous to our health. It could come down at any moment and hurt someone. So to answer your question, Chloe, fixing this roof must be our first priority."

Chloe grinned into the camera. "And that's exactly what we'll tackle first, right after this message."

There was a short pause and then the stage manager said, "And . . . we're clear. Great job, guys. Ten-minute break while we set up the next shot."

The stage manager took our hardhats and Chloe slipped her arm through mine as we walked down the steps. "What do you think?"

"That was amazing," I said, still tingling from my experience on camera. "I don't think I embarrassed myself too much, did I?"

"You were great, Shannon," Wade called from the driveway. Sean gave me a thumbs-up.

I flashed them a grateful smile. "Thanks, guys."

"They're right," Chloe said, giving me a quick hug. "You were fantastic."

Blake strolled over from the catering table. "Good job, ladies."

"Thanks, Blake," Chloe said. "You and Diego are up next."

"We're ready," he said, and winked before walking away.

Chloe glanced my way. "You want to rehearse our next lead-in?"

"Let's do it."

We strolled along the walkway running lines together.

"So let me ask you," I said. "Once we've finished all these lead-ins and explanations, do we get to work on actual demolition and construction?"

She frowned a little. "Well, we'll mostly be starting the projects and then the crew will actually move in to handle the heavy lifting. It's basically to save time. But don't worry, we'll get plenty of chances to destroy things."

I clapped my hands. "Goody."

"That's my favorite part, too. But it just saves a lot of time if the crew takes over after we've done the initial explanations and demonstration."

"So they get to do the fun stuff." I heard the disappointment in my own voice and who could blame me?

"Pretty much. Like what we just did. We

tore off a little siding and ripped off the molding, did some scraping and poking to show all the damage. Later the cameras will film the crew doing the actual demo. They'll completely remove the outer layer of the front of the house. And that's pretty much how it goes, inside and out, all the way through the next few shows."

"I guess it makes sense to do it that way for television. I mean, if I were doing all the work with my crew, it would take us months to finish this house."

"Exactly," Chloe said. "But we've got a crew of fifty guys standing by and that includes some really experienced carpenters and electricians and painters. They can do the work in less than a month, as long as we get the lumber, tile, supplies, and equipment to show up on a timely basis."

"More showbiz magic."

She grinned. "Yup."

"Chloe? Is that you?"

We both turned and watched in horror as Richie Rich strolled across the grass like he owned the place. He wore black slacks with shiny black patent leather shoes. He had his white polo shirt tucked in and the collar popped up. He just looked so slick, and not in a good-looking way. More like a refugee from the *Jersey Shore.* Not the actual place, but the tacky TV show.

"Hey, babe," he said. "I can't believe it. What're you doing here?"

Babe? And what a dumb question. Were we supposed to believe that he didn't know that Chloe Hammer, star of *Makeover Madness,* would be in town filming for two weeks?

Without a second thought, I stepped directly in front of Chloe. "I've got a better question, Richie. What are *you* doing here?"

Chloe maneuvered around me, whispering, "It's okay, Shannon."

"No, it's not," I hissed back at her.

"Hey, it's Shannon, right?" Richie's slow, smarmy voice was scraping my nerves like nails on a chalkboard. "You're looking good, girl. Long time no see."

"Not long enough," I said, low enough that only Chloe caught it. Hearing her giggle made me smile. But I had to wonder why guys like Richie were so clueless.

"Soooo, Chloe," he said, slicking back his hair. "I heard you were working here and figured I'd stop by and say hey. If you're not busy later, let's you and me go for a drink."

"Not even tempting," she said. "Go away, Richie."

"Aw, come on. We can drink to old friendships."

"Friendship?" She made a short gagging sound. "I don't think so."

"Why not? We had a good time back in the day."

I jumped in. "So you're not only icky, but delusional."

Chloe nudged me aside. "There were no good times with you and me, Richie. You took advantage of me and then threatened to destroy my family's reputation."

He frowned. "What in the world are you talking about?"

"I'm talking about the films we found in the Connolly house." She lowered her voice a bit, but Richie didn't miss a word. "Don't pretend you don't remember. You stole them and sold them for a lot of money. Then you threatened to blame it on my father if I ever told the police."

He squeezed his eyes shut as if he were trying to recall such a scenario ever happening. "Oh, yeah." He chuckled. "How do you even remember stuff like that? It was years ago. We were just kids. Get over it."

"Maybe I'd be able to get over it if you hadn't kept calling me and sending e-mails for the past ten years."

My mouth gaped. "Wait. What? He's been

calling you, too? And e-mailing? You didn't tell me that."

She winced. "I was going to mention it the other night, but there was so much other stuff to tell you, I just forgot."

"So he's been harassing you all this time?"

"Hey, back off," Richie said. "I was just trying to connect with an old friend."

"*Connect* is one word for it," I said. "Stalking is another."

"Jeez, lighten up."

"What a colossal jerk," I muttered, just loud enough to make sure he caught it.

Richie shot me a dirty look, so I knew he heard me. I gave him an evil smile. "Look, you are *not* an old friend of Chloe's. You are a creep and a liar. And you're a thief, too."

"And you're cramping my style." He bumped my shoulder to push past me and moved right up to Chloe. Lowering his voice seductively, he said, "Come on, babe. Enough with playing hard-to-get."

"This isn't hard-to-get, Richie," she said. "This is trying-not-to-hurl."

"You don't have to be insulting."

"Apparently I do." She growled in exasperation. "Look, I don't even want to breathe the same air as you, so I think you'd better go."

He gritted his teeth, growing annoyed. "I can't believe you're still pissed off about those stupid film cans. The owners never even knew about them, so what did it matter? Stop being such a tease and come with me for a drink. My treat."

"I was never a tease," she said through clenched teeth. "Now I'm asking you to leave quietly. Otherwise I'll have my crew physically remove you from the premises."

"Oh, yeah?" He stuck his chin out belligerently. "I dare you."

He really was an idiot. Every guy on my crew and even Chloe's gang of Hollywood elves were tough, strong men who worked hard every day. Richie wouldn't stand a chance.

"Don't push me, Richie," she said.

His eyes narrowed and his hands formed into fists. I thought, where was Rolly Wagner when you needed him? This guy had better back off. I started to move forward, but Chloe grabbed my arm.

Richie got the message. "You're going to be sorry you turned me down."

"I'm sorry I ever knew you."

He was clearly seething. "I can make sure you never work in television again."

Chloe moved right up into Richie's face. "And I promise to see you dead first."

■ ■ ■ ■

An hour later, we had finished taping four more segments on the front porch.

"It's going great, isn't it?" Chloe said. "I think I got a little burst of energy from Richie showing up."

"I'm glad for you," I said. "All he did for me was make my stomach churn."

"Sorry about that. But it just felt so good to confront him after all these years."

I could understand that. Most of the time I'd have loved to be able to tell off my old nemesis, Whitney Gallagher, but had to settle instead for dirty looks.

"I hated to see him attack you like that." I frowned. "He doesn't have any connections in Hollywood, does he?"

"Seriously?" She laughed. "You believed him? You think he could destroy my career?"

"No, but he's just so horrible." I struggled to explain. "People like Richie have a whole different brain physiology and I can't figure out what makes them tick. Makes it difficult to deal with them."

She shrugged. "You said it yourself, Shannon. He's a freaking sociopath."

"I did say that, didn't I?" It sounded even scarier now that I'd seen him in action.

"Yes. So just stop worrying and let's get to work on our next segment."

I gazed at the porch. "We're running out of wood to tear off this poor house."

She glanced around. "There's still so much work to do, it's hard to narrow down the focus."

"I've got a great idea," I said in triumph. "Let's rebuild the front porch steps."

She knelt down to study them. "That's perfect. This whole time I've been afraid of falling right through them."

"Me, too. I had already planned to redo them, even if it wasn't filmed for the show. Lots of homeowners would like to know how to rebuild their own steps, right?" I had already asked Wade to cut planks for the steps in the unlikely event that he had some spare time. Not surprisingly, he had them ready by the time we were set to film the segment.

"For now, we'll keep the sides open," I said, pointing to the edges of the staircase. "But eventually we should cover the openings with a piece of marine-grade plywood and maybe paint them a contrasting color."

"That would be fun," Chloe said. "I'll make sure to tell our viewers that. And we should add a railing on each side to make them safer and more attractive."

"That's going to look great."

The director agreed with our plan and for the next hour, we talked it out and blocked the scene. Then Chloe and I started working and it was like the old days, when we both worked on our dad's crew. We were still a good team. Only this time, we were talking to the camera, explaining our actions as we worked. By the time we stopped filming three hours later, the Bloom house had a brand-new front stairway.

I pounded the last nail into the bottom plank and then Chloe gave her final lines to the camera. "All that's left to do now is stain and weather-seal the wood and add the finishing touches, like a thin piece of molding along the sides and a pretty railing that matches the porch rail. And that's how you rebuild an old staircase. On our next show, we'll take you inside the Bloom house and, among other things, we'll show you the secrets of updating an old powder room."

"And . . . we're clear," the stage manager shouted. "That's a wrap for today, people."

Chloe and I grinned at each other as applause broke out from the crowd still gathered on the sidewalks and along the driveway.

"That was so good," she said. "But I'm exhausted. I wish I hadn't promised Peggy

I'd come over tonight because all I really want is a hot bath and a pizza."

"Me, too. In that order." I gave her a sympathetic look. "Can you postpone the dinner with Peggy?"

"No, I need to get it over with."

"I understand." Chloe planned to tell Peggy the whole story about the film cans that were stolen from her home ten years ago by Richie Rich. I just hoped she didn't experience a burst of guilt and offer to pay Peggy for the films. That payment needed to come from Richie.

"Hey, who's that?" Chloe asked, staring ahead.

I followed her gaze and almost groaned out loud. A thin woman wearing a black sequined top, black leggings, and black stilettos walked toward us, stepping gingerly on the grass.

"Kill me now," I muttered. "It's Whitney Reid Gallagher."

"I can't believe I didn't recognize her. Oh no. Looks like she's headed our way."

"Of course she is. And here we were having such a nice time." The only thing worse than finding another dead body was having to deal with Whitney Gallagher.

"Why is she all dolled up?"

"Because . . . it's a day of the week ending in 'y'?" I shook my head. "I don't know why. She's just weird."

From the corner of my eye I saw Mac approach quickly behind Whitney. And then Wade dashed over from the opposite side of the house. *My heroes,* I thought fondly. Were they here to save me from evil queen Whitney?

Apparently not, because they came to a stop a few yards back as Whitney continued her relentless toddle toward me on those stiletto heels that kept getting stuck in the dirt beneath the soft grass.

So the guys were just here to watch the show. Well, Whitney and I were usually capable of delivering a doozy.

"Whitney," I said when she halted in front of me. "Always a pleasure."

"Don't pretend you're happy to see me," she said.

"Okay, I won't." I turned and walked away.

"Don't you dare walk away from me," she said.

I laughed as I turned around. "So what do you want?" I had a feeling I knew, but I would wait for it.

"I want your slutty sister to leave my cousin alone."

"Hold on there," I said, waving my finger

toward her. "You're going to want to rephrase that, before I shove your face in the dirt."

She sputtered. "What did you say?"

I was willing to put up with a lot from Whitney. Mostly because I simply didn't care what she thought about anything — though I continued to wonder how sweet, affable Tommy put up with his venomous wife. But there was just no way I would stand there and watch her turn her talons on Chloe.

"You heard me," I said. "Right in the dirt. Although I'd really hate to ruin that sparkly top you're wearing." I paused, tipped my head to one side, and studied her. "I'm kidding. I'd *love* to ruin it. Because seriously? Who wears freaking sequins to a construction site in the middle of the afternoon? Not to mention those ridiculous shoes."

"They're Jimmy Choos," she protested.

I shook my head in disgust. "I bet he never meant them for hiking boots."

"Fine," she said, tossing her hair back. She took a long, deep breath. "Let me rephrase what I came here to say. Your sister *propositioned* my cousin and I won't have it."

"No one would proposition Richie!" Chloe shouted. "That's totally gross."

I patted Chloe's arm while staring daggers at Whitney. "Excuse me? *You* won't have it? Well, here's what *I* won't have: your horrible little cousin telling lies and making up stories about my sister. *He's* the one who begged her to go out with him and she turned him down flat."

She laughed. "Oh, right. He's rich and good-looking. No woman turns him down. No way."

"Yeah, *way,*" I said. "I was here. I heard him. But you don't have to take my word for it. My crew was here and saw the whole thing. He made his move and got shot down. And you know why she turned him down?"

She sniffed, thrusting her nose in the air like a bad actress. "Of course I know why. Because she's a low-class townie."

"No," I said. "Because he's a flaming jackass. He's never told the truth in his entire life and my sister wouldn't be caught dead with him. And another thing. The fact that he went whining and crying to *you* speaks volumes. The guy can't even fight his own battles. What a pathetic coward."

She gasped dramatically. "How dare you?"

I pointed to all the people lined up on the driveway. "You ask anyone standing here. They all saw and heard it for themselves. So maybe you should go find your smack-talking little cousin and wash his mouth out with soap for lying to you. Because he's making a big fat fool out of *you* as we speak."

"You're impossible," she said, stomping her foot and driving her stiletto so deep into the grass that now she was standing lopsided. I admit it. I laughed.

"I should've known you'd be crass and rude," she said. "Just the type of behavior I expect from a *townie.*"

I could hear Chloe growling as though she might tear Whitney's arm off and beat her with it. I personally was on the verge of ripping the woman's hair out of her skull, so I sucked in a few lungs' worth of air to calm down. On a side note, I knew what the expression *seeing red* meant, because Whitney Reid Gallagher had driven me to that state. Not for the first time.

It took me a few more seconds before I could trust myself to speak, but finally I did. "As long as you put so much stock in the fact that you're better than me and my family because we're townies, Whitney, let me explain something to you. Your three children are townies. Your husband is a townie. You've been living here almost twenty years and you know what that makes you? A townie."

Her face was pale and turning ghostly, but I was on a roll and kept going. "My sister, on the other hand, has lived in Los Angeles for the past ten years, which makes her anything *but* a townie. And you know what the dumbest word in the English language is? It's *townie.* So the next time you feel like calling someone a name that you believe makes them less of a human being than yourself, you might think again, because all it'll do is make you look as stupid and mean as you look right now. *Townie.*"

I grabbed Chloe's arm and we flounced away from her, over to the catering table where Emily stood applauding quietly. "Well done, my friend."

I curtsied. "Thank you." But I was still shaking with anger. I took a second to look over my shoulder and snorted when I saw Whitney bent over, tugging her heel out of the ground.

Chloe hugged me so tightly, I was afraid I'd lose consciousness. "I love you so much."

"I love you, too, honeybun."

"That was the best speech ever," Mac murmured in my ear.

I looked up and beamed at him. I wasn't sure he was right because as comebacks went, it wasn't my most brilliant. But I had to admit that after all these years of putting up with her insults, calling Whitney Reid Gallagher a *townie* had felt really, really good.

Chapter Ten

That night, Chloe went over to her friend Peggy Connolly's house for dinner. I knew my little sister wasn't looking forward to confessing to Peggy's family what had happened to the film cans that were stolen from the family, but she knew it was the right thing to do.

Those stupid film cans! Every time I thought about them, I pictured that smarmy Richie Rich and all the years of grief he had caused my sister. I hated him so much right now. But I brushed off those negative feelings and tried to concentrate on something more positive instead. Namely, the fact that my sister was the most courageous person I knew for having the guts to face the Connollys and confess everything.

"Chloe," I said, just before she walked out of the house. "If they want to be paid for the films, you should tell them to go after

Richie. Please don't offer to pay them yourself."

"I won't, I promise. They can hunt down Richie and squeeze the money from him. Good luck with that, though."

"True. He'll probably deny taking them anyway." I gave her a hug. "Love you. Good luck."

"Thanks," she said. "Love you, too."

I heard the truck engine start and a few seconds later she drove off. Now I was alone in the house with too many ways to keep busy, and I didn't want to do anything but chill. Chloe had planted the idea of a hot bath and a pizza in my head and it just wouldn't go away.

I had hoped that Mac would come over for dinner tonight, but he had a very important poker game to go to. Some of his old Navy SEAL buddies played serious cards once a month and there was no way I would expect him to cancel his plans. Besides, the thought of spending the evening alone with a pizza and a glass of wine was growing more appealing by the minute.

Jogging upstairs, I started the bathwater and tossed in a gallon of fragrant bath salts. Just before I climbed in, I called to order a pizza and a salad to be delivered from Bella Rossa. They were busy but promised to have it here in half an hour, so I pinned up my hair, set my phone alarm for twenty minutes, and slid into the hot, bubbly water.

"Oh, bliss," I said, and sank down until only my head was above the water.

When the timer went off, I jolted. Completely disoriented, I looked around. I was in the bathtub. I had to work to recall how I'd gotten here.

"Wow, I fell asleep hard." *Hard?* I was lucky I didn't drown.

Robbie barked happily and I realized that he and Tiger were sitting on the bathroom rug, watching my every move.

"My lifeguards. Why didn't you guys wake me up?"

Robbie barked again, enthralled to be having a conversation with his human. Tiger ignored us both and began to lick her paws.

Still a little discombobulated from the nap, I forced myself to pull the plug, then stood up and dried off. I climbed out of the tub and walked into my room to throw on clean sweatpants and a thick henley.

When the doorbell rang, I was already downstairs feeding the pets.

"Pizza pizza!" I cried as Robbie barked like a crazy hound.

I peeked through the curtain and saw the kid on the porch holding a pizza box and a small bag. At that moment I was pitifully grateful that I'd thought to order dinner before I stepped into the bath. Sometimes I was even smarter than I thought I was.

After fixing a plate full of pizza and salad and pouring myself a glass of Cabernet, I settled into the couch to watch television while I ate.

I couldn't recall ever being this exhausted after a long day of construction work. Okay sure, there was also a murder investigation going on, but to be fair, that was nothing new for me. So why was I extra tired today? Was it possible that Chloe's job was even more grueling than my own?

"Oh no." I could never admit it to her!

"But it's true," I mumbled after taking another delicious bite of sausage, onion, and mushroom pizza.

Maybe it was the stress of being on camera, because to be honest, I had barely done any actual construction work all day. As soon as I would start to hammer a nail or pry off a piece of wood, the stage manager would yell that we were done with the shot. And that was when the crew guys — and gals — would move in and do the actual work. It was bizarre. Of course, we did manage to build a set of stairs at the end of the day. But that wasn't particularly hard work.

So why was I completely worn out?

For now I put all of those thoughts out of my mind and concentrated on my pizza and salad — and catching up with my favorite TV show.

An hour later, when I was sufficiently stuffed and the latest episode of *NCIS* was over, I stowed the leftovers in the refrigerator, tidied up the kitchen, gave the kiddies fresh water in their bowls, and climbed the stairs. Lest I forgot, I had another six a.m. call time tomorrow morning.

I crawled into bed, joined by Tiger and Robbie. "Good night, everyone," I murmured and fell asleep almost immediately.

It seemed like only minutes had passed when my alarm clock blared, waking me up. It was still dark in my room and all I really wanted to do was tug my quilt up over my head and go back to sleep. I groaned loudly at the unfairness of it all. Had I really slept the whole night? I hadn't even heard Chloe come home.

I hit the alarm to stop the noise — but it didn't stop.

"What the heck?" I hit it again before I realized that it wasn't the alarm clock blaring. It was my phone ringing.

It took me a few seconds of fumbling with the phone before I answered, "Hello?"

"Shannon?" My sister's voice, sounding panicked. "I need help."

Well, that woke me up fast enough.

"Chloe?" I jumped out of bed and checked the clock. Almost midnight. "Where are you?"

"Shannon, can you call the police?"

"Honey, what's wrong? Did you have an accident?"

"No. I mean, no. It's not . . . um, I'm at the Bloom house. And there's someone on the front porch."

"What're you doing there?" It took me a few seconds to figure out what she'd just said. "Wait, someone's still working at the house?"

"No," she said. "Nobody's working. He's not . . . I think . . . Oh God, Shannon, he's not moving. I think he's dead."

I called Eric Jensen and told him about the body on the Blooms' front porch. Then I begged him for a ride because Chloe had my truck. I had almost considered riding my bike across town if Eric had refused, but by now it was after midnight so that seemed like a really bad idea. He agreed.

I dressed quickly, wearing the same sweats and henley I'd put on after my bath, along with warm socks and tennis shoes and a heavy jacket. While I waited for Eric, I called Chloe back to let her know we were on our way. Then I called Mac because I knew he would want to know what was going on. He was just wrapping up his poker game and told me he would meet me at the Bloom house.

Within minutes of picking me up, Eric was cruising through the town square toward the Bloom house with me in the passenger seat. I gazed at his masculine face, silhouetted by the streetlamp. I knew I was taking a chance, but I had to ask. "Did you get the final results from Chloe's coffee cup?"

He flashed me a long look and I wondered if he would bother to answer me. Finally he gave a short nod. "Yeah. It was definitely Dilaudid. They must've really wanted her to O.D."

"That makes me sick," I said, rubbing my stomach at the thought of someone doing this to my sister. "Did you talk to Chelsea?"

"She had no idea how the stuff got into the coffee or where it came from." He shook his head. "I pressed her and she started crying."

"Bet you loved that," I murmured.

"Yeah, it always makes my day when I can get a woman to cry. Anyway, we've got a warrant to search her hotel room, so stay tuned."

"Sounds good. Oh. I just remembered something else." I pulled the makeup bottle out of my purse and repeated the story Josie told us that morning. "Something might've been added to Chloe's makeup to hurt her or poison her. I know it's farfetched, but I thought I'd better give it to you for testing."

I watched him clenching and unclenching his jaw. He'd been doing a lot of that lately. "I'll take care of it."

"Thanks, Eric." I put the bottle in the cup holder between our seats.

Seconds later, he zipped into the Blooms' driveway. I jumped out of the SUV and took off running toward the front porch.

"Shannon," Eric shouted. "Don't go near that house."

"I won't. I'm just going to Chloe." I knew he was concerned about evidence, but all I cared about was my sister.

"Chloe," I yelled, and that was when I saw her huddled at the bottom of the steps. She stood and ran to ward me and I pulled her into my arms. "Are you all right? You scared the life out of me."

"I'm sorry," she said, sounding distressed. "I didn't know what to do. I was going to call 911, but I guess I panicked and pressed your number first. I'm sorry I woke you up."

"Don't worry about it," I said, smoothing her hair back. She was shaking and her eyes looked a little wild. "You did exactly the right thing. Eric's here and everything will be okay."

Eric joined us then. "Chloe, are you all right?"

"Yes, thank you, Chief. I'm fine. I'm sorry we had to call you, but . . ."

"Don't be sorry," he said, and surprised us both by wrapping his arms around her in a warm hug. "You must've been awfully scared."

"Yeah, I've got to admit I was."

A moment later, he let her go. "I have to ask, did you touch anything?"

"No, I promise."

"What were you doing here so late?"

She took a deep breath as if to brace herself. "I had dinner with a friend and I was on my way home, but I decided to stop and talk to Blake first. We didn't get a chance to really talk all day and usually we spend a few hours going over the show rundown and figuring out our lines, you know? And I missed that. I missed him."

"I understand," Eric said kindly.

I nodded. "Me, too."

"Anyway, I came here looking for him,

but he wasn't in his trailer. So I thought I would walk over to the house, thinking maybe he would be here checking out the work we did earlier. It's something he would do. And that's when I saw Richie."

I gasped and looked past her, even though I couldn't see the body in the shadows. "It's Richie?"

She looked miserable as she nodded. "Yeah. I couldn't tell at first, but yes. It's him."

Eric had belatedly pulled out his notepad and pen and was frantically writing everything down that Chloe had said. He looked up to ask, "Who's Richie?"

"Richard Stoddard," Chloe said, scrubbing her hands up and down her arms. "We call him Richie. He was here earlier today."

"He's the guy who got punched by Rolly Wagner," I explained.

"And he's Whitney Reid Gallagher's cousin," Chloe added.

Eric gave her a long, questioning look. "You're sure it's him?" he asked, gazing up at the body on the porch. "Did you go up there and look at his face?"

"No, I swear I didn't go near him. I got halfway up the stairs when I saw a big lump. It was too dark to see what it was, so I used my phone flashlight. And . . ." She shook her head and exhaled heavily. "I could tell it was him from his hair and the shirt he was wearing."

"The white polo shirt?" I asked.

"Yes." She glanced at me. "His collar was still popped."

I almost snorted but saved myself.

Chloe continued. "So I scrambled back down the steps and ran to the truck to call Shannon. I waited in the truck until she called back to tell me you were on your way. Then I walked over here and waited for you on the steps."

"Okay, good," he said, still writing. "Thanks."

Another police SUV zoomed around the corner and parked behind Eric's SUV. I recognized Tommy's car and watched him get out and jog over to meet Eric. He hadn't taken the time to change into his uniform but wore jeans and a heavy leather bomber jacket. Eric was still dressed in his uniform because he'd been working late at police headquarters.

Tommy jogged across the lawn and when he reached us, Eric touched his shoulder. "I didn't realize the victim is related to you. If you'd rather sit this one out, I'll understand."

Tommy glanced at me, then back at Eric.

"Who is it?"

"Richard Stoddard."

Tommy blinked and took a few slow breaths. "Whitney's gonna flip out."

"Yeah." Eric ran his hand through his hair in frustration. "Sorry, man."

Tommy took one last deep breath and nodded with determination. "I'm cool. Let's do this."

Car headlights flashed and seconds later, I recognized Mac's car. He drove slowly past the scene and parked a few houses down.

"That's Mac," I explained to Eric. "I called him to let him know what was going on and he insisted on meeting me here."

"The more, the merrier," Eric said dryly. He turned to my sister. "Chloe, I'm sorry, but I'll want to ask you some more questions after I see what happened to your friend Richie."

"He was no friend," I muttered.

Chloe shot me a look. "I understand, Chief. Take all the time you need. I'll wait right here."

"Yeah, we'll be here," I said.

Eric gave Tommy the heads-up and the two of them climbed the porch steps.

As soon as he left, I whispered, "Sorry about that 'friend' comment. Probably not helpful."

"It doesn't matter. I'm sure he'll find out that Richie and I had a big fight this afternoon. Plenty of people saw it, after all." She rested her head on my shoulder. "I hope you've saved up enough money to pay my bail."

"That won't happen," I insisted.

I glanced up at Tommy and Eric and wondered how they could see anything with just one small flashlight. The moon was almost full tonight, but it was covered in clouds.

Sure enough, a few seconds later, Tommy dashed down the steps and jogged over to get a light tree from the back of his SUV. We watched as they set it up on the porch, running a cord into the house for electricity. Suddenly the porch, or at least the section of the porch where Richie lay dead, was as bright as daylight.

Mac walked quickly across the grass. "How are you doing?"

"I'm doing okay, but I'm not so sure about Chloe. Finding bodies used to be my thing, but it's quickly becoming a Hammer sisters thing."

He gave her a hug. "I'm sorry, Chloe."

"Thanks, Mac. Must be my lucky day." She said it lightly, but I could tell she was agonizing over the situation. I couldn't blame her.

He sat down beside me on the step. "Do we know who it is?"

I gave him a weighty look. "It's Richie Rich."

His mouth dropped open. "You're kidding."

"Nope."

Another cop car arrived and we watched Mindy Payton and Dan Brackman come running toward the house. Eric gave them their orders and a minute later, Dan raced down the porch stairs and crossed the street. I assumed he was checking out the dressing room trailer where Blake had slept the night before.

"Guess they're looking for Blake," Chloe said. "I'd be surprised if they find him in the trailer. I knocked when I first got here and nobody answered."

I looked at Mac. "Let's move a few steps higher so we can hear what they're saying."

"Great idea," he said with a grin.

The three of us moved incrementally so we wouldn't draw Eric's attention and be exiled to the driveway, where we wouldn't be able to see or hear a thing.

A minute later, Dan came back, racing up the steps to the porch. "Chief, the door was unlocked and the place was empty."

"What do you mean, empty?" he asked.

"No humans inside."

Eric frowned. "Is it still a mess in there?"

"No, it's pretty clean now."

"That's weird," Chloe whispered. "The door was locked when I knocked earlier."

"Maybe someone unlocked it after you came over here," I said. "But you're right. It's weird."

"I'm going to go check it out," Mac said, and dashed off.

"Mac was in there with Blake for quite a while yesterday," I said to Chloe. "He would know how it looked."

"But how did it get unlocked?" Chloe wondered.

"Are you sure it was locked? Maybe it was just stuck or something."

"No, it was locked. I knocked a bunch of times and I shook the handle to make sure."

"I believe you. It just means that someone came along and unlocked it after you. Or, someone was inside the trailer and didn't answer when you knocked. Either way, someone came along after you left. But where did they go after that?"

"And who was it?" she asked. "I haven't seen anyone around here since I arrived. I mean, it's dark, but I still would've heard or seen someone."

"Unless they were trying not to be seen."

A few minutes later a van pulled up and Leo Stringer climbed out of the driver's side. He carried a large, heavy-duty silver briefcase containing his forensics tools and equipment across the lawn to the steps.

"Hi, Leo," I said.

"Shannon. Awfully late for you to be here."

"You, too."

He shrugged. "Duty calls." Climbing the steps, he joined the cops, who were still staring down at the body of Richie Rich as if waiting for him to sit up and tell them who killed him.

I looked up and saw Mac hurrying toward us. "What did I miss?" he asked.

"Leo just arrived," I said. "So what did you find in the trailer?"

"It's still unlocked and it's definitely been cleaned. No sign of Blake."

That was a mystery for another time, I thought. But maybe Blake had decided to go sleep at the B and B. That made a lot more sense than sleeping in a small trailer. Aloud, I asked, "So what was Richie Rich doing here? His car must be around here somewhere. But why would he even come here?"

"I was just about to bring up the same

question," Chloe said.

"And who hated him enough to kill him?" Mac asked.

I exchanged a look with Chloe. "There were legions," I said. "He was a nasty piece of work."

"Yes, he was," she murmured.

I thought of everyone who'd tangled with Richie over the past two days. Rolly Wagner, of course. And his wife. There might've been others. I suddenly recalled Chloe's friend and producer, Suzanne, having a chummy conversation with Richie. I made a mental note to mention that fact to Eric.

Mac reached over and squeezed Chloe's hand. "I guess you had your own issues with him."

"Most definitely. But I didn't kill him."

"Of course not. No one thinks you did." I glanced anxiously at Chloe, who looked even paler in the eerie light of the moon and the reflected light from the porch. I decided to change the subject. "So how was Peggy?"

She was clearly happy with how their visit had gone. "She's great. She has an adorable family. Two smart kids and a good-looking husband. He's a teacher, did you know that?"

"I did. We're not really friendly, but I

know he teaches at Lighthouse High. And Peggy's a pharmacist, right?"

"Yes."

"Did you talk about the films?"

"Yes, and you'll never believe it, Shannon." She smiled with a mixture of delight and relief. "She told me that her great-grandfather hoarded dozens of those film reels all over the house. But never in plain sight. When they tore down their garage a few years ago, they found over a hundred film cans hidden in the rafters and even inside the walls."

"You're kidding," I said. "That's crazy."

"That takes hoarding to a whole new level." Mac shook his head in amazement. "So after all these years and all the pain you went through to wrangle them, they still had tons of them gathering dust?"

"Yes, and Peggy wanted nothing to do with any of them. She already knew about that foundation I told you about. The family donated them all years ago." Chloe laughed. "She said that even though she didn't care about the money, she would be happy to taunt Richie Rich with threats of a lawsuit, just to see him squirm." Chloe cringed, realizing what she'd said. "Oh, but she was just kidding."

"Of course she was."

"Shannon."

Eric's voice was so close, I almost jumped. I'd been so wrapped up in Chloe's story about the film cans, I hadn't heard him come down the steps.

"What is it?" I asked.

He held up a white cloth that was wrapped around a deadly-looking, blood-soaked crowbar. "Does this look familiar?"

I felt my eyes widen and I swallowed nervously. "I guess it could be one of mine."

"There must be a thousand crowbars that look exactly like that one," Mac protested, and I could've kissed him for standing up for me.

Eric went on. "Dan said you were using a crowbar for some of the shots this afternoon."

"That's true. But I'm positive I put mine back in my toolbox." Was I positive? I couldn't even remember now.

Eric persisted. "Where is your toolbox right now?"

"In the back of my truck."

"Let's go take a look."

I glanced at Mac, who looked grim. Dang. There was nothing I hated more than the feeling of knowing I might be a murder suspect. It was something you just never got used to and that was an understatement.

Mac and Chloe tagged along and I felt somewhat relieved to have them with me on the long trek to my truck. The only way I could prove without a doubt that I wasn't the owner of the murder weapon was if my crowbar was still in with the rest of my tools. We got to my truck and I opened the box.

The truck was parked under a streetlamp but Eric held up a flashlight so I could plainly see that the crowbar was not on the top shelf of the toolbox where I always kept it. I closed the top and latched it, and turned around to face him.

"Don't you want to look inside the other compartments?" he asked.

"I don't have to," I said, feeling sick to my stomach as I stared up at him. "The crowbar only fits in the top section. It's not there."

On the way back to the house, Eric ran ahead to talk to Leo and his officers while I walked more slowly with Chloe and Mac.

I glanced at Chloe. "Did you see the crowbar on the porch when you climbed the steps earlier?"

She winced. "Not exactly."

"What does that mean?"

Her face was a mask of anguish and it almost broke me.

"What is it?" I asked.

She sighed. "The crowbar wasn't on the porch, Shannon. It was . . . it was stuck in Richie's neck."

"Oh, the joy," I muttered, feeling even sicker than I did a minute ago. Given the amount of blood that had soaked into Eric's white cloth, I had to assume that Richie's killer had managed to sever one of the carotid arteries in his neck with the curved, double-tongued sharp end of the crowbar.

"How could this have happened?" Chloe whispered.

"If you remember putting the crowbar back in the toolbox," Mac reasoned, "then someone obviously stole it sometime after that."

"Right," I said. "But who? And when? And how did it wind up getting stuck in Richie's neck?" And how did the cops decide it had to be mine? I wondered. Maybe there were still flecks of wood stuck to the metal. Who knew?

"There must've been a hundred people watching us this afternoon," Chloe said. "Including the cops who were there for crowd control. They all saw you working with the crowbar and many of them probably saw you put it away in your toolbox."

Mac nodded. "So how do we whittle that

number down to the number one or two most likely suspects?"

We were silent for a moment, all wrapped up in our own troubled thoughts. Sadly, none of us were coming up with answers.

"Who had it in for Richie?" Mac asked finally.

"Me," Chloe admitted.

"And me," I said.

He gazed from Chloe to me. "Did anyone else on the crew even know this guy? Besides you two, I mean."

"He probably wasn't familiar to the crew or production staff, but lots of Lighthouse Cove people knew him," I said. "Richie grew up here. There must be plenty of people in the crowd who've done business with him."

"And don't forget he knew Bree," Chloe said.

"Don't remind me," I said, rolling my eyes. "Oh, and Suzanne."

"Suzanne?"

"Yeah, I saw the two of them talking together. They looked awfully friendly."

"That's weird. But Suzanne would never hurt anyone."

I shrugged, then remembered more possibilities. "What about the Wagners?"

"That's right," Chloe said. "They had that

big fight early yesterday morning."

I looked at Mac. "Rolly Wagner attacked Richie Rich."

"How did I miss all the excitement?" Mac lamented.

I patted Mac's back sympathetically. "You were stuck inside the trailer with Blake."

"Yeah." He scowled. "So tell me everything that happened."

"Apparently Richie sold the Wagners their house and then promised them that the house would be featured on the show. When it didn't happen, the Wagners showed up looking mad enough to kill. As soon as they saw Richie, Rolly punched him out."

"Amazing," Mac said, and I knew he was regretting that he'd missed the whole scene.

"There was definitely no love lost there," Chloe said, then added, "He almost punched out Tommy, too."

"That's right." I pictured the scene. "And then Eric slapped a pair of handcuffs on Rolly Wagner and sent him down to the station for questioning. And Mrs. Wagner was whining and moaning the whole time."

"I'm really sorry I missed it." Mac flashed a wicked grin. "But it sounds like we've got ourselves a first-class suspect."

Chapter Eleven

The next morning, despite four hours of sleep, Chloe and I woke up and showered and made it back to the Bloom house in time to start work. Thanks to our lack of sleep, we didn't look like the most dewy-eyed starlets in the reality show galaxy, but we made up for it in sheer perseverance. Despite Richie's murder hanging over us like an ax.

The entire front porch had been cordoned off with bright yellow police crime scene tape. A uniformed officer stood guard at the bottom of the stairs.

"Hi, Mindy," I said.

"Hey, Shannon." She gave me a sympathetic look. "Sorry about this, but it's Chief's orders."

Of course Eric had closed off the latest crime scene. I should have expected it. "Is the rest of the outside of the house closed off, too?"

Mindy shook her head. "Nope. Just the front porch and the inside."

"Okay, thanks." I turned to Chloe. "What are we supposed to do now?"

Chloe's shoulders dropped. "I was hoping and praying they'd be finished with the porch area, but I guess it wasn't meant to be."

"And they probably aren't finished inside the house yet, either." I gazed up at the gables and then walked around the side of the house. And almost ran into Blake.

He grabbed my shoulders, chuckling. "Sorry about that. Good morning."

"Good morning, Blake."

"I was just checking out the back of the house. Figure we'll be stuck working outside for another day or two."

"I was doing the same." I took a deep breath and forged ahead. "Hey, where were you last night? Chloe said she came looking for you but couldn't find you."

"Oh, I went and stayed at the bed-and-breakfast." He shook his head. "Couldn't face another night in that trailer."

"I don't blame you. The Hennessey House is so nice."

"Beautiful. Jane tells me you did a lot of the repair work and I've got to say, it's stunning."

"Thank you. Coming from you, that's a great compliment." I leaned one shoulder against the house. "So anyway, Chloe told me that she missed talking to you so she stopped by hoping to catch you in the trailer."

"Yeah. I talked to her a few minutes ago and heard all about how she found that guy's body. I'm sorry I wasn't here for her. Sounds pretty gruesome."

"It was."

Just then Chloe came jogging around the corner. "There you are. What's up?"

I pointed up toward the roof. "I was thinking that if I can get the boom lift delivered in the next hour or so, we could do some stuff up in that gable."

Blake raised an eyebrow. "You've got a connection to a boom lift?"

"It belongs to my company, but we rent it out. I'll have to make a few calls."

"Do it. We can definitely use it all over this place."

"I will."

"Sounds good." Blake gave a salute and walked off toward the catering table. I caught a glimpse of Chelsea standing by the donuts and her face lit up at the sight of Blake approaching.

I sighed and got back to business. "So

what do you think?"

Chloe stared up at the third floor where the roof peaked. "We'd definitely need a boom lift because we can't possibly get up that high with scaffolding."

"No way." I'd found that scaffolding was good for going maybe twenty feet up a wall, but after that, it was too big a risk. For one thing, we wouldn't be able to attach it to the house securely enough, and for another, we'd still need twenty or more feet to reach that gable.

"Wow," Chloe said, straining her neck to get a look at the wood carvings that decorated the frame of the gable. "I never took a good look at those panels. From a distance they look so distinctive."

I looked up, too. "Yeah, but up close they're sort of washed out and gray."

"Are those spoon carvings?" she asked.

"Yes." We shared a knowing smile. My sister and I had been trained by the best — our dad — to appreciate the intricacies of lost carpentry. "Aren't they cool?"

"Fantastic."

"But even from down here, I can tell that they're caked with old paint and dirt. It'll take a lot of work to get them looking pretty again."

The designs in the wood panels were

called spoon carvings because they looked as if they might've been carved by a sharp spoonlike tool. The tools used were actually curved whittling knives whose original purpose was to make — you guessed it — spoons. These knives came in various rounded shapes and sizes, and the unique crescent-shaped designs they produced in wood furniture and in the panels of many Victorian homes came to be known as spoon carvings.

Chloe considered the task before us. "We might have to use a heat gun to clean the paint out of those crevices."

"Ah, I love my heat gun."

"That just sounds weird," she said, laughing as she looked over at me. "And how sad is it that I completely understand your feelings? But since you probably use one a lot more than me, you'll be in charge when we start that project."

"Yes, boss. And once we clean out the old paint, we'll probably need ten gallons of wood filler to smooth out all the cracks and gaps."

She continued to stare up. "It looks like those panels were once painted white, but the color is just gone. It's like it's disintegrated or something."

"I don't think the exterior of this house

has ever been repainted." I looked over the façade with an inner sigh. I hated to see glorious old homes completely neglected. "Which means it's been sun-baked and weather-beaten for over a century."

She sighed, too, but with a sense of coming satisfaction. "It's going to look beautiful when we're finished."

"Absolutely."

She pointed up. "Those scalloped cedar shingles covering the third-floor exterior are peeling and falling apart."

"We can't fix them," I said. "They'll have to be removed and replaced. We'll need the boom lift for that, too."

"Yeah."

She studied the cedar shingles, then gave me a skeptical look. "That peak has got to be at least forty feet high. Will the boom lift arm reach that far?"

"It'll go more than fifty feet up."

"Yay!" she said, and did a quick little feet shuffling happy dance. "Let's get it over here."

"You sound psyched. I'm glad."

"I really am psyched about the boom lift. Is that a reasonable thing? Or will I need a ride to the loony bin?"

"In our family, completely reasonable. And I think you're fine, anyway. Just a little sleep-deprived."

"For sure."

We walked back and forth along the side of the house and stopped when we got to the bay window. "We could do something with this."

Chloe nodded. "Viewers love bay windows."

I took a closer look at the structure. "These window frames need to be rebuilt."

"Definitely. And look, some of the glass is cracked along the edges. We'll add double-paned windows."

"And this weird copper awning above it will have to go." I studied it for another few seconds and shrugged. "It was obviously added to keep the rain from getting inside the windows."

She considered that for a moment and nodded. "Yes, it has a purpose, but it was an awkward choice. It doesn't suit the rest of the exterior."

From where we were standing, I turned and looked at the thick copse of trees along the property line. "This is a beautiful view from this window."

"And remember? Inside it's got that archway leading to this bay window that makes it feel like a little alcove." She smiled.

"We could fashion it into a cozy reading nook."

"That sounds wonderful."

"Oh, Shannon. We could build a window bench."

"I love it," I said. "We can check it out once we're allowed to go back in the house."

"Okay," Chloe said. "You call and get the boom lift over here and I'll go talk to Blake and Diego."

"Sounds like a plan."

The filmed segments worked so well, it was like we'd all been doing this our whole lives. I enjoyed watching the camaraderie among Chloe and her co-stars. They treated me like one of the gang, too, which I appreciated.

The only snag was that I couldn't get hold of the boom lift until sometime tomorrow, so we dedicated a big portion of the afternoon to working on the bay window. Blake explained how to reframe a window and then Diego showed some techniques for adding extra decorative molding or replacing any molding that was damaged or decayed for any reason.

"And . . . cut," the stage manager shouted as Suzanne approached. She grinned at Diego, who was still slapping wood filler on the piece of molding he was working on. "Dude, I said *cut.* Save it for the camera. Take a break."

We all laughed.

"Hey," he said with a manly shrug. "I'm dedicated to my work."

"You're just showing off," Chloe said, grinning.

Blake smiled when Josie the makeup girl stopped and ran a tissue across his forehead followed by a soft, dry makeup brush. "It's getting a little warm out here. Guess I worked up a sweat."

"That's what I'm here for," she said.

"Hey, Suzanne," Chloe said. "I can't find my rundown. What's up next?"

The tall woman flipped a page. "You're up on the extension ladder, removing that awning thing from above the bay window."

"Oh, good. I hate that ugly thing." Chloe frowned at it. "It just doesn't look like it goes there at all."

Suzanne glanced at me. "Shannon, you mind holding the ladder?"

"Not at all." Actually, with all the weird stuff going on around here, I felt better taking charge of my sister's ladder. "Should I do any talking?"

"Yes. Chloe can explain why she's removing the awning and then you can wing it.

Maybe tell a story or whatever. Or hey, talk about ladder safety."

"Ladder safety. I love it."

"We'll be on a wide shot, so don't worry about whether the camera can see you."

I really wasn't worried, but I said, "Okay, thanks."

Ten minutes later, Blake and Diego carried the extension ladder over and set it up along the side of the bay window. Chloe and Diego and I stood next to it.

Suzanne motioned to the stage manager, who pointed to Chloe and said, "And . . . action."

Chloe looked into the camera. "Right now we're about to remove that ugly green copper awning that the owners placed over the bay window. We think it was meant to keep the rain from coming in the window, but it's about a hundred years old and falling apart. And once we replace these windows, the rain won't seep in like it used to."

She climbed up eight rungs while Diego and I held each side of the ladder.

I watched and waited until Suzanne pointed at me and that's when I started to talk. "Most homeowners have an extension ladder in their garage, even if they just use it for putting up Christmas decorations once a year. There are a few safety rules to follow when using an extension ladder. First, see these things at the bottom?" I knelt down and patted the base of the ladder. "These are called 'shoes' or 'feet' and they often have a nonskid surface on the bottom so that wherever you set your ladder, it won't slip or slide. So always make sure that they're flat on the ground."

I stood up. "Another thing to remember when you're climbing the ladder: it's good to have three points of connection. So for instance, if your hand is moving up to the next rung, make sure your other hand and both feet are connected."

Standing at the foot of the ladder, I demonstrated the movement.

"It helps if you can get someone to hold the ladder for you," I continued, smiling at Diego. "And always make sure that you hear those rung locks click into place." I pointed to the locks. "That will ensure that the ladder won't collapse with you on it. Nobody wants that." I glanced up at Chloe. "How's it looking up there?"

"This awning has been here for so many years that the screws holding it in place are completely rusted." She turned to the camera. "I might have to get some rust spray to remove the rust if I can't get my power drill to connect to the head."

"That's a pretty common problem with these old houses," I said.

"Yeah," Chloe said, clutching the power drill. "I'm going to —"

All of a sudden it felt like an earthquake had hit. The ladder shook. Chloe lost her balance and screamed.

I jolted as the ladder collapsed on itself.

"Chloe," I cried, looking up to see her arms whirling around as she plummeted down. Before I could reach out to her, Diego took one step forward and caught her in his arms.

"Oh my God," I cried. "Are you all right?"

She couldn't catch her breath. Diego held her tightly, staring wide-eyed. We all froze for what felt like an hour, but was only a few seconds. What had happened?

Diego swallowed nervously. "Can you stand up?"

Chloe nodded, still breathing heavily.

He set her down gently and her legs wobbled, but she managed to stand on her own.

Blake ran over to Chloe. "What the hell happened?"

"The ladder broke," I said, then thought, *Duh.* But how? I wondered.

Chloe managed to speak. "It happened just as I was reaching out to try to get the drill bit to fit the screw head. I was off balance and couldn't catch myself."

"Jeez, Chloe." Blake ran a nervous hand through his hair. "You took ten years off my life, and I can't afford to lose them."

"Right there with you," she murmured.

He leaned in and studied her expression as he rubbed her back. "Are you sure you're okay?"

"Yeah." She exhaled in relief. "I'll be fine."

I was watching the exchange. My heart was still slamming in my chest as part of my brain went over everything that might have happened if Diego hadn't reacted so quickly. I had set the rungs in the extension ladder myself so I knew they'd been locked. And yet — the locks had failed. The ladder had collapsed and there hadn't been a thing I could do about it besides watch my baby sister fall.

Was this just an accident? Or was someone trying once again to hurt Chloe? And if so . . . who? And why?

"We've had this ladder for years," Blake was saying, "but it was meant to last forever. I really don't get it." He shook his head. "I'm just glad you weren't hurt."

"You and me both."

He studied her for another long moment, then gave a brief nod. "Okay, guys," he announced. "Everyone's alive. Chloe's fine. Let's take a break."

Most of the crew walked off toward the catering tables.

I stared up at the ladder for a while. It hadn't been taken down yet, but it no longer extended farther up the wall, having retracted completely. I shook my head. After my spiel about safety, I felt pretty stupid. So once everyone had left the area, I got up close to see if I could figure out how it happened. The rope-and-pulley action looked like it was still functioning, so I took a look at the rung locks. Both of them had snapped in two. "That's impossible," I whispered. They were hard-cast aluminum and meant to last at least twenty years if not forever, as Blake had said.

But I looked closer and realized that both of the locks had been sawed almost in half from the inside. And someone had filed down the jagged surface so you wouldn't notice the saw marks. They were clearly intended to break at the slightest bit of pressure. An attempt on Chloe's life? But that couldn't be, because whoever had sabotaged the ladder couldn't have known which of us would be climbing the thing. Or could they?

I didn't say anything but pulled my phone out and took close-up pictures of each of the rung locks. Then I sent them by text with a short message to Chief Jensen.

Eric showed up ten minutes later. I tried to ignore the looks on the faces of the crew as I greeted him. They were probably getting tired of seeing the police always around here, but I didn't care. I walked him around to where the ladder had been moved onto its side and was leaning against the house.

We knelt down and I showed him the sawed-off rung locks. "I don't know if Chloe was the intended victim, but she's the one who does most of that kind of work on the show. Because she's quick, you know? Diego is the muscle and Blake is the talker. Still, in fairness, it could have been any of us on the ladder today."

"I've seen the show a few times but I never realized the tasks broke down like that."

"Chloe pointed it out and I've noticed that they pretty much stick to that formula." I stood, still a little shaky and worried about the might-have-beens. "We used the ladder earlier today and it worked fine. So either it hadn't reached its breaking point yet, or someone did this during our lunch hour."

He stared at the rung locks. "We might be able to get some prints off this surface." He sighed. "It was obviously done with the intent to hurt someone. We just have to figure out who did it and why."

I looked over at the crew milling around the craft tables and wondered just which one of them might want Chloe dead.

"I'm tempted to shut down the entire production," Eric said.

"No!" I cried. "I mean, of course you can. But I hope you won't."

"I won't," he admitted. "For now. I know everyone is depending on these shows to attract some good attention and new business to the town. But that doesn't mean I won't take action if something else occurs."

"I appreciate that," I said, as we walked slowly around to the front lawn. "But look, if you shut it down, how will we ever find out who killed Bree Bennett and Richie Rich?"

His eyes narrowed on me. "And by 'we,' I know you mean the police."

"Absolutely." I nodded briskly. "Yes."

"Good. So I'll allow the production to keep rolling, but just to warn you, I'll be making a few changes."

"What do you mean? Are you planning to bait the killer? Can I help?"

"No, and no. Just let that thought go, Shannon."

"All right, all right." My jaw was starting

to hurt from clenching my teeth so much lately. "But whoever sabotaged that ladder had to be the same person who killed Bree and Richie."

"I'm not willing to agree with you yet," Eric said. "But I do know that your sister is in danger."

Despite Eric's dire words, I managed to sleep well and woke up feeling a lot more refreshed than the day before. I planned to keep an eagle eye on Chloe today whether she liked it or not.

As we stepped onto the property, I felt a little gun-shy. We had already found two bodies at the Bloom house and I was scared to death we might find a third. Not to mention, I was still traumatized after watching my sister tumble off a ladder.

Chloe and I walked up the walkway and stopped at the bottom of the front stairs. "Everything looks copacetic."

"Thank goodness," Chloe said. "No bodies." Clearly she was feeling the same sense of anxiety that I was.

"And no yellow tape on the door."

"Does that mean we've been cleared to work inside today?"

"I hope so," I said, but then remembered Eric Jensen's words. I still wondered what "changes" he had in mind.

We walked back across the lawn and crossed the street to the hair and makeup trailer, where Josie worked her magic on both of us. I had to admit I was enjoying this luxury lifestyle.

A half hour later, we stopped at the catering table for a cup of coffee and a quick chat with Emily and her helpers.

"How are my girls this morning?" she said.

I smiled. "Much better than yesterday."

"I'm just hoping we get through this day without any mishaps," Chloe said after a quick sip of coffee.

"Me, too," I said, smiling at her. "Please don't try flying again."

She grinned. "But I'm so good at it."

I gave her a sideways look. "And Diego is so good at catching you."

"He definitely qualifies as hero material."

Emily smiled. "He's a lovely man."

"Good morning, you two."

I turned and saw the owner of the Bloom house standing a few feet away. "Margaret!" I gave her a quick hug. "I haven't seen you in a few days. How are you?"

"I'm wonderful." She glanced around. "I can see changes happening already."

I chuckled slightly. "Well, it's slow going but things should start to pick up."

"Good. I just wanted to make sure you were all right. I heard you took a fall."

"That was Chloe. But she's fine."

"Thank goodness. Well, I won't keep you. Just wanted to check in."

"I'm glad you did. Help yourself to coffee and a donut."

Her eyes sparkled with anticipation as she stepped closer to the table. "Don't mind if I do."

"Chloe."

I felt a strange chill as my sister and I turned and saw Eric Jensen looming a few yards away.

"Good morning, Chief," Chloe said.

I didn't like that look in his eyes but I greeted him, too, trying to keep things light and breezy. "Hey, Eric. Is the porch still off limits?"

"No, you're cleared to use it. And they should be finished inside the house within a few hours."

"Good." I nodded. "Thanks."

"Chloe." His voice sounded more strained than I'd ever heard before. "I'll need you to come with me down to the station."

"What for?" I demanded, before Chloe could say a word.

"Shannon, it's okay," Chloe said softly, her attitude much different than the last time he had shown up to drag her down to police headquarters.

"No, it's not." I scowled at Eric. I couldn't lie about it. Eric taking Chloe down to the station a second time felt like a personal betrayal. He had to know she was innocent. "Why are you taking her? What's going on?"

He held up his hand. "We just want to ask her a few more questions."

"You can ask them right here," I said.

"No," he said firmly. "I need to record her answers and I want a more private setting." He glanced around. "This won't cut it."

I gave him a death glare and was pleased to see the discomfort in his eyes even though he didn't budge on his demand. "Then I'm going with you."

"Shannon, no," Chloe said. "I'll be all right."

"I know," I said, with another hard look at Eric. "Because I'll be with you."

Chloe sighed. "Look, the sooner I go, the sooner I can get back to work."

"*We* will get back to work. I'm going with you as your legal counsel."

Eric looked as if he might've wanted to laugh but knew I would kill him if he did. "You're not a lawyer, Shannon."

"Do I have to be a lawyer?" I asked, then

answered my own question. "I don't think so."

"Why would I need a lawyer?" Chloe asked sensibly, her tone casual as she reached out and squeezed my arm. "I'll be okay. And while I'm gone you can follow up on the boom lift. We'll need to use it today. And by the time it arrives, I'll probably be back."

I glared at the police chief. "Will she?"

He hesitated, then said, "You might need to take her place for a few hours."

"Are you kidding me?" I might've screeched the words. It happens when I'm a little overwrought. Like when my sister's about to be dragged off to the big house by the cops.

Yes, I was being dramatic, but I was scared witless. Why did Eric want to interrogate Chloe? Was it connected to Richie's death? Or did it have something to do with Bree?

Unfortunately, Chloe was connected to both of them and not in a good way. That didn't mean she would ever hurt either one of them. Eric had to know that.

"Look," I said, trying to sound rational. "You know Chloe is innocent. She wouldn't hurt a fly." I moved closer and lowered my voice. "You know she was the victim yesterday. Why aren't you talking to Rolly Wagner? Or Mrs. Wagner. She's whiny but I'm willing to bet she packs a wallop. And they both hated Richie. And they hated Bree, too. In fact, half the staff hated Bree. And one of them probably slipped a roofie into all those water bottles to keep Blake from coming to Bree's defense."

"Shannon," Chloe said. "Calm down."

But I was on a roll. "I saw the production manager talking to Richie the other morning. And she also had a very suspicious conversation with Blake the other day. And now that Bree's gone, they've made her the producer. You should talk to her. Her name's Suzanne. Maybe you should haul her off to jail instead of Chloe. In fact, I've got a whole list of people you could take with you. Just not Chloe."

"I've already spoken to Mr. and Mrs. Wagner," Eric said calmly, "They have an alibi for both nights."

"Oh, really?" I frowned. "Well, somebody's lying."

"And just because the producer talked to Richie is no reason to arrest her."

"Does she have an alibi? And by the way, did you see how tall she is?"

Chloe choked on a laugh. "Will you relax, Shannon?"

"I'm not sure I can."

"Just chill," she said, and for the first time, real impatience colored her tone. "I'll be back in a little while." She wrapped her arm around my shoulders and we walked toward the driveway.

Once again, Chloe was trying to comfort me while she was the one being carted off to police headquarters. It just went to show that she was way too good a person to be treated this way.

I watched helplessly as Chief Jensen opened the back door of the SUV and cushioned the top of her head as she climbed inside. As if she were a hardened criminal! I knew in my gut that Eric going after Chloe was the biggest mistake he could've made. She was a victim, lest he forgot! And she was as innocent as the day was long.

If this was all the cops were doing to try to find the killer, they were wasting their time. But apparently I was the only person who realized it. Which meant that it was now up to me to track down the real killer.

As Eric drove off with Chloe in the back seat, I suddenly felt adrift. How long would he keep her at the police station? How long would he interrogate her? I had been in that interrogation room. They had kept me there for hours. I knew how frustrating and demoralizing and unfair it could be.

"I should be there with her," I mumbled, and turned to head back to the house. But my feet, of their own accord, took me straight back to the donut table and walked me closer to the box of cream-filled maple bars. What else could I do but take one?

"Those are my favorites," Emily said.

"I thought you liked the napoleons best."

"I do," she said. "And the crullers, and the maple bars, and the tartlets, and the eclairs. They're my children and I love them all the same. How can I favor one above the others?"

"You are a strange woman, Emily Rose."

She laughed. "I consider that a compliment."

"I meant it that way." I took a bite and swooned from the intoxicating blend of luscious creamy custard, fluffy doughy wonderfulness, and maple-sugared yumminess. "You have the best job in the world."

She gazed at me. "I always thought *you* had the best job, love."

"Sometimes I'm not so sure." I wiped my chin with my napkin. "I mean, I love my job. I do. But then comes the day when I walk into an old Victorian house that's just begging to be rehabbed, and I find a dead body. And then I'm not so sure about the job I do."

She came around the table and gave me a warm hug. "I'm sorry Chloe was the one who found Richie Stoddard."

"She found Bree Bennett, too."

"I know."

I twisted my lips in a wry smile. "Seems to run in the family now. Who knew?"

With her arm around my shoulder, she led me away from the table and away from the crowd. "Come to dinner tonight. I'll call the girls and we'll have a fun evening of wine and pasta and giggles."

It felt as though I hadn't seen Lizzie or Marigold or Jane in weeks. And right then, the thought of going another day without seeing my posse, my inner circle, my girls, was almost too much to fathom.

"I would love that," I said, leaning into her. "Thank you, Emily."

"And you'll bring Chloe with you."

"I will." But then I frowned. "If they let her out of jail in time."

"She's not in jail, Shannon. She hasn't been arrested," she said with more assurance than I felt. "Eric just wants to ask her some questions. He's a smart man and like you, he's very good at his job. He might have a compelling reason for getting her away from here."

I gaped at her. "What do you mean?"

"He's trying to find a killer."

"Of course, but —"

"And Chloe did have that fall yesterday."

"Yes, but —"

"I've got to get back to the table, love. I'll see you tonight at seven."

An hour later, I had filmed two more segments with Blake and one with Diego. I had to admit it was great fun to work with Blake. He had a corny sense of humor that I loved, and he really did know how to blather on cue. It was a real gift.

But wow, the man was a first-class klutz. He dropped the hammer *twice* and that was when he was just standing there! He didn't even bother to try to pound a nail. Chloe was so right about his incompetence with tools.

Thank goodness for Diego, I thought. He was a talented carpenter and he could get the job done *fast.* He was fun to work with, too, in an entirely different way from Blake. Diego might not be a great talker, but dang, the man *looked good.* His smile was like a gift from the gods. And he had snatched my sister out of midair, so I was predisposed to like him.

But maybe his good looks hid a sinister

streak. He was so strong, he could've easily shoved a crowbar into Richie's neck, cutting his artery. He could've dragged Bree across the floor and effortlessly knocked her out or strangled her — or both.

I was giving myself chills. I forcefully shook off those thoughts and as soon as we took a short break, I grabbed my phone and texted Chloe. But there was no response. I stared at the empty screen and wondered if they had confiscated her cell phone.

"Oh, jeez," I whispered. Emily was right, it wasn't like she was under arrest. She probably just turned off her phone while she answered questions. Still, my head was ready to explode. As soon as we broke for lunch, I intended to drive over to the police station and make sure my sister wasn't being flogged.

Glancing around, I noticed that the crowd size was even bigger than yesterday. I wondered if the news about a second body being found at Bloom house had brought out the lookie-loos. Usually when people heard about a killer on the loose, they stayed inside and locked their doors. But not in Lighthouse Cove. Here we couldn't get enough of the gory stuff.

Someone could make a fortune selling soft drinks and popcorn, I thought, as I scanned the faces of the crowd. Was the killer watching me at this very moment?

I had to rub my arms to chase away the shivers that slithered through me at that grisly thought. And like the sun coming out from behind a dark cloud, I caught sight of Mac standing with Wade and Sean over by the stacked lumber. He saw me looking and smiled so warmly, I wanted to sigh. *How did I get so lucky?* I wondered. He blew me a kiss and I almost melted. I blew one back to him and he reached out and caught it, then slapped his cheek, and we both laughed. It was a sweet moment and I couldn't wait until I could hold him close and just talk for a while.

"Hey, Shannon," Blake called. "Let's work on this next segment."

I gave Mac a final wave and a smile and then jogged over to the side of the house, where Blake and I strategized for a few minutes. Diego joined us and Blake gave him his cues.

While I could admit to enjoying these guys, I still missed Chloe. As we waited for the countdown to start the scene, I had an abrupt and overwhelming burst of guilt hit me. Was I betraying my sister by having too much fun with her co-stars?

"And . . . action!"

Luckily the camera was on Blake. I sucked in a breath and let it go, then did my quickie arm-shaking routine to get rid of the guilt and calm my nerves.

Blake gazed down at me from the second step of the *new* extension ladder. He didn't dare go any higher because along with his lack of coordination, he had a fear of heights.

"What do you think, Shannon?" he asked. "Can we clean out those old cedar shake shingles?" He glanced into the camera. "Say that three times fast."

I laughed. "It's going to be a dirty job. And it would be almost impossible if we didn't have this little miracle worker."

The camera zoomed out to include the articulated arm that was now stretched up to the third floor.

"Our extension ladder will go thirty-two feet up the wall. But this baby" — I patted the motor on the boom — "can go up to fifty feet in the air and hold two workers. It's called a boom lift and it features an articulated arm that stretches and expands to reach anywhere we want to go. We'll be able to get up there and rip off those old cedar shingles in no time flat."

"Then let's get 'er done," Blake said.

"And . . . cut."

Blake stepped out of the shot. "Good luck."

"Thanks." I climbed onto the boom platform and the first thing I did was check to make sure that the guardrails were secure. Bob the cameraman climbed on after me. He wore a headset and would convey the director's cues to me.

Wade would be on the ground operating the lower controls that kept the motor running and moved the lift cylinders up and down. I would take care of the upper controls that would allow me to rotate the platform or move it forward and backward and up and down.

"Everybody set?" the stage manager asked. I gave a thumbs-up and twenty seconds later, she counted down to action.

"And here we go," I said to the camera, and we slowly climbed forty feet up to the third story, where we could see the cedar shake shingles peeling off the wall. Bob held the camera on me with the house behind me.

"A common feature of Victorian homes," I said, as the platform rose slowly, "is the many different styles of exterior façades, all in one house. So you saw the horizontal clapboard siding on the first story, and here's the second story where they've used the same clapboard siding but painted it a contrasting color. And finally we get to the third story. As you can see, it's covered in these cedar shake shingles."

Bob zoomed in to get a close-up of the ratty old shingles.

"These are in bad shape," I said, scraping at a row of shingles. They peeled right off and fell to the earth below like confetti at a party.

"When we were on the ground looking up," I continued, "these shingles didn't look too awful. But now that we can see them up close, you can see what's going on here. This is the sort of damage that will cause water to seep into your home. And it'll raise your heating costs because the wind and cold will breeze right through."

Another row of shingles bit the dust. "So while it may be costly to make these repairs," I said, "it will save you money in the long run."

I knocked yet a few more shingles off, then turned back to the camera. "Once Diego and I remove these shingles and patch and prime the wall beneath, we'll be replacing these old shingles with a classic clamshell-style shingle that I think will look beautiful on this home."

"And . . . cut," Bob said. "Good job,

Shannon."

I grinned. "Thanks, Bob. Ready to get back on terra firma?"

"Yeah." But he revved up his camera so he could get more shots of the world from forty feet up in the air. "We'll use these as transition shots throughout the programs."

"That'll be nice," I said. "This really is a gorgeous property."

"And I love how it's surrounded by woods. You just don't see much of that in Los Angeles."

I pushed the controls and we started our descent. Bob kept the camera rolling until we were settled back down on the ground.

"That was fun. Thanks, Shannon."

"You bet," I said, and watched him walk back toward the equipment truck. I checked my watch. Almost noon and time for a lunch break. Which meant it was time to go check on Chloe.

I had stowed my purse in Emily's catering truck so I swung by to grab it, then headed toward the street to get my truck. But before I could make it to the sidewalk, I heard someone shouting my name.

"Shannon Hammer! Get back here."

I turned and saw Whitney Reid Gallagher storming toward me. She was wearing sneakers today so I figured she'd learned her lesson with her stilettos.

I sighed. I really didn't want to deal with her special brand of baloney again today.

"What do you want now?" I asked.

"My cousin died because of you." She was screeching and I wondered if she had taken an extra dose of mean pills today. "I know you had something to do with it! You hated him and you hate me and it's all your fault."

"You're wrong," I said, "but I'm sure that won't stop you from spreading that vicious lie all over town."

"Every time a murder happens anywhere in town, you're right there." Her eyes were wide and angry. "So why aren't you in jail?"

"You're obviously crazy or maybe just high," I countered. "So why aren't you in rehab?"

She frowned. "That's just stupid."

"I don't think so. I think you've lost your last marble."

She stomped her foot. "You've always hated me and this time you took it out on my poor cousin Richie. I know exactly what's going on here."

I had to ask. "What's that?"

"This is an attack on me."

She was so ludicrous, I had to laugh. "Yeah, it's all about you, Whitney. Everything is all about you. Two people are dead, someone was drugged, my sister's been attacked at least twice, but it's all about you."

"But why else would you be so awful to poor Richie?"

I just goggled at her. Even Whitney couldn't be that dense. "Because he was a schmuck?" But that was a mean thing to say, even to Whitney. "Listen, I'm sorry he was murdered. No one deserves that. But I had nothing to do with it, and neither did my sister."

"Hey, you," a woman nearby said loudly. "Did I hear you say you were Richie Stoddard's cousin?"

We both turned and saw Mrs. Wagner standing a few feet away. I almost didn't recognize her without her angry, hulking husband, Rolly.

Whitney was certain she had a sympathetic ear so she sniffled loudly and said, "Yes. He was my cousin. The poor man is dead because of *her.*" She pointed her finger at me.

Mrs. Wagner grabbed my hand and shook it firmly. "In that case, I want to thank you, miss!" she said. And to Whitney, she snapped, "Richie Stoddard deserves to rot in hell!"

And with that, the woman turned and sashayed down the sidewalk.

Whitney's mouth hung open and she blinked in shock. Maybe I did, too, because I never in a million years would've expected the lollygagging Mrs. Wagner to be my champion. Happily though, the older woman distracted Whitney enough for me to take a chance and sneak away, dashing down the street to my truck.

I climbed into the truck, locked the doors, and drove away.

On the drive to the police department, I thought about Mrs. Wagner and how she stepped right up to give Whitney some grief. I was so grateful, I was almost willing to take her off my suspect list. Almost. Her husband, however, was still on the list, right near the top until further notice.

Ten minutes later, I pulled to a stop in the city hall parking lot next door to the police department.

I climbed out of the truck and slammed the door shut.

Staring at the façade of the police department, I had a lightning-bolt realization. I suddenly knew who had snitched to the police about Chloe's run-in with Richie Rich.

It had to be Whitney Reid Gallagher.

Who else could have done it? Whitney was married to the assistant chief of police, namely Tommy, which made it super convenient for her to drop the hint without even leaving the house. She'd probably even mentioned the subtle death threat Chloe had made to Richie. Although calling it a *threat* was a stretch.

Whitney had known every little detail about the confrontation between Chloe and Richie. That had to mean that the sniveling coward had gone directly to his meaner, tougher cousin Whitney to whine about it. And then shortly after that, Whitney had shown up at the Bloom house and accused Chloe of propositioning him.

Which was still so absurd, I began to snicker — in spite of Richie turning up dead as a doornail.

I walked into the station and waved to the desk sergeant, another Lighthouse High alumnus. "Hi, Kevin."

"Hey, Shannon. You here to pick up your sister?"

My eyes lit up at the good news. "Yes. Is she cleared to go home?"

"I think so. Let me check." He typed something into his computer and saw something that caused him to frown. He glanced up at me and winced. "Sorry, Shannon. Guess I should wait to hear from the chief before I open my big mouth like that."

"Oh." That didn't sound good. "What's wrong?"

"Uh, nothing. No worries. I mean . . . hmm. Give me a minute, will you?"

"Sure. I'll wait."

He picked up the phone. "Yeah, Chief. No. Yes. Okay." He flashed me a hopeful smile, paused another moment, then said, "Yes, sir," and hung up the phone.

"Go on back, Shannon. The chief wants to see you."

"Oh." Was that a good thing or a bad thing? "Thanks, Kevin."

I'd been here enough times that I knew the way to the end of the hall where Police Chief Eric Jensen had his office. The door was closed, so I knocked.

"Come in."

"It's me," I said, walking in. I didn't sit down because all I wanted to do was get Chloe and get out of here.

"Have a seat."

So much for that plan. I sat down. "What's going on?"

"I don't want you to panic."

"Really? Because when someone says 'don't panic,' it's a pretty clear indication that you should *panic.*" I glared at him. "What did you do?"

"My job."

"Eric . . ."

"Look, I warned you."

"Warned me about what?"

"That I was going to make some changes on the film set."

"Like what?"

"Don't freak out, but I'm holding your sister in jail overnight."

CHAPTER TWELVE

I jumped out of the chair. "What?" Again, a little shrill, but who could blame me? "Why?"

Eric waved both hands in a calm-down motion. "It's for her own protection, Shannon. I think she may be a target."

Well, that was like throwing a bucket of ice water in my face. "A target? You mean, of the *killer*? Do you know why?"

He scowled. "She knows something or saw something."

"If she did, she wasn't aware of it."

"It happens that I agree with you, and so does Chloe." Eric frowned even deeper. "But someone out there thinks she's onto them or witnessed something incriminating."

I frowned, too. It made sense and I really wished it didn't. I hated the thought that Chloe was in danger, and having Eric say it out loud made it all the more real. "This is like a bad movie."

"Again," Eric said softly, his voice deep and dangerous. "Agreed. The ladder was the last straw. Somebody's trying to hurt your sister and I'm here to stop them."

"Okay. I appreciate that." I paced in front of his desk. "But how long does she have to stay here? And why in jail at all? My house is safe enough. And let's face it. It's prettier. More comfortable. Better food. Friendly pets."

A hint of a smile curved his mouth briefly. "I'll grant you it's not as pretty here, but our beds aren't bad. We've got memory foam."

I just stared at him. "You're scaring me, Eric."

"And as far as food goes, I was planning to order a pizza from Bella Rossa."

I nodded. Heck, now I wanted to stay in jail. "That's hard to turn down. But look, this is crazy. She should come home. You can assign someone to stay with us. Or you could sleep on the couch. Or I could ask Mac to come over. Or all of the above. I don't care. But please, not jail. It's just wrong. Everyone in town will think she's guilty of something. It could cost her her job, Eric."

"It's safe here."

"It's primitive."

He looked hurt. "We have running water."

I peered at him for a long moment. "Have you arrested my sister?"

"No."

"So she can leave anytime."

"Yes."

"Then I'll just go get her and we'll be going."

"She's staying. Voluntarily."

"What?"

"She's safe here, Shannon," he said softly. "She wants to stay."

All I could do was shake my head. When Eric Jensen's voice revealed how kind he could be, there wasn't a woman alive who wouldn't go along with him. I smiled briefly, but then brought it back to the real topic. "Who do you think is behind the murders?"

His brow furrowed. "I've narrowed it down."

So had I, I thought, but I wasn't about to share my theories with him. He would only tell me to buzz off.

"But I'm not ready to make an arrest. Not yet."

"Well, why not? You're willing to keep Chloe in jail but not willing to arrest someone? Come on, Eric. What aren't you telling me? Make an arrest so I can take my sister home." Did I sound as aggravated as I felt? I was trying to be nice. He was the police chief, after all. And more than that, we were friends. But this was really pushing the limits of friendship.

"Just let it go, Shannon."

"Not much chance of that. We're talking about my sister. I'm not going to let it go."

"You need to trust me."

"Really?"

He stared at me for a long moment. "Would you like to see her?"

I let loose a frustrated groan. "Of course I want to see her."

"Come with me."

I followed Eric halfway down the hall until he stopped and unlocked a heavy steel door. "This way."

I glanced around. We were in the section of the building that housed the jail. I stared at the iron bars in front of me and counted four cells.

I spotted Chloe right away, sitting in a comfortable chair and playing with her phone.

"Chloe."

"Shannon!"

I glanced back at Eric, who didn't seem inclined to leave us alone. So I ignored him. "Eric says you're not under arrest, but since you're sitting in a jail cell, I'm calling him a liar."

"It's okay, Shannon," she said. "Eric's been a real sweetie to me. And I feel safe here."

A sweetie? I wasn't feeling that generous toward him. "But I could keep you safe at home."

She shook her head. "It's too risky."

I turned to Eric. "This is your fault."

"Don't yell at Eric, Shannon."

I frowned. "I'm not yelling. Yet."

Eric grinned. "I'll leave you to it, then."

He walked away and when the door shut behind him, I gripped the bars of Chloe's cell. "What is going on? I'm really worried."

"Me, too," she said, as she pushed her chair closer to the bars. "First I got sick from that coffee. And then there was that weird thing with my makeup. Eric said they found some kind of poison added to it that seeps in through your skin. And then I fell off the ladder. It was rigged to break and I can only assume that I was the target. So I'm starting to believe Eric's right. I think I might be in danger."

"Danger from who?"

The door opened and Eric walked back into the hall carrying a chair. He set it down in front of Chloe's cell and walked away.

"Thank you," I murmured, and sat down.

"He's so nice," Chloe said, with an indulgent glance at the hall where Eric had stood a few seconds ago.

"I used to think so," I muttered. "Now I'm not sure."

"I know you're kidding. He's your friend." Chloe pulled her knees up to her chin and wrapped her arms around her legs. "And he's promised he'll stay here tonight so I'll feel safe. He's going to sleep in that cell over there."

"Oh." I nodded soberly. "Like a slumber party."

She rolled her eyes. "Very funny. I know it sounds weird."

"It doesn't just sound weird. It *is* weird."

Sighing, Chloe said, "Look around. This place is a fortress."

I glanced back at the steel door. "I get that."

"No one can get to me in here. And Eric's providing a pizza, so I don't have to worry about starving, either." She took a deep breath. "Look, you should go back to the Bloom house and work for a while. I'll be fine. Just keep your eyes open."

I gave her my best steely-eyed stare, but she didn't budge. I finally relented. "Okay. But are you sure Eric has your best interests at heart?"

"Yes." She sounded absolutely certain. "Right from the start he told me that he thinks I'm in danger and he's promised to keep me safe."

Fine, then. I could trust Eric to keep his word and he was so tough, no one would get past him to hurt Chloe, so that was something. "I'm happy about that part."

She sighed. "There's something else. Eric found out about my confrontation with Richie and that's another reason why he decided to bring me to the police station."

I didn't like the sound of that. "Did he say how he found out?"

"No."

Scowling, I said, "I'm pretty sure Whitney was the snitch. She probably told Tommy, who passed it on to Eric."

"That makes perfect sense," she said. "But strangely enough, Whitney didn't mention the part where Richie had threatened to ruin Dad's business."

I was fuming again. "I'll make sure Eric knows that part."

"Oh, I already told him."

I grinned. "That's my girl. Then I'll just make sure Whitney knows."

"Did I mention that Eric's really nice?"

"Once or twice."

"Yeah. So when the ladder thing happened, it freaked him out." She smiled a little wistfully and I wondered if Chloe was actually interested in Eric. "He said he thought about it all night long and then this morning, he decided to bring me in, to keep me safe. But then he found out about my and Richie's big fight." She shrugged. "So that added to his worries. Someone saw us fighting, then killed Richie to frame me."

"Does Eric have a clue about the killer?"

"I think so, but he's not sharing the info with me."

"And who might've sabotaged the ladder? And the coffee? And the makeup?"

"He wouldn't say. Said he's still investigating some leads. But I feel like he's got his eye on someone. He mentioned baiting a trap."

"But how can he bait a trap with you in here? You need to be out in the world to be the bait in the trap. Not that I'd ever want you to be used as bait to catch a killer. I would seriously smack him if he even considered it for a half second."

She shrugged. "Maybe he's using some other kind of bait."

My eyes widened. "Maybe he's thinking *I* can be the bait."

"No way," she said. "Don't even think that."

But the more I thought about it, the more sense it made. I was pretty sure Eric wouldn't do that, but I didn't care. I was ready to expose this murderer and I knew exactly who to ask for help.

"I don't like that look in your eyes." Chloe watched me warily.

"Don't worry," I said, and realized I sounded like my sister. "I mean it. I'll be fine. And so will you. I'll check in with you later."

She sighed. "Please don't forget."

"I won't." I stood and gripped the bars separating us. "Love you, Chloe."

"Love you, too."

Back at the Bloom house, I went through the motions, hoping I wasn't a total dud when the camera was on me. I couldn't think straight, knowing my sister was stuck in that cell and I was here trying to catch a killer.

Blake and I were going over more possibilities for the bay window while everyone took an afternoon break.

"Is Chloe still being questioned?" Blake asked, checking his watch. "She's going to miss the whole day."

"I know." I brushed dust, dirt, and peeled paint off the windowsills. "But she's one of the few people who knew both victims, so the police have a lot of questions for her."

He scoffed. "They can't possibly think Chloe had anything to do with the deaths."

"I'm sure they don't. I mean, she was attacked herself." I shrugged. "They're just trying to get answers and apparently she's got plenty of them."

"Oh. You think she knows something?"

"Probably not," I said, waving away his concerns and giving him a big smile. "But she's a talker, in case you never noticed. And she's super observant. Nothing much gets past Chloe."

"You know, the other day they had me in there for a few hours, too," Blake admitted.

"I guess that makes sense since, well, they always say the spouse is the best suspect, right? I mean, so they say."

"Yes," he murmured. "So they say."

I smiled. "Especially when you're married to an executive producer who likes to fire people."

He chuckled fondly. "Yeah. Bree was a pistol. But I loved her. I still do. God, I miss her."

"Of course you do."

"The day she died . . ." He began to choke

up and had to stop to compose himself. He swallowed carefully and wiped his eyes, then continued. "I had been drugged and could barely think straight. But I rallied once I got to the police station. Not that I was much help."

"Did you know Richie Stoddard?"

"Who?"

"The other victim."

He frowned. "What'd you say his name was?"

"Richie," I said. "I would've thought you knew him. He was the real estate agent who submitted the Wagners' house to be on the show."

"That was strictly Bree's territory," he said with a shrug. "I never get involved with the home owners."

"Probably a good policy. But anyway, when they didn't make it onto the show, they got really angry with Richie."

He nodded slowly. "Do you think they had something to do with Bree's and Richie's deaths?"

"I don't know. Mr. Wagner was really bent out of shape. But murder? Hard to say." I made a point of staring at the bay window and reaching for my tape measure. "You know, I saw Richie at the inn the first day you all set up the production offices over there. I thought he might've been there for a meeting with Bree."

"It's possible," Blake said. "She handles all the decisions about which houses we'll be working on. I mean, she *handled* all that."

Nodding, I kept talking. I wanted Blake to open up more and I also wanted to let him think that just maybe there was more going on than he knew. "Richie was absolutely certain Bree was going to choose his clients' house. Guess he was wrong."

"Bree made a point of never making promises. She had her reasons for choosing the houses she chose and was just as likely to change her mind ten times before she settled on one."

In for a penny, in for a pound, as my dad used to say. I tried to keep it casual as I brought up the sticky subject. "So Chloe mentioned something about a new show she was going to be working on."

He looked surprised. "What new show?"

"Something for one of the big networks, I think."

He pursed his lips as he thought about it, then sighed. "I was sworn to secrecy. But since you already know about it, you should hear the whole story. Truth is, Bree was talking about firing Chloe. The network wanted me and Diego to star on the show. To give it sort of a father-son angle."

I would've snorted with laughter but managed to stay serious. "I thought everyone liked the male-female thing that you have with Chloe. A lot of women watch these shows and they can relate to someone like Chloe."

"They like to see men, too," he said, with just a touch of defensiveness.

"Well, sure." *Duh,* I thought. But still, the father-son angle? He was being ridiculous.

"They're looking to shake things up a little. Our formula was getting a little stale and in television you've got to keep things fresh or you'll die. And Chloe is cute, but they wanted a more macho dynamic."

"Huh." *Macho dynamic?* Was he kidding? *Makeover Madness* was the highest-rated home improvement show in cable history and while Blake was popular, I liked to think that most of the credit went to my sister. "Chloe wasn't fired, Blake. She *did* have a discussion with Bree about the new show, but she didn't get fired."

He flashed me a patient smile. "You're her sister so it's a little difficult for me to say this. But Bree was planning to fire Chloe right after we finished this set of Victorian-themed shows." He shrugged again. "But then Bree died. So who knows what'll happen? Maybe Chloe will escape the chopping block. Lucky break for her, right?"

I blinked hard. "Are you actually insinuating that Chloe would benefit from Bree's death? Because that's what it sounds like. And that's crazy."

"That came out wrong," he rushed to say. "I'm sorry. All I'm saying is . . . I don't know." He wiped his forehead with his sleeve and shook his head. "I don't know anything."

"Look, I don't blame you for lashing out because you just lost your wife, but you couldn't be more wrong." My teeth were clenched so tightly, I worried that they would crack. "In case you haven't noticed, Chloe's been the victim of at least three attacks."

He stared blankly. "Three?"

"Yes. I don't know if it's the same person who killed your wife, but whoever's trying to hurt her will have to get through me first."

He took a deep breath. "You're a good sister."

"So is Chloe."

Blake nodded. "I'm glad I got a chance to talk to you. I'm still trying to process everything that's been going on around here. It's . . . not easy."

"I know."

He patted my back. "Hang in there, kiddo."

"You, too."

He walked away, leaving me totally confused. I'd been fuming inside earlier and now I didn't know what to do or how to feel about Blake Bennett. Did he really believe that if Bree were still alive, she would've fired Chloe for real? Had he really implied that Chloe had the very best motive for killing Bree?

Okay, yes, Chloe had admitted that she actually *had been* fired the day before she got here. But she had explained that Bree was always firing someone. Even Blake.

And who knew if Bree had told Blake the truth? The woman was a master manipulator, telling half-truths or pure lies to get people to do what she wanted. Or maybe she did it just to watch them squirm. She hadn't been a very nice person.

And I was right back where I'd started, with no real answers to any of my questions. But I vaguely remembered Chloe mentioning that the network bosses would be showing up here at some point to see how the filming was going. Would they use the opportunity to announce the stars of their new show?

I moved to the next window and went through the motions of measuring its size, taking deep breaths as I went. Blake could spin this any way he wanted, but we all knew the truth would come out from the network. I was sure they wanted Chloe. And I wondered what Blake would do when he heard that.

Funny how a minute ago when we started talking, Blake was insisting that Chloe couldn't possibly have anything to do with the murders. But as soon as I mentioned the network show, he was suddenly accusing her of murder.

Could Blake have murdered his wife? I couldn't quite believe it, having heard from everyone, including himself, that he loved her so much. And also, I'd seen firsthand what a klutz Blake could be. Sure, he could've used sheer brute strength to knock Bree over the head with a pipe wrench. But how could he possibly have driven a crowbar with such precision into Richie's neck?

I supposed sheer desperation could've done it. Maybe Blake looked in the mirror one morning and saw a man who was aging quickly and who knew the reality of the television business. Very soon he would no longer be in demand. Of course, I had to admit the crowds still loved him, but how long would that last? Would the network turn down all of his popularity in favor of the youth and beauty they would get with Chloe and Diego?

Who knew how network brains operated?

I was sick and tired of listening to myself think, but I couldn't seem to stop coming up with more scenarios. I certainly didn't want to get into another argument with Blake, but he really did seem the most likely suspect. But then, what did he have against Richie Rich? Had he suspected him of sleeping with his wife? Maybe. Chloe and I had both suspected, but then quickly discarded that possibility. But why? What little I knew of Bree Bennett made me think she would be willing to sleep with another man in order to get something from him. Had she flaunted her assignation in front of Blake? Or maybe Richie had bragged about it. Or even tried to blackmail Blake. Knowing what he'd done to Chloe, I wouldn't put it past Richie to try it.

Was anyone else on the production staff involved with Richie? I'd seen Suzanne talking to him, but that could've been about anything. She seemed way too nice and smart to have had anything to do with Richie.

Maybe the two deaths were completely

unrelated. Could there be *two* killers roaming the film set?

No. That was what my gut told me. Someone had killed both Richie and Bree and now they were tormenting my sister. Why? Who had something to gain from any of it?

The only conclusion I could come up with was the same one I'd been thinking all along. Blake. But he'd been drugged the night Bree died. And sure, Richie was a jerk, but why would Blake be meeting him on the Bloom house porch in the middle of the night? And why would he try to attack Chloe?

I needed to run all these theories past Mac. He would be able to talk through it with me. But I wouldn't see him until tomorrow, so instead, I jogged off to find some breathing room. And ran into Suzanne instead.

"Shannon, just the person I wanted to see," she said. "How's Chloe doing? I'm really worried about her."

I pasted a smile on my face. "Chloe is okay. She's just answering questions and she should be back to work anytime now." I was making it up as I went along since I had no idea how long Eric would keep her there.

"Oh, thank goodness. The past few days

have been difficult for everyone. With Bree gone, things are so crazy, and then Chloe gets taken away. I'm just so grateful that you're such a pro at this stuff. You're doing a fabulous job standing in for her. But frankly, I'm about to lose it." She shook her head, exhaled, and grinned. "But hey, I put up a good front, don't I?"

I couldn't help but smile. The woman had a lovely, self-deprecating sense of humor. I just hoped she wasn't a cold-blooded killer. "I'm glad I ran into you because I wanted to ask you something."

"Sure. Ask away."

"I saw you talking to Richie Stoddard the other day. Are you friends with him?"

She frowned at first, but then nodded slowly. "You mean, the guy who got killed?"

"Yeah."

"I've never met him before in my life. He stopped to ask me about Chloe. He said he went to high school with her and was wondering where she was staying in town."

"And you told him?"

She grimaced. "I gave him her phone number. But judging by your question, I'm wondering if I did the right thing."

"Don't worry about it. You would have no way of knowing if he was telling the truth or not."

"I'll admit I was a little frazzled when he approached me. I figured since there were extra show rundowns on the catering tables, anyone could easily look up our phone numbers. So I went ahead and wrote it down for him since he said he was a friend. I'm sorry if I blew it."

I squeezed her arm lightly. "Don't give it another thought. I was just wondering." And hoping and praying that Suzanne really was as good a friend to Chloe as my sister thought she was.

Except for our lines for the camera, I avoided talking to Blake for the rest of the day. Once we finished for the day, I drove home, took a shower, and dressed for my evening at Emily's. I spent some extra time nuzzling and playing with Robbie and Tiger. The house felt depressingly empty without Chloe, but I knew she would be home in a day or so, as soon as we could figure out who was trying to hurt her.

"You made it," Emily said when she answered her front door.

I laughed. "Did you think I wouldn't?"

"I just know you're really busy. Come in."

I handed her the bottle of wine I'd brought and walked into her beautiful home. "You've added more furniture. It looks fantastic in here." I had helped refurbish the place when Emily first bought it. It had always been known as the Rawley mansion and old Mrs. Rawley had haunted the place until Emily and Gus moved in. Now they all lived in peaceful harmony, for the most part. I was pretty certain the ghost of Mrs. Rawley had a crush on Gus.

I walked past the archway leading to the dining room and ventured a peek inside. Immediately the chandelier above the table began to sway.

"She knows you're here," Emily said, smiling.

"Hello, Mrs. Rawley," I whispered. "I hope you're happy."

The chandelier took one last swing and came to a stop. "Is that a yes?"

"Yes," Emily said softly. "We're all very happy, especially when Gus is home."

"Is he here? I told him I owe you two a dinner out on the town one of these nights. He's been so amazing with all the television people."

"Gus loves cars, which means he loves driving." She grabbed my arm. "And before we go any further, I want to thank you again for hiring Niall. I don't think I've ever seen him so happy."

"It's my pleasure. I haven't even worked with him yet, but all my guys think he's brilliant and talented. And fun."

"Oh, he's fun, all right." She rolled her eyes as only a sister could.

I smiled as she led the way into the front room. I was overjoyed to see that my friends were all here.

"Shannon, you made it." Jane jumped up from the couch and gave me a hug.

"Here's a glass of wine," Emily said, handing me a glass of my favorite Pinot Noir.

Lizzie and Marigold were admiring a new quilt Marigold had brought with her. Her quilts were made by her Amish friends and family back in Pennsylvania and she sold them at Crafts and Quilts, her shop on the town square.

Lizzie walked over and hugged me. "I feel like I haven't seen you in months, but I know it hasn't been that long."

I smiled as I slipped my arm through hers. "I've missed you, too."

"I'll see you this weekend for the book signing, won't I?"

"Absolutely," I said. "Chloe is really excited about it." Even though she was currently in jail, I thought, wincing. She had probably forgotten all about the book signing.

Jane's eyes grew wide. "Is it true she's spending the night in . . . ?"

I glanced around at their concerned faces. Of course they would've heard. This was Lighthouse Cove, home of the instantaneous gossip machine. News here traveled faster than the speed of light.

"In the slammer?" I finished Jane's sentence for her. "So you've all heard. Yes, it's true. She's in what I like to call protective custody." I made air quotes with my fingers as I said it.

"Tell us everything," Lizzie insisted.

"But first," Emily interrupted, "let's go sit down and eat."

"Excellent idea," I said, feeling suddenly famished.

She led the way to her huge, beautiful kitchen where an old-fashioned farm table held platters of two kinds of pasta and a big green salad loaded with veggies.

"This looks beautiful."

"Please sit," Emily said to me. "Put some food on your plate and then spill your guts."

I did as I was told, relating all the latest news about the show and the murders and Chloe. My friends gave me advice and warnings. We discussed the suspects and everyone took votes on who did it.

All in all, the evening was exactly as Emily

had promised. Wine, pasta, and giggles. And good friends. I had missed these girls so much and I wished beyond anything that Chloe could've been here with us. It made me even more determined to get together with the girls and Chloe at least once before she went back to LA.

And just thinking about Chloe leaving made me want to cry. But I took a sip of wine instead and fortified myself with the knowledge that my sister would be visiting us a lot more often after this.

"I think your instincts are right about that Blake Bennett," Lizzie said. "The fact that he can't hammer a nail makes me think he's got issues."

"You mean, he's compensating for something?" Jane asked.

Lizzie nodded and turned to me. "Don't you think so?"

"It's possible," I said. "But really, all I know is that somebody killed two people. And it wasn't Chloe."

"No, of course not," Lizzie said. "But if not Blake, who else could it be?"

"Suzanne," Emily chimed. "Anyone as tall as she is must have psychological problems." She glanced around the room. "I'm kidding."

"Of course you are," I said with a chuckle.

"Although I did spend some time trying to figure out how she killed both people and poisoned Chloe's coffee."

"Wow, Shannon," Lizzie said. "Your mind is a dark place."

"I know. But seeing all of you brightens it up a lot."

"Aw," Emily said, reaching over to squeeze my hand. "You brighten up our lives, too."

"Let's get back to the tall woman," Jane said, quickly adding, "Not that her height is an issue."

I chuckled. Jane and I had always been the two tallest girls in class, which had made us the target of ridicule for some reason.

"But," Jane continued, "Suzanne sounds like a real pro at multi-tasking."

"Oh, definitely," I said.

"That's a skill that would be useful in planning murder. And with Bree's death, she gains a powerful new job title and a big raise in pay — not to mention, she wouldn't have to work with toxic Bree anymore. Sounds like a major motive to me."

"But why would she want to hurt Chloe?" I wondered.

"She thinks Chloe knows something," Jane said.

"Or *saw* something," Marigold suggested.

"Who else is on the suspect list?" Lizzie asked.

"Diego?" Marigold suggested. "I mean, I can see him killing Bree, but how does he even know Richie?"

Jane sipped her wine. "Maybe they met somewhere. Maybe Richie was blackmailing Diego."

Emily frowned. "With what?"

Jane shrugged. "I've known Richie forever. He's never played by the rules. Maybe Diego has a dark past that Richie found out about and decided to use it to make some money."

"But why?" I asked. "What's the connection between Richie and Diego?"

"Bree?" Marigold suggested.

"Or just money," Emily said.

I frowned at that. "But Richie had plenty of money."

"Not really," Jane said. "He liked to show off, but he wasn't as rich as everyone thought. He just wasn't a good businessman. He was living on the money as it comes in."

"How do you know that?" I asked.

"Well, first of all, I know everything," Jane said, biting back a grin.

"That's true," Lizzie said with a nod.

"And second, we go to the same bank.

Not that I've actually hacked into his records or anything, but I happened to be there a few months ago when the bank president started yelling at Richie about his overdrawn accounts. Everyone in the bank could hear him."

"Whoa." Richie didn't have money? I would have to think about this.

Marigold spoke up. "He was supposed to be in charge of some big charity gala last year and they always rake in the dough. But with Richie in charge, they lost money. I mean, a serious amount of money. I think they're still investigating."

"Um, if Richie was having sex with Bree, maybe he took a video of them together." Lizzie's voice was quiet, but firm.

"Ew," Marigold said, making a face.

"Ugh," I said. "I don't even want to go there."

Jane chuckled. "But it would make a great blackmailing tool."

Lizzie nodded. "And an excellent motive for murder."

"You can say that again," Emily murmured.

We all sipped our wine for a moment in silence. Then I shuddered. "Yuck, that image! Is there a way to bleach my brain?"

"Mine too, please," Jane said, and we all

laughed.

"My money is on that personal assistant of Blake's," Emily said. "She follows him around like a puppy and clings to him whenever she has the chance. It's sad."

"Do you think they're sleeping together?" Jane asked.

Lizzie raised an eyebrow. "Brings new meaning to the term *personal* assistant."

"Chelsea?" I thought about it. "It's pathetically obvious that she's in love with Blake."

"Another perfect motive for murder," Jane said.

I couldn't agree more.

I still blamed Chelsea for lacing Chloe's coffee, and I had my suspicions about whether she had also tainted Chloe's makeup. But there was no way she could've damaged the extension ladder. I sighed. Until Eric finished his investigations, I could only wonder and worry, which was so *not* my style. No, it was way past time I took some action. And I knew just the person to help me with that.

On the drive home, I called Chloe. "How's it going?"

"I'm actually very cozy and feeling fine."

"Did you have pizza?"

"Yes, and Eric even smuggled a split of

Cabernet into the cell for me."

"Sounds like a party."

"It was actually nice. He's so interesting and easy to talk to. Did you know he studied drama in college?"

"Seriously?" I smiled. Our chief of police probably wouldn't be pleased to know Chloe was spilling his secrets.

"How was work today?" she asked, changing the subject.

"I had a long talk with Blake," I said.

"He's so nice, isn't he?"

"Sure he is." I was getting the feeling that Chloe thought everyone was nice. I couldn't agree, but I didn't want to say so. "I hope you don't mind, but I brought up the network show. He tried to convince me that you were the one being fired because they actually wanted to pair Blake with Diego."

"What?" Wow. Who knew that our shrill voices sounded so much alike? "He's delusional."

"That was my thought, too. Delusional, or he's just plain lying. He said the network was looking for a more macho dynamic."

"What a crock." She paused for a moment, then added, "You know, it really bugs me that he said that. Not only because it's a complete fabrication, but because he said it to *you.* He had to know it would hurt you."

"I was furious, but I tried not to show it."

Chloe had a point, though. Had he said all of that on purpose just to get me mad enough to tell him everything I knew?

"I know you're good friends," I said, "but he's quickly becoming my favorite murder suspect."

"Maybe we're not as good friends as I've always thought," she said. "But I still can't picture him killing anyone, let alone Bree." She sighed. "I just hope we get some answers soon."

I came to a stop on the north side of the town square. "Do you know anything about Diego's background?" I asked.

"Not much. I know he was going to college when Bree discovered him. He was premed, believe it or not. His father was a carpenter. And Diego used to build houses with his church group when he was in high school. That's how he knows so much about construction." She chuckled. "Guess I know more about him than I thought."

"He seems like a sweet guy." But a premed student would know chemistry, I thought. He could probably figure out how to poison someone by applying tainted makeup to their skin.

"I think so, too," Chloe said softly. "He's not a good suspect for murder, either, Shan.

Really, I can't think of anyone I know who would kill Bree and Richie. Let alone try to kill me, too."

"It's always hard to picture someone you know doing something like that."

"It sure is."

I didn't say anything else because I didn't actually agree with her. From my experience, *anyone* could make a good suspect for murder.

She yawned. "I'm going to go to sleep now."

"Okay, sis. Sleep well."

"Thanks, sis. Love you."

"Love you, too." Seconds after I ended the call, my phone rang. I was stopped at the corner of Main Street and Blueberry Lane so I took a quick look at the screen and answered. "Hey, Mac."

"Hi, Shan."

I smiled at the nickname. Until Mac came along, it was only my family who called me that. "I was going to call you. I just left Emily's a few minutes ago. I had dinner with the girls."

"Hope you had a fun evening."

"The best," I said, smiling.

"Glad to hear it. Where are you now?"

"Three blocks away from my house."

"Okay, I'm going to stay on the phone

with you until you get home."

"That's nice. It'll take me at least a whole minute."

"I'll take it," he said.

As I drove, he told me what he'd done tonight and a minute later, I pulled into my driveway and came to a stop.

"I'm home," I said. "Will I see you . . . Wait. My gate is open."

I stared at the gate, swinging slowly back and forth in the light breeze. Had I left it open? No, I never did. Had Chloe come home at some point and forgotten to latch it? But no, she wouldn't have done that and also, she hadn't come home yet. She'd gone straight to the police station from the film set. And it probably wasn't Dad, either. Everyone knew to close the gate because Robbie liked to use the doggie door to come out and play.

"Shannon," Mac said. "Don't get out of the truck. Stay on the phone with me. I'm calling the police from my home phone. And then I'm on my way."

Tommy showed up ten minutes later and Mac arrived ten minutes after that. They did a thorough search of my house and yard, but found nothing. When Tommy finally left, Mac stayed, determined to spend the night just in case the open gate was not a fluke. And I was happy to have him.

I poured us both a half glass of wine and we sat at the kitchen table.

"I think I'm more upset that you guys *didn't* find something."

"It's possible that the wind blew the gate open," he said. "But with everything that's been going on, it's good that we got the cops to come check. Better to be safe than sorry."

"I know." I wasn't sleepy so we stayed up for a while, talking and laughing. I told him all about Chloe hiding out in a jail cell, and then I brought up my conversation with Blake.

"You were trying to bait him, weren't you?" he said.

I blinked, all innocence. "Is that what it sounds like?"

He chuckled. "Yeah. I guess I don't blame you, but I'm begging you not to do that unless I'm around."

I smiled. "Will you be there tomorrow?"

"Yes. And I'm sticking close by you."

"Good. Because I don't trust Blake Bennett." I frowned. "And I don't trust his assistant, Chelsea. And I can't honestly be sure I trust Suzanne. Or Josie, although she's been nothing but wonderful. Still, Chloe was attacked twice in her makeup trailer." I twisted my lips in a frown and gazed at him. "Actually, I don't trust any of them right now, so I have a feeling I'll be doing a lot more baiting tomorrow."

Mac spent the night and woke up early enough to make me breakfast. It was like heaven to spend an extra hour with him, especially over French toast, bacon, and coffee. When it was time for me to leave, he said he would drive home to shower and change clothes, but promised to get to the set as soon as possible and stay there all day. My hero.

I was crossing the lawn to get a cup of coffee when I spied two familiar faces in the crowd. The Wagners.

I bypassed the coffeepots and walked straight over to talk to them. "Hi, Mrs. Wagner. Do you remember me?"

"Sure I do. Call me Lolly," she said.

I almost swallowed my tongue. Was that why her husband claimed she was lollygagging? Maybe it was an inside joke between the two of them, although they didn't come across as jokesters. And yet they were *Lolly* and *Rolly.* It was all I could do to keep a straight face. "Lolly. That's an unusual name. I'm Shannon."

"My name is actually Lola, but I never

thought it suited me. So I changed it to Lolly."

I grinned. "Well, that does seem to suit you."

"I think so, too." She turned and elbowed Rolly. "This is my husband, Rolly. Honey, this is the girl I told you about. The one I saw yelling at that silly cousin of Richie Stoddard's."

"Ah." He regarded me with suspicion for a moment, then burst into a big smile. "Well, thank you. Any enemy of Stoddard's is a friend of mine."

What did it say about me that I liked them both for saying that? "Can I ask you why you were so angry with Richie? What did he do to you?"

Rolly began pounding his fist into his palm. "Don't get me started."

Lolly patted his arm. "Don't blow a fuse. She just asked a simple question." Lolly looked at me. "He sold us a house that's full of mold."

"Mold?"

"He never disclosed it," Rolly said.

"We didn't find out until we started getting sick all the time. We had a plumber doing some work on our basement bathroom and he discovered the mold."

"Are you sure it was already there when

you bought the house?"

Rolly scowled. "I went and checked the public records and found that it had been disclosed by the previous owner, but Stoddard removed it from the papers we signed."

"That's awful," I said. "And illegal."

"You're telling me," Rolly grumbled. "We can't even live there anymore."

"We were going to sue him," Lolly said, "but then he promised we'd get a free home makeover from the show."

"And he lied about that, too." Rolly bared his teeth. "Maybe it's cruel of me to say so, but I'm happy he's dead. I didn't kill him, but I'll gladly shake the hand of whoever did."

CHAPTER THIRTEEN

"Today we're going to work on this scaffolding platform," I said to the camera. "We've got some loose siding on the second floor and we'll be removing them and treating the subsurface to help guard against future water damage." I talked as I walked, pointing up at the house.

The scaffolding had been rigged that morning, mostly by my crew, and it ran the entire length of the side of the house, at least fifty feet long and fifteen feet high.

As the camera ran, I pulled myself up onto the scaffolding, grabbing the pipes like they were monkey bars. Actually, climbing these always made me feel like a kid again. Chloe and I had grown up on jobsites, so this was old hat to both of us.

Once I was safely up on the scaffolding, I said, "This wide horizontal board I'm standing on is called the platform." I grinned as I stomped on it with my boot.

"That's what I call it, anyway. Some builders also call it a bridge."

I said a few more brilliant words, then we stopped filming so that Bob the camera guy could climb up to the platform and get some close-ups of me and the damaged wood. His camera was carefully hoisted up to him by two of his assistants.

"Once we start working inside the house," I said to the camera, "we won't have as many issues with rotten wood. But as you can see, here on the outside, we've got dozens of problems. The good news is, once we've replaced the wood and painted the entire house with a good oil-based paint, it should stand for another hundred years."

We finished filming for the day and while the crew shut down the set, I sat on the front steps and wondered what to do next. I'd been so busy that I hadn't had a chance to bait anyone all day. Which was sort of a weird thing to think about, but honestly, I needed to figure out who killed Bree and Richie so I could spring my sister from the comfort of her jail cell.

I stared at the activity going on across the driveway where my guys were helping the film crew break down the scaffolding and straighten things up for the day. I noticed Mac was there, too, and felt a burst of pride that he was so willing to jump in and help where it was needed.

Earlier that afternoon, Eric had given the okay for us to go back inside the house and I for one was glad and relieved to hear it. I watched Mac stacking the scaffolding planks and knew I had some time to kill before we left for the day. The sun was beginning to drop behind the trees, casting long shadows across the property. That was when I realized that what I really wanted to do was take a little self-guided tour inside the house. I wanted to get a feeling for the layout of the rooms and gather ideas for the various projects we would do in the next week or so. I stood and crossed the porch, unlocked the front door, and walked inside.

Gazing around, I had to smile. This old home was just as impressive as I remembered from the first day Chloe and I had walked in and found Bree's body.

I spent a few minutes strolling around the living room, then moved into the dining room, where I stared at the wall of rich, dark wood paneling and sighed. It was positively droolworthy — if you were inclined to drool over beautiful mahogany paneling. I was.

A built-in hutch with dozens of drawers held pride of place in the center of the wall. A large mirror was built into the wide space under the cabinets and above the gold-veined Carrara marble countertop. I couldn't wait for Chloe to see it.

I'd called Chloe first thing that morning just to check in. She was still fine, but I thought she sounded a little on edge, as if she were already tired of being in Eric's protective cage. And who could blame her? We needed to sort this out fast and spring my sister. It was just wrong that an innocent person was languishing in jail because a guilty person wanted to kill her. Which brought me back around to my list of suspects.

I thought about Rolly and Lolly Wagner. Never in a million years did I ever think I would feel sorry for them, but I did. I wanted to help them, but mold was a tricky problem. Getting rid of it was a costly and lengthy procedure, but they really deserved some help. Maybe I would see if Chloe could get the show to donate some time or money toward the project. And if not, I would call in some favors and get the work done.

I heard footsteps above me and wondered who in the world was walking around up there. The house was getting darker by the minute. I looked around for a light switch and flicked it on, but nothing happened.

The old chandelier hanging from the ceiling wasn't working. Undaunted, sort of, I crossed the foyer and took a few steps up the stairs, then called out, "Hello?"

The footsteps quickened and I felt chills skitter across my shoulders. A figure appeared at the top of the stairs and I almost went running.

"Oh, Shannon, it's you."

"Suzanne?" I could hardly breathe, wondering what she was up to. "What were you doing up there?"

"Now that we're allowed to come inside the house, I wanted to take a quick look around. This place is amazing, isn't it?" She descended the stairs, passing me on the way. She stood on the foyer floor while I remained one step higher. At least we were eye to eye now. Sheesh.

"It's beautiful," I said. "I guess we had the same idea."

"Well, I'll leave you to it. I still have to finish the payroll before I leave for the day."

"That's important."

She chuckled. "Oh, yeah. I'll be in deep doo-doo if I don't get it done."

She walked out and I breathed in relief. Gripping the handrail, I realized it was wobbly and was glad it wasn't me. "Someone will kill themselves grabbing on to this," I muttered, and knelt down to study the problem. The wood itself was in really good shape so I wouldn't recommend replacing it. After a few minutes, I decided that all it would take to fix it was to reattach the railing more securely to the newel posts. The balusters were loose, too, and could probably be pulled right out of their sockets. But again, the wood was firm and strong so I figured we would just glue each spindle back into its place and that would solve the issue.

I wandered back to the dining room. I tried the light switch and the two ornate sconces on either side of the built-in breakfront twinkled to life, casting a romantic glow on the room.

I was able to get a better look at the room now and saw how the wood glistened in the light. I opened and closed some of the breakfront drawers and marveled at how smoothly they moved in and out. For a decrepit old mansion, this room was in pretty good shape.

More footsteps echoed against the marble foyer floor. I was calmer this time since it made sense that some of the staff or crew would want to see the house after being kept outside for so many days.

I turned in time to see Blake walk past

the dining room entryway. "Beautiful house, isn't it?"

"Yes," he said. "Bree always picked the best ones." He kept walking through the foyer and at some point he stopped because I couldn't hear his footsteps.

It was fully dark outside by now and I just hoped some of the crew was still working outside. I decided to ignore Blake and continue examining the hutch. I couldn't wait to get Chloe working on this wall of drawers and mirrors. It would be a stunning backdrop for the show.

I bent down to take a closer look at the mirror. It was in near-perfect condition, which was a minor miracle. As I stared into the mirror, I realized that I could see Blake behind me. He had returned to the foyer and was gazing up at the ceiling. I knew what he was looking at. It was the still-lovely chandelier hanging from the center of an elaborately decorated plaster ceiling rose. I had admired it myself a few minutes ago.

As he ambled around the foyer, checking out the features, he casually tossed a hammer up in the air and caught it each time. Knowing Blake, I worried for the marble floor and hoped he didn't drop the hammer. I was so wrapped up in the beauty of the breakfront and the mirror that I didn't pay much attention at first, but then the realization hit me. I continued to watch him through the mirror as he tossed the hammer up again and again. And caught it every time, almost the way a talented professional bartender would twirl a bottle before pouring a shot. For a man as clumsy as Blake, it was astonishing.

And that was when I knew something was very wrong.

Blake glanced into the dining room and saw me. He took two quiet steps toward me, but then realized I was watching his every move through the mirror. Our gazes met, and I knew he knew that I had figured it all out.

No one as klutzy as Blake was supposed to be would ever be able to master the trick of tossing a hammer and catching it like that. All he had ever been capable of doing with a hammer was dropping it. Or so I'd been led to believe.

I stood up and turned around to face him squarely. "Hello, Blake."

He nodded, still clutching the hammer. "Shannon."

"You lied about Bree firing Chloe."

"No, I didn't." He shook his head and gave a short, hard laugh. "She fired Chloe and everyone else at least once a month."

"Including you."

"We had a fiery relationship."

"But she was firing you for real. The network didn't want you working on their new show."

"Sorry, kiddo." Shaking his head sadly, he gave me a look that most people reserved for delusional, elderly relatives. "I know it's hard to accept, but Bree was trying to dump Chloe."

I laughed. "Right. How long do you think that story's going to fly?"

"What's that supposed to mean?"

"It means that when the network people show up next week, we can ask them who they've chosen for the show."

His eyes narrowed. "What are you talking about?"

"Ah. I guess that was something that Bree didn't tell you. She certainly told Chloe. Turns out you don't know everything after all, Blake."

"You're lying."

"Am I? I guess we'll see who's telling the truth when the network bigwigs show up."

"I knew they were coming, of course," he said, and I could see him clenching his jaw. "They're coming to see me."

"Oh, really?"

He clutched the hammer even more tightly

as he walked toward me. I suddenly wondered if anyone was still working outside. Was Wade waiting to go over the schedule for tomorrow? Had Mac decided to go home? Maybe he couldn't find me and figured I had left for the day. I was on my own.

Blake tossed the hammer again and caught it like an expert juggler. I had thought he was a weakling and a klutz. Apparently I was wrong. I glanced around for some kind of weapon to use against him, but there was nothing. It didn't matter; I was younger and stronger. I worked hard every day and I was in good shape while Blake had only pretended to work all these years.

I wanted to kick myself, knowing that all day long, either Mac or Wade had been no more than three feet from my side. My own personal bodyguards. Even my dad and Uncle Pete had shown up, moving through the crowds, keeping an eye on me and everything else around them. And now, here I was, all alone with a crazy person holding a hammer.

He approached me by circling the perimeter of the room, cutting off my access to escape out the front door. I circled in the same direction to the other side of the room. I stayed as far away from him as possible while watching his every step. He kept narrowing the circle while I tried to push it farther out. I had suddenly realized that I *did* have a weapon I could use against him, if only I could get to it. I would have to make it to the foyer staircase. Those wobbly balusters weren't exactly lethal, but if I could yank one of them loose, I could use it to defend myself against that hammer he kept tossing around.

"Why did you kill Richie?" I asked.

He stopped momentarily, looking surprised. Guess he didn't realize I could multi-task, talking while he stalked me.

"Tell me why, Blake."

He shrugged. "He slept with my wife."

Sounded reasonable enough. But there had to be more. After all, he'd also killed his wife. "I guess that's one reason. But a lot of people sleep with other people's spouses. Did you have to kill him?"

He snorted. "Did you ever meet him?"

"Yeah."

"I rest my case."

I sighed. He had a point. Richie was an abhorrent human, but did he deserve to die? The jury was still out.

"I probably would've let him live," he continued. "But he thought he could blackmail me. He actually wanted money to keep quiet about the fact that he had cuckolded me. I agreed to meet him here the other night to give him the cash."

"And you killed him instead."

He grunted angrily. "He was a scumbag."

Still walking, still watching him, I was also curious. "Why do you pretend you can't even use a hammer?"

"Why should I do all the tedious stuff?" He demanded. "I worked for years doing grunt work. I paid my dues." He scowled. "Bree used to ridicule me and give me grief about it. Sometimes I really wanted to strangle her. But I decided to bide my time."

He took another two steps and so did I. At the opening to the foyer, I stepped back, moving toward the staircase. He followed and kept talking. "I was the one who got the network to come look at our show. I set up the whole deal and then found out that she was going to cut me out. Me! Hell, I made this show. Without me, Bree would have been nothing. She thought she could just get rid of me? I wasn't going to let that happen."

Show business really was dog-eat-dog. "I take it you drugged yourself."

"That was a stroke of genius, don't you think?" He smiled and took another quick side step to his right, watching me carefully.

"If I was drugged, I couldn't be blamed for anything. I was a victim, too."

"Smart." Actually, it was, and I didn't like admitting it. I was close enough to the staircase that I leaned against and quickly ripped one of the balusters from the railing. I waved it at him like a sword and he laughed.

"Now I'm scared." He tossed the hammer from one hand to the other, showing off his skill.

I walked backward, pushing open the doorway that led to the kitchen. "So you killed Bree," I said, "and you killed Richie. You tried to kill Chloe or at least injure her."

I slammed the door shut and moved back into the dining room. Blake ran around to the living room and stopped under the archway between living and dining rooms. "You're not as clever as you think you are."

"I was going to say the same thing about you." I clutched the spindly baluster, ready to fight off his hammer attack. "Why did you try to kill Chloe?"

"I don't have anything against Chloe, but I need her out of the picture. As long as she's around, the network will want her. I was sure that overdose would do her in, but she's a tough one."

Infuriated, I fought to keep my voice calm

while inside, I was boiling. "Yes, she is. Much tougher than you."

He shrugged. "But I'll win in the end. After I take care of you, I'll be going after her."

I gazed at him. "Did you try to go after her last night?"

"What're you talking about?"

"Did you come to my house looking for her?"

He paused, then probably figured he might as well confess all of his sins. After all, who was I going to tell? "Yeah, I came by. But nobody was home and that damn dog kept yapping so I got out of there."

"My dog doesn't yap," I protested. But Robbie did have a good, loud bark. And clearly he had saved the day, driving a vicious killer away from the house. I planned to treat him to the most expensive food on the market from now on.

For now, though, I had to keep this vicious killer focused on me. "You can't keep killing people, Blake."

"I don't plan to. But I can't let you live. You know too much. I'm going to have to shut you up."

"So your plan is to kill me here and then . . . what?"

"The woods surrounding this house will

hide my getaway. I've got a truck parked on the far side of the trees and I'll be able to make it to the highway before anyone knows I'm gone. I'll lay low for a few days, then go take care of Chloe."

I was starting to shake from the chills I felt. I believed every word he was saying and wondered why none of his co-workers had ever realized what a cold-blooded threat Blake Bennett was.

"You can try," I said, hoping my voice didn't betray my fear. "So much for your career in showbiz."

He chuckled. "I've got plenty of cash stashed away. And there's a nice little house waiting for me on a Caribbean island that no one will ever find."

"So you've worked it all out." We continued to circle around the room and when I got to the archway by the living room, I made a sudden detour, dashing over to the bay window and smashing it with the baluster. I hated the idea of hurting the house, but we planned to replace those windows anyway.

"That won't do you any good," he insisted. "Everyone's gone home."

I refused to believe that, but now I was stuck in a corner. The small alcove by the bay window was a dead end. I had nowhere else to go. Blake laughed as he clearly realized the same thing. "Nice move. Now you're stuck."

And suddenly I saw a sight that made me want to shout and scream for joy. I coughed to clear my tight throat. "I should warn you, my boyfriend is standing right behind you with a two-by-four."

He laughed again and it sounded like a cackle. "Yeah, right. Nice try. Trying to make me turn around? Take my eyes off you? I'm not falling for that old trick."

"No, not you. You're too smart for that."

"Sure am." Blake took one more step toward me and raised his hammer.

Mac moved quickly and the wood floor creaked beneath his feet. I winced at the sound as Blake whirled around and faced him, wielding the hammer like a bludgeon.

"No!" I screamed and ran at Blake, smashing the baluster into his head. It wasn't enough to knock him out but it stunned him and Mac used the moment to take a swing at Blake. The two-by-four hit him squarely in the gut, causing him to gasp and fall to his knees.

I let go of the breath I'd been holding and cried, "You did it!" I took a running leap and flew into his arms. And he caught me, like any good superhero would.

"No, sweetheart," Mac said. "You did it."

I would've kissed him right then, but we had a villain to restrain. I let go of Mac for the moment and when Blake tried to stand, Mac used his foot to shove him down again. He grabbed the hammer from Blake and flung it across the floor, out of harm's way.

"You are the most wonderful man in the world," I whispered.

"And you are the bravest woman."

"Thank you for being here."

"Hey, I couldn't let you have all the fun," he said.

We heard sirens approaching. "Did you call the police?"

"Wade did," he said.

"Oh God." I was still breathing heavily. "I thought you'd left. I didn't know what to do."

"You were doing pretty well there on your own," he said.

"I just tried to keep him talking. I was scared to death."

"I'm sorry, baby," he whispered. "Eric called a little while ago to let me know that he'd settled on Blake Bennett as his prime suspect. He was on his way over here, but meanwhile, he asked me to give Blake a bit of room to see what he was going to do."

My mouth gaped. "So I really was the bait?"

"Well, not for long. We saw Bennett walk into the house and I knew you were already inside. So I came inside through the back door and was able to hear every word he said."

"I'm so glad."

"Your father and Uncle Pete wanted to come inside with me, but I talked them into guarding the front door so Blake couldn't escape."

"Even more brilliant," I said.

"Come on in, guys," Mac shouted. And Dad and Uncle Pete stormed into the house and stood sentry over Blake.

That's when I grabbed hold of Mac and kissed him with every ounce of love and gratitude I had welling up inside me. And he kissed me right back. With his arm around me, I rested my head on his shoulder. A minute later, the police pounded up the front steps and ran into the house.

I kissed Mac again. "Let's get out of here."

The line of people went out the door of Lizzie and Hal's bookshop on the town square.

Inside, Lizzie had arranged a beautiful spread of cupcakes and champagne with little takeaway baggies filled with plastic tools and an adorable pink measuring tape. It was the perfect touch for Chloe's book signing.

Chloe was blown away by the crowd. It looked as though every single person in town was here and she must've signed three hundred books. I couldn't have been prouder.

Dad and Uncle Pete were there, along with every teacher Chloe ever had in school, including the principal of Lighthouse High. I almost laughed when I saw her walk in. Having Mrs. Fielding show up at her book signing was something Chloe would remind us of forever.

But when Eric Jensen walked into the store, and I saw how her eyes lit up like stars, I knew we had trouble.

I turned to Dad. "Did you see that?"

He was frowning. "You don't think . . ."

Uncle Pete, who wasn't always aware of the underlying emotional current, looked from Dad to me and back to Dad. "Is Chloe going to move back home?"

Dad and I stared in shock at each other. "This was not on my radar," I said.

"Well," Dad said, nudging me away. "Scope it out, work the room, get back to me."

"Yes, Father." I strolled away laughing. And walked right up to Eric Jensen. "Why is my sister looking at you like that?"

He smiled, and I could see the answer in his eyes.

"Really?" I said. "One night in jail and this is what happens?"

He laughed and gave me a big hug. "She makes me happy."

And just like that, I turned to jelly. My eyes started watering and I sniffled until he finally handed me a tissue. Leave it to Thor to have me weeping like a baby.

"Thanks." I blew my nose, then scowled at him. "Way to bury the lead, Eric."

He held up both hands. "The plan was to keep things quiet for a while. So you didn't hear anything from me."

"I didn't hear anything from her, either."

"Really?" he said, looking a little dazed. "Because she likes to talk."

"Well, there is one nugget she shared, something about you in drama class . . ."

He groaned. This was going to be fun.

I laughed again, gave him another hug, and walked away to find Mac. Things were moving and shaking in Lighthouse Cove and I couldn't wait to see what tomorrow would bring.

ABOUT THE AUTHOR

A native Californian, *New York Times* bestselling author **Kate Carlisle** worked in television for many years before turning to writing. Inspired by the northern seaside towns of her native California, where Victorian mansions grace the craggy cliffs and historic lighthouses warn fishermen and smugglers alike, Kate was drawn to create the Fixer-Upper Mysteries, featuring small-town girl Shannon Hammer, a building contractor specializing in home restoration. Kate also writes the *New York Times* bestselling Bibliophile Mysteries featuring Brooklyn Wainwright.

The employees of Thorndike Press hope you have enjoyed this Large Print book. All our Thorndike, Wheeler, and Kennebec Large Print titles are designed for easy reading, and all our books are made to last. Other Thorndike Press Large Print books are available at your library, through selected bookstores, or directly from us.

For information about titles, please call:

(800) 223-1244

or visit our website at:

gale.com/thorndike

To share your comments, please write:

Publisher
Thorndike Press
10 Water St., Suite 310
Waterville, ME 04901